Stiletto S[...]
Silver [...]

CW00741730

A GREAT COLLECTION OF
EROTIC NOVELS FEATURING
FEMALE DOMINANTS

If you like one you will probably like the rest

A NEW TITLE EVERY MONTH

Stiletto Readers Service
c/o Silver Moon Books Ltd
109A Roundhay Road
Leeds, LS8 5AJ

http://www.electronicbookshops.com

If you like one of our books you will probably
like them all!

Stiletto Reader Services

c/o Silver Moon Books Ltd
109A Roundhay Road
Leeds, LS8 5AJ

http://www.electronicbookshops.com

<u>New authors welcome</u>
**Please send submissions to
STILETTO
Silver Moon Books Ltd.
PO Box 5663
Nottingham
NG3 6PJ**

THE RICH BITCH
by
Becky Ball

CHAPTER ONE

Jason stood close to the end of the long polished dining table, his thick cock erect and pulsing in excited little spasms. The foreskin was rolled back along the great shaft to expose the huge, bulbous head. He was totally naked save for the black bow tie around his neck and in his hands he held a silver serving tray. Draped over his forearm was a starched linen napkin with ornate initials in red embroidered on the corner. Dutifully he stood erect and dutifully silent beside his mistress.

Arabella, seated and fully dressed, ate with her right hand; her left hand rested between Jason's thick muscular thighs from the rear, her fingertips teasing at the rear of his firm ball sac.

In the large dining hall of the manor all was silent, just the occasional chink of a fork against plate and the odd whimper of delight from Jason to break that stillness.

At thirty two years old, Arabella was in prime condition. Tall and slim, with jet black hair that fell to her shoulders and deep, dark smouldering eyes, her appearance fitted perfectly her title of 'Lady.' Well educated at only the best of schools, refined and socially acceptable within the upper circles of society in which she moved, Arabella was every bit the Lady of the Manor. Being extremely wealthy too helped tremendously to maintain the luxurious and carefree lifestyle that she led.

She didn't flinch or show even the faintest hint of surprise or revulsion as Jason grunted and then sighed loudly. His cock twitched in excited little jerks to pump forceful spurts of thick sperm jetting onto the polished surface of the table close to her plate.

Almost casually Arabella removed her hand from between Jason's thighs, picked up her cotton napkin and dabbed carefully at the side of her mouth.

"Well Jason?" her polished accent demanded.

5

"Madam," he said loudly, "I apologise and will clean the table immediately."

Arabella sat back in her chair, crossed her legs and smoothed her delicate hand over the tight riding jodhpurs that she wore.

"Unacceptable!" she stated firmly and then softened her tone. "Totally unacceptable."

"Yes Madam."

"Face me!" she snapped.

The servant turned as directed, his semi-erect cock swinging down between his thighs and a little string of sperm hanging down from the eyehole.

"Have I not told you before to control yourself?"

"Yes, Madam, you have indeed."

There was an air of hopelessness in her voice as she reprimanded the tall muscular man.

"Yes! Yes I most certainly have Jason. You know full well that following dinner I like nothing better than to suck a cock and taste sperm - you have deprived me of such pleasure today."

His voice was low and full of remorse.

"Madam, I apologise."

"Huh!" she snorted in derision, her anger beginning to spill out. "And what good is an apology to me now?"

He didn't reply but stood erect and silent awaiting the further lashing of her harsh tongue.

"You will be punished! Most severely punished - now get out and send Paul to me this instant."

"Yes Madam," he muttered and walked quickly away.

***

The small coffee house in the large shopping mall was bustling with mid-morning customers. Natalie and Claire seated themselves at a table close to the wrought iron railings. It was more a meeting place than a coffee shop; a place for the young

6

and elderly alike to gather and gossip. A place for weary shoppers to rest their feet and bags during their spending sprees, the coffee shop was always crowded.

"Guess what," Claire said with a hint of intrigue in her voice. "Received an invitation the other day - from Arabella - remember her from the sixth form at...."

"You too?" Natalie interrupted. "I got one from her yesterday."

Claire rummaged in her handbag as she spoke.

"A reunion perhaps."

"Must be, although that bitch always thought herself too good to associate with the likes of us. I'm surprised that she even remembered our names."

Claire handed the card across the table, turning it so as to read it at the same time as her friend.

"There we are. Friday the eighteenth at 8 am."

"That's morning," Natalie pointed out. "Must be an error."

Claire read the invitation card again and shrugged her shoulders.

"It says 8 am. but it must be wrong."

"Are you going?"

Claire sat back, pausing to order two cappuccinos from the waitress hurrying past.

"Might be fun. Be good to see some of the old faces again - remember that skinny girl? Redhead she was, can't remember her name."

Natalie wasn't listening; she was totally absorbed in reading her own invitation card.

"Did you say the eighteenth?"

Claire's head turned, following the progress of a youth in a pair of tight jeans that pulled harshly across his firm backside. She sighed wistfully and giggled.

"What? Sorry, other more important things to view first."

"My invitation is for the twenty seventh."

Claire looked at her friend quizzically and reached across

7

to take the card.

"You're right. That's over a week later. What the hell is going on?"

"Search me, that rich bitch always was a bit dizzy, she never could count."

Claire was unconvinced, Arabella was anything but dizzy. Cold and calculating with a sharp mind and a twisted outlook on life perhaps but never dizzy. When it came to socialising Arabella had excelled, cold and aloof at times she may have been, but hugely popular at parties and gatherings. It was her charge; the time in her life when she really came alive, all of her social events were planned with almost military precision and nothing left to chance. Claire couldn't see Arabella making a mistake such as this.

"Wonder if Amey got one?"

"Or Louise," Natalie added; now sharing a little of her friend's concern.

Claire stood and picked up her handbag.

"Simply have to know, I'll phone Amey now."

" But your coffee! It'll get cold."

Claire wriggled past the backs of the chairs close to their table.

"The phone box over there," she nodded to indicate the direction. "Two minutes and I'll be back."

"Well?" Natalie asked eagerly as her friend returned.

Claire slumped heavily back down in her chair.

"Different date and even a different month. I phoned Louise too, different dates yet again."

Natalie looked bewildered.

"So what the hell is going on?"

Claire shrugged, her gaze distant and detached.

"Haven't the faintest idea - but I mean to find out."

***

With a thick mane of blond hair, his flashing blue eyes and muscular build Paul looked the epitome of health and fitness. A thick neck and broad shoulders, his deeply sculptured chest and stomach all bore testament to his regular workouts in the gym. Bulging biceps and heavy thighs added to the overall appearance of sheer power that he possessed. Like Jason and all of the mistress's servants, he wore a black bow tie around his neck as standard dress and was otherwise totally naked.

He was seated now, his backside perched on the very edge of the dining table and his legs splayed one either side of Arabella's chair. He was rested back and supporting himself on his outstretched arms, his stiff cock jutting out in front.

Arabella's delicate hand gripped his pulsing shaft, her fingers closing around its great girth, the red nails standing out in deep contrast to the pale skin of his cock. Her left hand stroked lightly and sensually at his powerful thigh, her fingers kneading and feeling in a rhythmic exploration of pure delight.

Paul groaned deeply and tensed his body as her thumb rubbed lightly across the top of his glans; the velvety head throbbed its delighted response.

The mistress lowered her head, her blood red lips making just the lightest of contact with the eyehole of his cock. Moving her head from side to side she smeared his drop of lubrication with her soft pouting lips, massaging it lovingly all around the bulbous dome. Throughout, Arabella sighed and moaned her pleasure as his obvious excitement increased. Her left hand slid up to cup his swollen scrotum, her fingers teasing as she cupped his balls tenderly in her palm.

Paul grunted, his thighs twitched in involuntary spasm in reaction to her teasing touch. His head slunk back; eyes closed and mouth open as he bathed in the sensations washing over him. He gasped as her soft warm mouth enveloped the head of his cock to take it into her wet, warm cavern. The blond servant cried out as her tongue flicked lightly across the very tip in sensitive teasing that brought him close to his peak.

9

That cry turned to a low animal-like growl as the very tip of her tongue drilled down into the tiny eyehole of his pulsing cock.

Arabella received a terrific jolt low in her vulva as his thick, warm sperm jetted into her mouth. Gripping contractions pulsed her internal muscles to produce delightful little spears of electric sensation. Her nipples tingled and her anus gripped as spurt after spurt of his thick cream shot deep into her throat. She mewed contentedly as his orgasm shook his body to emit further little jets of sperm in erratic surges. Some spilled from her lips as she used her tongue to lap and taste every last drop of sperm from the blond Adonis.

At length she sat back, both her hands resting on and caressing lovingly at his thighs.

"Your first dinner duty as my newest servant isn't it Paul?"

"Yes Madam," he replied throatily.

She smiled broadly dabbing at her mouth with the napkin.

"And most certainly not your last," she muttered softly to herself.

***

It was almost a standing joke between the four girls, a different colour and style of hair for each of them. Claire was the brunette with a short but neatly cropped style, Louise tall and blond, Amey petite and auburn haired whilst Natalie had fair hair but darker than blond. They sat around the lounge in Claire's home sipping coffee and discussing the possibilities as to Arabella's invitations.

"It all sounds very mysterious and exciting," Amey giggled. "A bit like the famous five stories."

The others shot her an incredulous stare and giggled in derision then resumed the normal dissecting of the information to date. Louise took it upon herself to summarise.

"Okay then, Arabella has invited us all...."

"All at differing times and dates," Amey interrupted.

10

Louise ignored her interruption and continued.

"But not to one function. The dates are spread across four months, one of us each month - so why?"

Natalie shifted her seat on the settee to sit on her legs.

"I never trusted her at school and I don't feel inclined to trust her now."

"Couldn't we simply phone her and ask?" Amey said brightly.

Claire offered her view.

"Tried that, spoke to her this morning. She was very evasive on the phone."

"See! Told you so," Natalie added.

"It gets even more mysterious though," Claire continued. "She wouldn't divulge a thing but said instructions would be sent shortly."

"Huh!" Louise snorted in disgust. "Instructions indeed! Just who the hell does she think she is to instruct us?"

Claire's calming voice added a probable solution to her friend's question.

"How to get there I think she probably meant."

Louise nodded silently, flushing slightly at her impetuous outburst.

"I still don't like it," Natalie stated.

Claire sighed heavily.

"So what do we do then? Accept or refuse?"

"If you, Claire," Amey offered, "as the first of us invited, go along next month and if it should be bad - tell the rest of us."

"Thanks," Claire said sarcastically."

"I think she has a point," Natalie chipped in. "One of us has to be first and could keep the others informed - what is Arabella likely do to us anyway? Eat us for God's sake!"

"Probably," Louise muttered.

"It was an invitation after all and not a command," Amey said in a rare moment of sensibility. "We don't have to go."

Claire sat silently for a few moments pondering the possi-

11

bilities.

"Okay!" she stated firmly. "I'll accept and see just what the rich bitch is up to."

The subject changed and much chattering and giggling followed, Claire however, sat silently, an indefinable feeling gnawing away inside her.

***

Her long stiletto-heeled boots clicked noisily on the stone slabs of the terrace as Arabella stepped out onto them. She paused at the top of the wide stone steps and stretched lazily. Her favourite black leggings hugged her slim hips and pulled tightly across the firm swell of her buttocks. At the front, they followed the contours of her firm mound and pulled satisfyingly close to her labia, the bump of her clitoris prominent near the top. They did so emphasise her slender thighs and long legs to almost perfection she felt, they also added to that commanding air that she carried about her.

A light tee shirt in white pulled harshly across her chest to show the swell of her ample breasts to good effect and to leave a couple of inches of bare midriff at the hem. Her long nipples pushed hard against the flimsy material to stand out in prominence from the swelling orbs.

Below her all were ready, standing in two lines on the emerald green lawns of the lower terrace. Ten in all, young, male, all powerfully built and well endowed, she liked her servants so very much. Naked and silent they awaited her arrival; Paul being the latest recruit had never seen a punishment ceremony and it was partly for his benefit that it was being held today.

Her expression became serious as she looked beyond the two lines of naked servants to the whipping post beyond. Jason, the premature ejaculator was tied securely to the heavy wooden cross. Naked and facing the framework he was stretched and bound as if in reverse crucifixion.

Slowly and deliberately Arabella moved down the steps, the riding crop in her hand striking nosily against the side of her boot as she moved between the two lines of men. It thrilled and excited her to have such command, the thought of these fit young men all wanting her pushed her level of arousal higher still.

Their hungry eyes roamed her body as she moved past them, searching and probing at her breasts and buttocks, her thighs and her thinly veiled pussy. Bolts of electric sensations shot through her at the thought and she slowed her pace to take full advantage of them.

"Jason," she announced loudly as she reached the whipping post and turned theatrically, "is guilty of robbing your mistress of her after dinner pleasures."

She slashed the crop back and forth menacingly in the air for effect.

"Today," she raised her voice above the wind blowing across the large estate, "he will be rewarded for that failure."

She stepped to the side, positioned herself and adopted a set and firm stance. She adjusted her body, weighed the crop in her hand and pulled her arm back.

Jason's body locked rigid and a pained grunt came from him as the crop struck. A savage lash stung his bare buttocks to send a stripe of searing pain racing through his body and to his brain.

"Count to fifteen!" Arabella screeched excitedly and raised the crop high above her shoulder.

"One!" Jason shouted loudly and then yelped as the second blow cut across his taut buttocks.

"Two!" he shouted, his voice cracking with emotion.

Again Arabella lashed and then again in a series of harsh and meaningful swipes that thwacked down hard on his soft flesh. In time with his counting she rained the blows on him, each sickeningly painful stroke of the crop sent electric charges of sensation rushing through her. In a wild frenzy of high sexual arousal she stung him with increasing savagery, wield-

13

ing the crop deftly with her expert hand. At the fifteenth stroke she paused, her breathing laboured and excited, panting hard from her exertions. Her body throbbed with excitement, her clitoris was hard and pressing against the tight leggings. The material of her tee shirt rubbed across her sensitive nipples with each movement of her body to further excite her.

A glance around his front showed clearly that in his pain he had achieved orgasm, globules of his thick seed trickled down the central post and stained the grass below.

Her pussy was wet, her nipples firm and her hard clitoris throbbed its aching need for sexual release. Arabella was pulsing with excitement, punishment sessions always seemed to bring out the very best in her along with that compelling and irresistible urge to have a cock up inside her. Beating a man, punishing him soundly was made all the better by ten leering men wanting to have her body. They would be imagining what lay beneath her thin clothing, her silky soft skin and puffy pussy lips. Her firm breasts and rosy pink nipples, her taut little buttocks and her sweet little anus.

She moved quickly between the two rows of young men, pulled down her leggings and panties and got down onto all fours. A quick nod of her head to him brought Claude, the big athletic black boy, eagerly around behind her.

He positioned his big cock at the entrance to her pussy and pushed fully home up inside her. Both his hands gripped her hips to pull her slim frame hard back onto him as he began a frantic pumping into her. Large and powerfully built, he had an athletic body that glistened like ebony in the bright daylight, the stamina that he possessed seemed almost without end.

Arabella's mouth hung open, her head and body shaking in time with Claude's powerful thrusting as his hips crashed against her soft buttocks. It excited Arabella to be had whilst the others watched; their cocks rising to erection in need, all of them wishing that it could be them serving the mistress.

She arched her back, her head threw up and she began to

wail. A low and animal-like howling of deep satisfaction as the thick cock pumped urgently into her. Arabella met his thrusting, forcing herself hard back onto him to gain the whole length of his cock deep up inside her soft interior. Her body locked and shook in violent tremors of pleasure. She grunted and her head hung down between her arms, for a moment or two she fell silent and then screamed aloud as she came.

Claude pulled out of her, his huge cock rearing up to spurt a thick stream of his sperm onto Arabella's buttocks and lower back. He pressed hard against his mistress's backside and rubbed himself to a slow finish as he knew she liked him to.

Paul, never having seen such a spectacle moaned as his cock jerked. At first just a little dribble of his seed appeared then his cock jetted long spurts of his sperm forcefully out in front of him. Arabella noted Paul's great excitement, and it pleased her greatly.

***

Claire was alone, the red silk robe the only material covering her otherwise naked body as she picked up the thick manila envelope from the doormat. With a mug of steaming coffee in hand she settled herself at the kitchen table and tore the envelope open.

Different, weird even, the instructions from Arabella were precise if a little strange. A surge of excitement rushed through Claire's body as she read them aloud to herself. A tingling in her nipples and little flutters in her vulva made Claire pause to question her feelings. "Written instructions, that is all they are," she scolded herself. "Nothing remotely sexual about them at all."

Deny it as she might the excitement she felt was building within her, dippy Amey had for once been right.

Claire found herself squeezing her thighs together, squashing her enflamed labia around her hardening clitoris to massage it comfortingly.

15

On the appointed day she was to dress in the prescribed manner, make her way to a point outside of town where she would be collected. A sketched map was attached and a typed list of points added as where exactly to stand and which direction even that she should look in.

A sip at her coffee and a delighted shiver couldn't stem Claire's rising feelings of thrilling anticipation. She and Arabella had always got on well at school, the others saw her differently but Claire harboured a liking for the woman. Her hand rested now over her pussy, her fingers gripping lightly in a steady rhythm to try to feed the nagging ache that simply wouldn't leave her.

She wouldn't, Claire decided, say anything to the others. Okay she had agreed to share the information on the instructions once they arrived but now, now it all seemed so very different. She sighed aloud, shifting her thighs apart to allow her hand access to her pulsing clitoris. Claire looked apprehensively at the kitchen window and tried to make her rubbing movements less conspicuous.

As the wonderful sensations increased, she slid forward on her seat, stretching her legs out beneath the table. Her three fingers now rubbing steadily to circle and to press on her hard bud. Faster and harder she stroked herself, eyes closed and head back she moaned her pleasure to the silent kitchen.

She gave several little whimpers as her body shivered in light convulsions of pre-orgasm. Her legs locked straight, her back arched and she cried out as she came.

For several minutes she sat as she had finished, bathing in the warm and blissful state of post orgasm. Claire was mewing softly, her hand still rubbing slightly at her sex to savour every last ripple of sensation from it. Her eyes opened, she flushed and sat upright in the chair, embarrassed at her inability to resist her urges. She pulled her robe tightly across her body and ran upstairs to the shower.

***

The huge marbled bathroom was larger than most normal lounges. Pale grey tiles lined the walls with long mirrors fixed horizontally to give ample opportunity for someone to admire themselves fully. The large sunken bath, more like a small swimming pool had steps at one end that descended into the foamy suds that covered the water. It was on these steps that Arabella stood naked, her body glistening with droplets of water and streaks of creamy suds.

"Work the lather in well, Vincent," she purred in delight.

The naked servant stood close to her, his cock erect and twitching as he ran both hands lovingly over his mistress's body to soap her completely. His thick fingers roamed freely, rubbing across her breasts to excite her hard nipples, sliding down over the curve of her firm buttocks to slip between her legs.

"Unnnh!" Arabella groaned in delight as contact was made on her labia.

The fingers probed and searched as she shifted her feet apart to accommodate them. Her hand slipped around her side to grip and to hold his throbbing cock, her head rested back on his broad shoulder. One hand now fingered her pussy, the other covered one breast and pulled her back onto him as he squeezed and kneaded it.

"Fuck me," Arabella breathed urgently. "Fuck me now."

He pulled her onto him, manoeuvring his cock up under her buttocks and between her legs. The great head pushed into her inner lips and then on up inside her moist interior. His finger and thumb pinched and rolled her nipple, the other hand circled her waist to rub slowly at her clitoris. Vincent began a slow thrusting up into his mistress, sliding his cock almost out of her pussy before ramming hard back up inside her.

Arabella moaned her pleasure, her internal muscles gripping him momentarily as each inward stroke peaked. Her whole soft inside closing around his great length to feed back

17

total pulsing sensations from his firm rod.

Only moments he lasted before she felt the warm wash of his sperm deep up inside her. She came at that moment, air forcing from her lungs as she savoured the feel of his thick warm cock up inside her.

"Good, Vincent, very good indeed," she praised breathlessly.

"Thank you Madam," came the dutiful reply.

"Now, wash yourself and sit of the side of the bath, I have yet to eat," she said firmly and then softened her tone to a sensual drawl. "And you know just how hungry I can get."

***

Claire's husband Robert looked up from his newspaper in surprise.

"The whole weekend?" he questioned with a hint of suspicion in his voice.

Claire sat in the armchair opposite flicking idly through a magazine.

"Arabella, you must remember my telling you of her. Old school friend, she's holding a class reunion."

Robert grunted and resumed reading his paper.

"Fine by me," he said in disinterest. "I'll just go to the squash club and probably eat at mother's house to save me cooking."

Claire put the magazine aside, got up and moved to Robert's side, she sat on the arm of the chair and slid her arm around his shoulders.

"If I'm to be away for a few days," she murmured softly and tickled at his ear lobe. "Do you think that we might...."

Robert grunted again and shook his head.

"Not in the mood."

Claire suppressed her initial reaction and maintained the coaxing voice.

"But it has been some months now Robert since

18

you....since you...."

He threw the newspaper aside angrily and jumped to his feet.

"Since I couldn't get an erection!" he shouted.

Claire remained calm.

"I was going to say since you last made love to me."

"You know damned well that I can't!"

"We could try," she soothed. "There are lots of things we could do without actually....you know."

He paused thoughtfully for a moment then shook his head.

"No," he muttered. "No, I can't - I just can't."

Robert walked away through to the kitchen.

Claire sat as she was, a warm sensation moving to spread from her pussy out across her upper thighs. Her nipples began that familiar tingling and the excitement stirred once again within her. Her thoughts now were not on her husband but on her friend, her old school friend - Arabella.

CHAPTER TWO

She felt a tart, Claire hoped and prayed that no one she knew would pass and see her dressed so. Why the hell she felt compelled to comply with Arabella's wishes she didn't know - but she had.

In the remote country lane in the early morning, Claire shivered with the chill. Silence surrounded her and thick mist covered the surrounding fields to give an eerie feel to the stillness.

A short pleated skirt in navy blue that finished indecently high up her thigh was so out of character for her. Normally staid and proper, nothing above knee length would have been acceptable either to her or to Robert. Black hold-up stockings, sheer and sleek gave her, she felt, a wanton and alluring appearance. The crisp white blouse, long sleeved and tight around her bust and waist simply reinforced her whorish feel.

What she couldn't deny to herself was the pumping excitement that she gained from it all. A deep tingling of naughtiness and abandonment, almost a transformation of character. To be dressed so, to be here out in the middle of nowhere at seven in the morning and to be - well, what was effectively - under the command of her long absent friend. It was all so ridiculous but at the same time so very thrilling - sexually thrilling.

Claire faced the direction that Arabella had insisted she should, her nipples hardened in the chill air or was it excitement? A little of both she decided as she waited. The small suitcase by her feet contained mostly cosmetics and underwear, 'all clothing provided' Arabella's note had said, that fact simply added to the mystery and the thrill of anticipation.

"Madam," the deep voice stated from behind her.

Claire squealed in shock and whirled around in surprise, she hadn't even been aware of his approach.

The tall chauffeur stood impassively as she looked him up and down suspiciously.

"Madam Arabella's compliments, she asks that you allow me to transport you to her residence."

Claire was stunned, he was so young, so confident and so very, very - well - nice. His sharply pressed black uniform and cap gave his tanned face an almost irresistible look. The flashing blue eyes and wry, knowing smile made her insides melt in desire. She had expected Arabella herself but wasn't in the least disappointed. Claire took the opportunity as she followed to inspect every teasing move of his firm backside as it moved within his tight fitting trousers.

As they reached the black limousine parked further down the lane the chauffeur paused to hold up a blindfold.

"My apologies Madam but mistress insisted that you wear this."

A pumping thrill coursed through her as he moved close behind her to slip the blindfold over her head and fix it into

20

place. Shivers of delight rippled through her as she stood passively whilst his strong fingers touched at the side of her head. His closeness and the smell of his after-shave sent her vulva in to gripping little spasms of delight.

For what seemed an eternity she sat in darkness on the back seat of the limousine, the ride was comfortable and seemingly unhurried. It was an almost undetectable halt that the car slowed to and only the switching off of the engine indicated to Claire that that they had actually stopped.

Again the wonderful fresh smell of his after shave and body as he leaned close thrilled her, the light dazzling her eyes as the blindfold was removed. They were at the gates of a large estate, a long sweeping driveway stretched out before them to cut its way through lush green grassland to the trees beyond. Tall wrought iron gates attached to enormous stone pillars stood open to allow them access to the sprawling grounds.

The car moved majestically towards the central wooded area, Claire gazed in awe as the house came into view. Huge and old, it was a mansion that could have come straight from a Hollywood film. Wide stone steps led up from the gravelled parking area to the front of the house itself and high Georgian window frames painted in white stood out in contrast to the stonework. As far as the eye could see rolling hills and farmland surrounded the house in whichever direction one cared to look.

Claire stepped a little nervously out of the car, the chauffeur holding the door open indicated with a sweep of his hand the direction she should take. As she reached the top step of the front terrace and approached the huge front door Claire halted abruptly, her eyes staring wide in shock.

A powerfully built youth, totally naked except for a black bow tie and a half smile stood dutifully by the open front door. His enormous cock hung limply down between his thick thighs and he showed not the slightest hint of embarrassment. Huge chest muscles gleamed in the light, his firm backside jutted out temptingly and his bulging biceps gave a clear indication as to the power his body possessed.

Claire flushed bright red and hesitated. She averted her eyes from his cock but as secretively as she could her gaze flicked back often to the huge member.

"Follow me please Madam," the youth stated loudly and led off through the house.

Claire followed in stunned silence, her interest firmly fixed on the servant's firm naked buttocks as he moved unhurriedly through the corridors and out onto the rear terrace.

"Claire!" Arabella squealed in delight.

She was seated at a small wrought iron table surrounded by four ornately worked chairs and rose to her feet in greeting.

"Thanks for accepting. It is so wonderful to see you again."

Claire moved trance-like, guided by her hostess to sit and to settle herself on one of the patio chairs.

At a snap of Arabella's fingers the servant came close and placed a tray of drinks on the table before moving away. The stunned woman couldn't resist a fleeting peek at his thick cock once again, she shivered in delight at both the sight of it and the thought of it inside her.

"Nice isn't he?" Arabella said casually as she handed Claire a drink and settled herself lazily in her seat. Claire could only nod at first, her mind was still taking in the opulent surroundings and the fact that her servant could walk around totally naked as though it were normal and nothing out of the ordinary.

"Wonderful," she blurted at last.

"He's quite a good fuck too," Arabella said with a casual ease.

Claire almost choked on her drink.

"What?" she squealed in surprise. "You actually....have sex with him?"

Arabella smiled broadly and nodded.

"All eleven of them actually."

A casual wave of her hand brought Vincent the servant to her side. Arabella raised her hand to rest his thick cock lightly in the palm of her hand. Her slim, delicate fingers closed around its girth and kneaded the huge member casually.

"Vincent," Arabella said casually as she caressed him, "is one of my favourites, he does so respond to a good blow-job. Don't you Vincent?"

"Yes, Madam," he replied dutifully.

Claire sat spellbound, watching intently as the huge cock twitched and rose in hardness under the gentle coaxing of Arabella's hand.

"Like to try it?" Arabella asked casually as though offering a biscuit.

Claire flushed and shook her head. Her insides were taut with tension, she wanted so very badly to be doing exactly that but her sheltered upbringing and strict social code were too deeply ingrained in her.

His cock was fully hard now; the foreskin pulled back tightly and seemingly painfully along the thick shaft, the velvety head rounded and full seemed to pulse its excitement.

"Mind if I do?" Arabella asked politely and glanced at Claire for confirmation.

Claire simply nodded and watched in amazement as Arabella closed her soft lips over his bulbous glans and slid her mouth far down onto the thick cock.

Mewing her contentment, Arabella sucked and moved her head on him, her cheeks pumping in a steady rhythm of pure sexual greed.

Great stabbing sensations in her vulva brought Claire close to her peak as she watched the erotic act, her gaze flicking up on occasions to see the delight etched on the servant's face. Every nerve end in her body cried out to be in Arabella's place, she cursed herself for being so hesitant and reserved and then gave a stifled gasp as the man came to orgasm, shooting his seed deep into Arabella mouth and groaning loudly as she sucked hard to drain him.

Arabella, sat back smiling, her lips coated with a smear of his seed, she wiped them clean with a tissue and looked across at Claire.

"You haven't changed have you?" she said kindly. "Still the prim and proper Claire that I knew at school. But you are here for the whole weekend, perhaps after a little while you might loosen up a bit."

A guided tour of the house followed, it was truly enormous Claire thought. An indoor swimming pool to the rear side of the house built within a huge glass conservatory complete with sauna and small gymnasium. Games room, study, lounge and dining room all made up the ground floor. Upstairs was equally grand with many large bedrooms all ensuite with lavishly decorated bathrooms and accessed by the maze of corridors that ran the length of the house.

The two women rested now in the comfort of the lounge, Arabella lounging back casually with her feet up and resting lazily on the coffee table between them.

"You aren't getting any are you?" Arabella stated firmly to break the silence.

"Sex you mean?" Claire asked and shook her head slowly.

"Problems?" Arabella probed gently.

Claire flushed and shifted a little uncomfortably.

"Some," she said simply.

Arabella's irresistible smile broke, infectious as always it lightened the gloom.

"Use the servants, you are female and to them a mistress - order them to do whatever you want and they will obey."

That surge of excitement passed through her again, Claire desperately wanted to agree but still that in-built reserve was holding her back.

"Me! I couldn't - really I couldn't," she protested weakly.

"Why not?" Arabella demanded icily.

Claire was thrown momentarily by the harsh tone of her friend's voice.

"I don't really know - just not me really I suppose."

Arabella's tone was softer and coaxing, warm and sympathetic toward her hesitant friend.

"You want a good cock - a damned good shag don't you?"

A little shocked at Arabella's choice of words, Claire agreed.

"Yes of course but....well...."

"Guilt at being the unfaithful wife eh?"

"No!" Claire responded firmly and then softened her tone. "No, that's not it. I just feel that it should be private and you know....more loving than the way you did it earlier."

"Prudish then."

"Perhaps, but I couldn't bring myself to tell them to do it."

"Would you like me to tell them for you?"

Claire sat silently, the thought of that muscular youth lying on top of her, his powerful hips forcing her thighs apart driving his big cock hard into her pussy made her shiver.

"Well...."

"That's settled then!" Arabella clapped her hands in finality and stood up.

"I'll leave you to freshen up and unpack before lunch - that will be on the patio at about twelve - then we can look around the grounds together."

The third turning left along the long corridor, Claire recited to herself as she made her way to what was her bedroom for the weekend. The maze of turnings made finding her room all the more confusing because of the identical look of all the many doors.

It was so sudden, she didn't even have time to scream. The hand came around from behind to clamp hard over her mouth, the air crushed from her lungs as a strong arm pulled at her waist to pin her slight body back onto his. Claire was propelled forward at mind-blurring pace, her feet clear of the floor she was carried hurriedly into one of the rooms. A powerful hand clamped onto the back of her neck to force her face down on the bed and to push her face deep into the soft quilt. Her legs flailed uselessly against the powerful man as her blouse was roughly ripped from her body, the knee pressing down in the small of her back forced most of the fight from her.

She winced as her bra strap was brutally torn from her body to bare her back, she murmured into the bedclothes as her skirt was flipped up and her thin panties ripped unceremoniously from her body.

Claire froze as she felt the head of a cock nudging between the tops of her thighs. The knee was removed, the hand on her neck moved down to press hard in the centre of her shoulder blades. She let out a great gasp as the big cock pressed against the entrance to her pussy and pushed up inside her.

Wonderfully hard and warm, filling her so completely and stretching her little used pussy lips tightly around its great girth the feel of the cock thrilled her. As it began a steady pumping into her soft interior Claire moaned in delight. It felt so wonderfully welcome and horny. Gone was the guilt for she hadn't asked for this but knew that she needed it so badly. Her hands bunched into tight fists, gripping at the quilt as the sensations washed over her. Hard and brutally he rammed into her, jerking his hips on the inward strokes to force every last inch of his cock into her.

It was a high, a charge like no other, to be raped, had against her will and fucked so very savagely into the bargain. Claire moaned her pleasure, moving her buttocks gratefully upward to meet his pounding hips.

Great waves of exquisite sensation tore through her, her head felt light and her mind distant. Bolts of electric stabbing pleasure tore at her insides and then she came. Her little voice cried out, her back arched and she shuddered with each jolt of pleasure that shook her body. Claire gasped as his wash of sperm, warm and powerful shot up deep inside her body and then she slumped sated into the thick quilt.

In the misty stupor of post-orgasmic bliss it was Arabella's voice that she heard from somewhere seemingly far away.

"Cock at last eh? Don't forget now - lunch is at twelve."

26

Claire rested her head and allowed the blackness to envelope her.

***

Sitting at the little table on the terrace in the bright sunshine Claire looked out over the distant hills. She felt complete, better than she had in months. Her body seemed to glow and radiate her happiness, she felt like smiling and did so broadly. She wore jeans and ankle-boots, a baggy sweatshirt in pale cream and her hair tied back in a ponytail. Bathed and rested, she felt ready to take on the world, a whole new confidence bubbling away inside her.

"Oh my!" Arabella gasped as she came out of the open patio doors. "No need to ask how you are feeling- you look positively wholesome!"

Claire blushed under the compliment and felt self-conscious that Arabella both knew of her sexual encounter and had seen her virtually naked.

"Thought you needed a little help in getting to grips with him," Arabella said knowingly and sat herself down. "Good?"

Claire couldn't contain herself.

"Brilliant! Absolutely marvellous! The best...."

"Fuck?"

"Yes that...."

"Say it!" Arabella demanded. "Say the word."

Claire hesitated.

"Fuck," she repeated softly and then almost shouted the word once more. "Fuck! The best fuck ever!"

Arabella laughed loudly at the enthusiasm that Claire held in her voice.

"Thanks," Claire offered more seriously.

"My pleasure," Arabella giggled. "And not just a little of yours either I think. Ready for lunch?"

Claire sighed heavily.

"Famished, I could eat a...."

27

"Cock perhaps?" Arabella quipped and raised her eyebrows mischievously.

Both women giggled loudly like the two schoolgirls they had once been. Arabella laughed longer though and then her tone became serious.

"Not for us my dear Claire, the servants always eat first."

"Oh - sorry," Claire stuttered in confusion.

Arabella smiled and clapped her hands. She shifted forward on her seat and parted her legs, lifting her skirt to show her naked thighs and pussy beneath.

Claire watched spellbound as the big black servant, naked and erect came out to kneel before Arabella. His head dipped down between her thighs and his tongue began lapping greedily at her pussy. So engrossed was she in the scene before her that it was a moment or two before she was aware of the blond Paul standing before her.

"If madam would remove her jeans I will be able to serve her," he said politely.

At first Claire hadn't realised that he was addressing her and not Arabella. A powerful surge shot through her at the very thought. She stood slowly and unclipped her jeans to slide them and her panties down to the floor. Claire sat again as the blond servant pulled her jeans over her boots, folded them neatly and laid them carefully aside.

Almost automatically she parted her knees, gasping loudly as his big hands rested tenderly on her upper thighs. Claire drew breath as his soft warm tongue licked at the swollen labia, first one and then the other in an exciting alternating pattern. She tensed, her hands gripping his powerful shoulders as his tongue first probed at her soft inner lips and then pushed up inside her. Wild series of sensation tore through her, thrilling and exciting horny and so very, very pleasant.

Her hands moved to grip is hair, her hands pulling his head harder down onto her open pussy. She was panting hard, her mouth open in a silent pleading for release. The excited grunts and moans from Arabella spurred her on to grind her mons hard against his face.

Claire screamed in delight as he dragged his rough tongue over her hard clitoris in long cat-like strokes. So wonderfully powerful and so deeply satisfying. Harder she bucked against his face, a sadistic streak coming to the fore as she delighted in his mumbled discomfort. All that mattered to her was her own pleasure and she urged him frantically on toward her peak.

She screamed aloud, her body locking rigid and her thighs clamping tightly together around his head as she came.

Claire sat as she had finished, naked from the waist down and her knees wide apart. There was a new sense of freedom about her, no embarrassment did she feel, only the warm sun on her upper thighs and pussy.

"Now it's our turn to eat," Arabella giggled.

"Which one?" Claire asked confidently. "Which of them fucked me earlier?"

"Ah!" Arabella teased. "Have to know do you? Tell you what, try them all over the weekend and then you tell me if you can work out which one of them it was."

Claire grinned and her clitoris jolted in reaction.

"Mmm! Sounds a most interesting puzzle to solve."

Over a huge ham salad and bottle of white wine the two friends chatted non-stop about old times and the highlights of their times spent together at school. The subject changed eventually as Claire tried to steer the conversation back to the sexual arrangements at the manor.

"So how do you do it?" she probed. "You order the men around with such casual ease and never a word of dissent from any of them."

Arabella gave a sly grin.

"Because I am a good mistress to them. Why? Interested in learning?"

"Yes!" Claire blurted almost too readily. "Yes, yes I am."

Arabella stared deep into her eyes.

"It can be hard and painful," she warned. "You have seen nothing yet, simply - shall we say - the starters before the

29

main course."

"My god!" Claire breathed. "You mean there is more?"

Arabella giggled.

"Much more," she paused for effect. "But pain and discipline come first as do humiliation and suffering."

"How do you mean?" Claire asked naively.

Arabella sat back, crossed her legs lazily and spoke with ease.

"Bondage, spanking and all manner of punishments to be administered to the men."

Claire sat wide-eyed trying to take in what she was being told.

"But," Arabella continued, "you have to experience it all yourself first - otherwise how would you know what the men are experiencing and more to the point - what they are suffering."

Claire found herself nodding in agreement.

"Not sure about the kinky bits though, they don't sound very exciting to me."

"Before today, if I had asked you if being raped could be considered fun would you have agreed?"

A moment passed as Claire pondered the question.

"Point taken."

"It's the same with spanking and humiliation. Sounds not too nice at first but as you experience the thrill of command, the powerful pleasures of control and assertive training, the terrific orgasms that come with it all........!"

"Okay! Okay!" Claire calmed her friend. "I believe you - I'm convinced."

Arabella leaned forward across the table to tenderly hold Claire's hand.

"Such deep pleasures unknown," she breathed sensually. "All waiting to be discovered."

"Teach me," Claire breathed in response. "Teach me, Arabella, please."

"Could you take it I wonder? Would you serve and accept

30

all the pain and humiliation required as part of the training?"

"Yes," Claire said hoarsely.

"I wonder," Arabella whispered.

Claire gripped tightly on Arabella's hand.

"I would be, I am ready to accept it. I would serve, I would comply. Please Arabella I need it and want it. I have the taste and now I need more."

The lady sat back, a deliberate expression of uncertainty on her face.

"Let me think on it. I'll decide tomorrow."

Deflated, Claire nodded her reluctant acceptance and squeezed her thighs together secretly beneath the table.

***

The grounds were vast and they only covered the areas immediately surrounding the house that afternoon and evening. The stable block and servants quarters in a huge annex at the back, the potting sheds and kitchen gardens behind the high walls, the neat and well-maintained gardens to the front and the densely wooded area to the side of the house. Claire warmed more to Arabella as they walked and talked freely. She felt comfortable in her presence, as though the woman was and always had been a close and valued friend.

No area was closed to her and not one of her questions went unanswered, Arabella was the perfect host and mistress of her domain. Claire enjoyed the afternoon tremendously as she did the evening meal. With two naked servants to ogle and a hearty steak to help feed her rising hunger Claire felt warm and relaxed as she pulled on her pyjamas and turned back the sheets.

A knock at the door halted Claire and Arabella entered smiling broadly. She stepped back as two of her male servants walked in and stood facing Claire's bed. Without instruction they bent forward and placed their hands on the bed.

"Try them and choose one - you can't sleep alone here -

why, I should never forgive myself for such inhospitable behaviour," Arabella grinned.

She cupped one servant's balls in her hand and weighed them lightly.

"Come on!" she urged sternly. "Have a feel and make your choice."

Her pussy gripping in little light flutters, Claire moved behind the bending men and slid her hand beneath the balls of the first one. She gasped at the waves of sensation it produced in her. Arabella gripped Claire's pyjama bottoms and slid them down with not a hint of protest from the girl.

"Feel the other one then," Arabella directed and pulled the top up over Claire's head to leave her stark naked.

"This one," Claire's excited voice quavered as she teased at the second man's balls.

"Excellent choice, my dear," Arabella said gleefully. "Now kneel on the bed, Claire."

With heart beating fast and pussy moist, Claire complied. On all fours she positioned herself with back arched and buttocks high. She trembled in delight as the servant moved in between her parted legs and pressed his cock flat against the crease of her buttocks. His big hands gripped her hips and pulled her hard back against him.

Under Arabella's direction the second servant positioned himself on the bed in front of Claire with his long cock level with her head.

"But I've never...." Claire protested weakly.

"What? Sucked cock?" Arabella asked with casual ease. "Nothing to it. Just get it in you mouth for starters and take it from there."

Hesitantly Claire opened her mouth as the huge head of his cock moved inward. She closed her eyes and shivered involuntarily as the first contact was made. It felt as though her mouth would split open as he pushed gently inside her warm cavern.

It was warm, hot even and throbbing in excitement, his

cock felt so very big in her mouth yet so wonderful. Claire relaxed and took more of it into her, Arabella's soft coaxing voice eased the passage of the huge member into her mouth and Claire was grateful for her guidance.

He began to move, a slow and gentle fucking of her mouth. The long thick rod sliding back and forth between her soft inviting lips.

So pleasant now did it feel that Claire began sucking and using her tongue, the pounding excitement inside her building rapidly. She gasped and almost came as the man behind shifted his hips to locate the head of his cock at the entrance to her open pussy and then pushed in.

The incredible feel and thrill of two men at once was beyond description. Claire sucked harder and more greedily as the cock moved up inside her pussy to fill her completely. She felt a whore, a loose woman who would have any cock she could and the best part was, that she didn't give a damn. Claire mewed contentedly and pressed back against his hips as the cock began driving hard into her from behind. Wild pulses of sensation and pleasure filled her, her need was urgent and her responses frantic. So enthusiastic was her sucking and fucking that she didn't hear Arabella wish her goodnight and leave the room closing the door quietly behind her.

CHAPTER THREE

Claire had risen early, showered and dressed she stood on the patio looking out once again over the stunning panorama of the estate. Her pussy felt a little sore and her nipples were still tender from the two servants' eager attentions during the night.

In just one day and night Claire had experienced more sex than she had had in nearly a year and far better sex than she had ever had. To have two such good-looking men lying by

33

her side, their hands roaming her freely and taking her as they wished in an alternating system of virtually continuous sex. She felt so desirable and wanted, so sexually alive it almost hurt. Claire stretched lazily and turned back to the house.

She stopped in her tracks, stunned into immovable silence at the sight before her. The tall Arabella stood arrogantly, her feet planted wide and in her hand an evil-looking riding crop. Her black hair had been styled to hug closely to the sides of her head and cheeks, bright red lipstick and heavy mascara gave her a menacing yet sensual appearance. It was her clothing though that increased the sinister look of the tall Madam. A tight leather suit clung to her body like a second skin, pulling harshly across the swell of her breasts and down over the mound of her mons. The suit was so tight that it seemed as if her body had been painted to leave just her face and hands showing as bare flesh.

"Strip," Arabella growled menacingly.

It took a moment for Claire to respond, the shock of seeing Arabella dressed so had thrown her completely in her thoughts. There was confusion, conflict even, in her brain as she pulled her sweatshirt up over her head and slipped down her jeans.

Arabella looked so commanding and confident, so sensual and so bloody attractive. Why? Claire asked herself as she threw her bra aside, should she feel aroused at the sight of another woman?

Her panties discarded, Claire stood naked and unashamed before her tall friend. A ripple of nervousness gripped her, for Arabella's expression remained severe her stare harsh and uncompromising.

Arabella moved, her long slim legs seemingly endless as the tight leather hugged close around them. She circled Claire menacingly, inspecting her closely in an unnerving silence. The crop rested lightly on the top of Claire's right shoulder to sent a shiver of fear running through the girl's body.

"When I give you a command," Arabella said in a low

34

voice close to Claire's ear, "you will obey and you will obey quickly. Do you understand bitch?"

Claire gasped. 'Bitch!' To be insulted felt so good, demeaning and humiliating but so very exciting.

"Yes," she uttered softly.

Claire yelped as the crop stung her buttock, her hand instinctively clamped over the affected area to soothe and protect.

"Madam!" Arabella hissed venomously. "You will call me Madam!"

Claire swallowed hard. Fear ran through her body yet her clitoris jerked in response to add to the confusion in her mind.

"Yes, Madam."

"Louder!" Arabella shouted. "And keep your hands by your sides."

Instantly Claire moved her hands to stand rigid and motionless.

"Yes, Madam," she almost shouted back.

Again Arabella circled her menacingly, her look was one of distaste and displeasure with the girl.

"So. You want to learn do you bitch?"

"Yes," Claire said nervously and screamed as the crop stung harshly at the outside of her thigh.

"Madam!" Arabella screamed angrily. "Madam! You will call me Madam!"

"Sorry! Sorry, Madam," Claire uttered quickly with tears forming in her eyes.

The tone softened to a velvety coaxing but still contained a harsh threat..

"I will teach you bitch and you will learn or suffer the consequences. You most certainly will."

"Yes, Madam," Claire said quickly and loudly.

She tensed as the tip of the riding crop touched beneath her buttocks and slid gently between her thighs to tease at her labia.

"Was your hungry little pussy well fucked last night bitch?"

"Yes Madam."

The crop pulled rapidly away from her and Claire flinched in anticipation of the blow that she expected to land on her.

"Clive!" Arabella yelled loudly. "Assemble the servants immediately."

She turned again to face the trembling Claire.

"And who?" she demanded, "gave you permission to sleep with my servants?"

Claire looked at her quizzically.

"But you did....Madam!"

"Liar!" Arabella screamed loudly, her face close to Claire's and spittle spraying out in her anger.

The servants came out onto the terrace and formed a single line facing Claire. All were naked as was usual except for black bow ties around their throats.

"This bitch" Arabella announced loudly to the servants. "This worthless slut, has the audacity to call your mistress a liar!"

"No!" Claire protested tearfully. "I didn't mean that!"

Arabella whirled to face her.

"Didn't you?" she asked sarcastically. "What then did you mean, slut?"

Claire sobbed, she was confused and shivering in fear. It was all so humiliating and in front of all the men even more so.

"I don't know, can't think," Claire sobbed pitifully. "You're confusing me."

"Punished," Arabella sneered gleefully. "You will be whipped for your insults."

Arabella stepped back and raised the cop high above her shoulder.

"Oh God!" Claire whispered urgently to Arabella. "I need the toilet - badly."

Madam lowered the crop and tapped the tip against Claire's pussy.

"Huh!" Arabella announced loudly to the servants. "The

36

bitch is going to pee herself!"

Claire groaned in deep humiliation, her face bright red, she simply wanted to hide her face but wasn't able. Her hips jerked forward in reaction, a dazzling flash of shock hit in her brain as the pain registered. The searing agony in her buttocks then burned deep into her soft flesh.

"Suffer bitch," Arabella screeched. "Suffer for your wanton ways."

Claire's eyes locked wide and her mouth gaped open as the second lash stung cruelly at her tender backside. Her bladder throbbed its need to deflate, her pussy muscles clamping tightly in an effort to hold back the flow. Her body jerked as the third lash of the crop stung at her and then it happened. A slow trickle at first oozed from her pussy, the hot urine trickling down the inside of her thigh. A fourth lash of the crop bit home and Claire screamed before sobbing in humiliation as the urine spurted forcefully from her. Deflected by her labia, the warm flow sprayed her thighs and legs to puddle between her feet on the grey slabs of the terrace. Claire sobbed in great body jerking heaves, she just wanted to die.

The continuing lashes of the crop seemed unimportant now, numbed and distant even as she hung her head in shame before the watching men. The flow down her legs just simply too humiliating to accept.

It took her by surprise, no warning given by her body, the orgasm shot through her with the force of a tornado. Her body locked, her head threw back and she screamed as she came. Claire's knees buckled and she slumped to the floor panting hard in her pain and pleasure.

***

"So?" Natalie asked excitedly. "Tell me!"

Claire moved around the broad mahogany desk and eased the telephone lead over the blotter, then settled herself in the big leather chair. She held the receiver close to her face and

37

talked with great enthusiasm into the phone.

"Listen, Natalie. It is simply great! Can't say too much at the moment but when your turn comes - you will love it!"

Natalie's pleading voice came back down the line.

"You can't do this to me - we had an agreement! I need to know, the others want to know."

"Patience bitch," Claire said sensually.

There was a stunned silence and then.

"What did you say? What did you call me?"

Claire giggled.

"Only one night here and I've got to grips with the local phrases and terms already."

No reply came.

"Wait and see, Natalie. If I tell you it would ruin the surprise."

A pause followed and then.

"You're the bitch!" Natalie moaned playfully.

"See!" Claire giggled. "Getting into the swing of it already aren't you? Talk on Monday, bye for now."

Claire hung up and sat back smiling. She had discovered so much about herself in such a short time here. The pain from her beating as she reflected on it had actually been in a way, pleasant. Agonising at the time and a real shock to her but it had been so very horny too. The humiliation that she had suffered had been deliberate, she understood that now. Unpleasant though it had been the men here seemed to accept it with a casual ease.

The orgasm that she had experienced during her thrashing, well that was the stunning part. Orgasm from pain and humiliation, Claire would never have thought it possible. It had been so powerful and racking and had been made all the more intense by having an audience to witness her ultimate and usually private pleasure.

No doubt about it she thought, her levels of acceptance were changing - and for the better.

The marks on her buttocks were still sore but she bore

them with pride now. She considered them the price of learning and looked forward very much to the day she would herself graduate.

***

A thick rope pulled her knees in tightly together to make even standing a difficult operation much less walking. Her wrists were bound tightly behind her back and the elbows pulled painfully in together and tied equally as securely. The thick collar around her neck rubbed uncomfortably against her soft throat as Arabella pulled hard on the long leash attached to it.

"Stop dawdling slut and get a move on," Arabella snapped in irritation.

She swiped cruelly with the thin cane at Claire's outer thigh to bring a low grunt of pain in response.

The rough ground, stones and twigs all bit harshly into the soft soles of Claire's bare feet. The narrow track that led into the woods was dry and sun-baked giving little comfort to the shuffling motion of her legs that Claire was obliged to take. Stumbling and waddling Claire worked her legs hard to try to keep pace with her mistress.

She tripped, sprawling headlong into the thick undergrowth, sharp thorns tearing at her soft flesh. Only the ball-gag in her mouth muffled her cries of despair as she rolled to a sitting position in an effort to stand.

Arabella towered over her, the long boots finishing just above her knees to show her slender thighs to great effect. Tight little panties in soft pliable leather and cut high on her hip made her legs look even longer than they actually were. Her breasts, perfectly symmetrical and supported on what were just platforms rather than a bra were naked and exposed. The long rubbery nipples jutted out temptingly in hardness to portray her rising excitement. Little golden rings hung from each of her firm buds to glint brightly in the sunshine.

"You continue to mock me, don't you slut?"

39

Claire shook her head rapidly, her eyes wide with fear. The cane sliced through the air to cut hard into the soft thigh of the cowering girl. Twice more she lashed her before grasping her hair roughly and hauling her bodily to her feet.

"Keep up or suffer," Arabella snapped and strode off again pulling on the leash to drag the struggling Claire behind her.

At length they reached a wooden gate, about five feet in height and six feet wide it had three main horizontal bars and was of a heavy construction. Arabella drew Claire to a halt and removed the ball-gag.

"You, slut, displease me. Your constant failure to comply, your half-hearted attitude toward your training is unacceptable. Punishment inevitably follows such failure."

"Yes Madam," Claire responded dutifully.

Her knees released Claire was guided up to sit on and astride the top rail of the gate. About five inches wide the thick top rail slotted between her thighs and proved an uncomfortable seat for the young woman. The leash pulled Claire's head down close onto the rail in front of her and was tied off securely to leave the girl in a 'jockey' position astride the gate. With her buttocks high and her pussy pressing down on the thick wooden spar it was an ungainly and most precarious position.

At the first lash of the cane across her backside Claire realised the reason for the position. Her body jerked to crush and drag her hard clitoris on the rough surface of the beam. The sensations that it produced were electrifying, pain in her backside combined with the sudden jolt of pressure and pleasure from her clitoris made her pussy grip tightly. The second lash whilst harsher than the first increased those terrific sensations.

Claire's little body bucked in reaction at each hard lash of the thin cane, the feelings and pleasure simply increased with each sting as the sweet agony rose in intensity. Her mouth hung open and she fought for breath as the rate of stinging blows increased. Fast and hard they stung at her soft flesh until that warm wash of pre-orgasmic ripples flowed through her. She cried out, tensed her body and came to a shattering orgasm that saw her grinding her clitoris hard down on the wooden gate. She was lost in her own world of deep sexual pleasure as she rubbed herself frantically on the hard wooden spar. Claire slowed and rested, panting hard as the after shocks of pleasure shook her body in little gripping convulsions.

"You learn fast, bitch," Arabella said softly in compliment. "There is hope for you yet."

Madam's hand smoothed over the curve of her reddened buttocks, Claire gave an involuntary shiver as the woman touched her. The thrill of the caressing was tremendous, a gripping in her pussy seemed to urge Arabella's fingers to move towards it. She closed her eyes and steeled herself to receive a female touch on her pussy for the first time ever.

"Little bitch needs to learn patience," Arabella sang and withdrew her hand.

Claire let out a great sigh, not of relief but of deep disappointment.

***

Natalie almost ran across the wide shopping mall toward their meeting place in the coffee shop. She moved quickly between the rows of table, dodging customers and waitresses alike. The girl reached the table and sat, her eyes wide with interest her breathing hard and laboured.

"Well?" she asked between breaths as she laid her handbag and coat on the seat next to her.

Claire giggled, Natalie's eager interest amused her, the hungry expression on her face most comical.

"Fantastic! Truly fantastic."

"What was - what's it all about? Tell me you mean thing!" Natalie questioned excitedly.

"Sex!"

Natalie stared back, her eyes searching Claire's face for

41

signs of jest - there were none.

"Are you serious?"

"Deadly," came the curt reply.

They paused as the waitress placed two coffees on the table before them and then moved away.

"Sex such as you have never known - could never have even dreamt of. Wild and different, horny as hell."

Natalie still regarded her friend with a little suspicion.

"How so? How different?"

Claire sat back in her seat, lounging confidently.

"Sorry but that part you will have to wait for and see for yourself."

"But you can't leave me dangling! That isn't fair! My invitation isn't for well over a month."

"Be all the better when you do go then, won't it?"

Natalie realised that she would get no further on that approach.

"Just a hint then," she pleaded in a little-girl voice.

Claire leaned forward across the table and lowered her voice to a secretive whisper.

"Orgasms, orgasms so plentiful and powerful that they will send you to paradise and back."

Natalie swallowed hard, her eyes wide.

"Wow!"

"Pure sex in its rawest form - exciting sex and best of all," she said and paused for effect. "it's all laid on for you at the manor."

"Must admit," Natalie breathed in response. "A little of that certainly wouldn't go amiss. It's okay for you, you're married but me? I have to take what I can get and when."

"Being married doesn't automatically entitle you to regular goodies but the manor sure does. My pussy is still sore to prove it."

"Oh God!" Natalie moaned wistfully.

Again Claire used a low voice, controlled her own rising excitement.

"How does two beefy young studs both going at you all night sound?"

"Heavenly," Natalie giggled.

"Both at the same time?"

Natalie's mouth dropped open in surprise.

"Never!"

Claire nodded and smiled. She knew her friend well and could recognise the sexual arousal in her expression and manner. She felt that she could almost read Natalie's mind as her friend sat silently absorbing what she had been told.

The tone became lighter as Claire sipped her coffee and then stated.

"I'm going back next weekend - and the one after that and the next and the next...."

Natalie looked at her and then giggled mischievously.

"That good eh?"

Claire nodded and beamed a smile.

"That good!" she restated emphatically.

***

Robert wasn't amused, he stood up and positioned himself in front of the fireplace as he was prone to do when trying to assert his authority, his hands clasped behind his back, chest out and inflated with self-importance.

"Why the need to go again next weekend?" he asked almost disinterestedly.

Claire sighed to display her impatience with him and shifted in her seat to further show her displeasure at his questioning.

"Because it's a training course, I have explained this to you already"

"Huh!" he snorted in derision. "So our weekends now are to be ruined because of this course."

"We never do anything at weekends anyway," Claire countered. "You watch football, go to the squash club and gener-

43

ally laze around doing the least you possibly can."

He stood pensive for a few moments.

"Well I don't think you should go," he said firmly and in the best authoritative tone he could muster.

Claire looked up from the magazine she was idly reading.

"I couldn't give a fuck what you think!"

Robert was stunned and he flushed in anger.

"What did you say?"

Claire tossed the magazine aside casually and crossed her legs, her stare was direct and challenging.

"You heard me, I don't give a fuck what you think, I'm going and that's all there is to say about it."

"I won't have it!" he retorted angrily.

Claire stood slowly, walked over to her husband and brought her face close to his.

"Like it or lump it because I am going."

He held her stare for several seconds and then backed down.

"Well - if it means that much to you...."

"It does!" she stated firmly.

He had no reply and simply turned and walked away. His usual response to confrontation was to avoid it and retire to the kitchen.

Claire was wet, her pussy throbbing its need. The thrill of challenging him, of holding her ground and taking control was so powerful. To be assertive felt good but to control would be better, she simply had to further the thrill. She walked into the kitchen where Robert sat silently brooding at the table.

"Either you fuck me this week or I'll get someone else to do it for you," she said simply.

Again he looked shocked, his usually demure wife using such coarse language. It was so out of character for her, he was thrown, unable to cope with the change in her. He simply nodded his head in acceptance.

Claire moved to the table, planted her hands firmly on the surface and leaned close to him. Her tone was threatening

44

and full of menace, designed to assert her control over him.

"Was that a yes to you fucking me or my getting someone to do it for you?" she demanded.

He looked up solemnly, a pained and pathetic look on his face.

"Yes to....doing it with you."

The thrill was pumping in her, her clitoris hard and throbbing.

"Fucking me! Say it!" she demanded.

He hesitated.

"Say it!" she hissed threateningly.

"Fucking you," he said softly.

"Louder!"

He swallowed and then repeated the words at the top of his voice.

"Fucking you."

She stood upright and turned, as she reached the doorway he called to her.

"Would you? Get someone else to do it if I don't?"

She paused for a moment without turning and then replied firmly.

"Try me!"

***

It hadn't actually been as painful as Claire had expected it to be. She had dreaded it, since last weekend when Arabella had insisted she be pierced Claire had been both curious and a little frightened. She stood now before her long mirror in the bathroom turning the little golden training rings as she had to each day. At first she could hardly bring herself to touch them but now, days later, it actually stimulated her to do so. The initial swelling had reduced and so too had the soreness, now only pleasure came from her piercings.

Nice sensations came from the turning of the rings, sexual

feelings of naughtiness and thrill. She had discovered too that pulling on the rings sent electric sensation buzzing through her body as her nipples stretched. She took pleasure in watching her reflection, the slim fingers with the red painted nails working so deftly and seemingly naturally to excite her buds.

Claire turned and walked confidently into the bedroom, her naked body erect and her shoulders back to emphasis her breasts.

"Like them?" she asked Robert casually.

He sat naked on the edge of the bed, his eyes roaming her body and then fixing a stare at her nipple rings.

"Why did you have it done?" he asked in surprise.

"Because I wanted to."

Claire moved around him and sat on the bed near the top, her back resting against the headboard in a half-sitting position. She spread her knees wide and raised them to expose her pussy in a base and unabashed fashion.

"Tonight Robert, you will eat me."

He turned to face her, a questioning look on his face.

"You mean....? But I don't do that that....it's, well unhygienic - disgusting."

Claire gripped on a nipple ring with each of her hands and teased herself with little tugs.

"I'm waiting Robert," she hissed impatiently. "Perhaps that will get your little cock stirring into life."

Reluctantly he crawled across the bed on all fours to position himself between her thighs. He mumbled softly to himself and dipped his head down. His eyes closed tightly and his tongue peeked out hesitantly from between his lips.

Claire gasped aloud as the contact was made, his soft warm tongue dipping into her pink inner lips. It delighted her to see him shudder in revulsion as he complied with her wishes.

"Up inside," she moaned, "deep up inside me."

He complied, pushing his wedge of flesh far up inside her open pussy, his body shivering in revulsion.

Claire cried out in pleasure, not so much at his clumsy

46

technique but the way she had him doing her bidding. It thrilled her to see his naked body kneeling before her, his head moving and tongue lapping in an effort to please her. She felt all-powerful and commanding, half-sitting with her legs wide and pussy offered whilst he bowed before her. The sensations she experienced defied belief, so intense and thrilling. Claire twisted the nipple rings to bring yet another set of sensations rushing through her.

"My clit," she moaned in delight. "Do my clit."

He mumbled as his lips closed around the hard bud, he kissed clumsily at her clitoris in a desperate effort to please. At last his tongue came into use, flicking across the very tip of her little bud.

Claire shifted her hips and moaned, her back arching to accept the feelings. She tensed and groaned then came to a mild but pleasant orgasm that made her body shudder in little spasms of delight.

Robert raised his head and body, still kneeling he smiled at Claire, expectant of praise for his efforts. His cock was hard, twitching in little jerking movements of excitement.

"Not good, Robert, not good," she said. "You will practice your fumbled attempts nightly until you perfect it."

His hand gripped his cock to squeeze in pulsing little grips as his excitement grew. The shaft and head bloated in anticipation and expectation of pleasures to come.

"Yes!" Claire breathed urgently. "Yes, wank it. I want to see you wank yourself."

Robert looked back at her challenging glare and capitulated.

His hand began to move, sliding the foreskin back and forth along his shaft.

Claire groaned as she watched, her nipples tingling as she teased at herself with the rings.

Faster he pumped his hand, his eyes closed and head thrown back. He began moaning his pleasure as the sensations rippled through him.

"My pussy," Claire breathed sexily. "Did it taste good Robert?"

He nodded and groaned, his hips jerking in time with his pumping hand.

"Mmmm," she moaned softly. "I must get someone else to lick it for me too."

He came instantly, his sperm shooting forcefully out to splatter over her open pussy and upper thighs. On and on the jerking spurts continued until he gasped loudly and slumped forward onto his hands.

"No excuse now is there Robert?" Claire said. "Your little cock works fine in your own hand and will work equally as well up inside my pussy."

He simply nodded in response.

"Good," she said loudly. "I'm glad we agree. Now you may clean your sperm off me - with your tongue."

His head snapped up to give her a look of total revulsion.

"Or," Claire teased raising her eyebrows, "should I get someone else to do it?"

Without further hesitation Robert dipped his head once more between her thighs, his tongue out and eyes firmly closed.

CHAPTER FOUR

The heels on the shoes were so high that Claire felt she might fall forward. She had worn heels before but never like this; they were six inches and even standing in them was near impossible much less walking. The way the shoes forced her to tense her buttocks tightly pleased Claire for it had a corresponding effect on her pussy and the feelings were wonderful. Her legs too were shaped and sculptured by the awkward position of her feet.

A stinging flick with the long cane at the back of her calf

prompted her back to the present instantly.

"Head up girl!" Arabella snapped. "Back straight chest out."

Madam was seated, naked except for her long boots, on the lap of one of the servants. Her back to him, his hands had circled her waist to cup her breasts, he sat obediently fondling her firm orbs. His cock was buried deep up inside Arabella's pussy and she moved on him only occasionally with a slight jerk of her hips.

Claire complied, she forced her shoulders back and pushed her breasts out to stretch the thin chain that now connected her two nipple rings.

It had started the moment she had arrived at the manor that Friday evening. She had been ordered to strip off on the steps outside the front door and to walk barefoot through the house to the small gym. It was there that Arabella had introduced her to the shoes that now Claire struggled to stand upright in.

She stole the occasional sideways glance at Arabella's parted thighs, the way her labia were stretched wide to accept the thick shaft of his cock inside her pussy. She could see the thick underside of his cock, the main vein prominent in its excitement as it forced her shaven lips apart.

"Keep your bum in I told you," Madam snapped in irritation and lashed her cruelly with the thin cane.

The searing pain burned in her buttocks, an incredibly intense pain that seemed to linger long after the blow had landed on her tender flesh.

Arabella moaned in pleasure, the movement of her body as she had swung the cane had caused the cock inside her to touch the sides of her soft interior. A low and deep moan of pleasure came from her.

"Walk now," she coaxed.

Before Claire could even attempt the first step the servant gave a groan that was followed almost instantly by a gasp from Arabella.

"My servant has just shot his load up inside me," Arabella announced casually.

Claire gasped both at her words and the mental image of his beautiful cock spitting its seed within her body.

"And," Arabella continued, "without my permission."

Again a bolt of sensation shot through Claire. He would be punished that much was certain and the thought of that excited her so very much.

Arabella stood, the thick sperm dripping out of her pussy as she got to her feet. She turned and landed a stinging slap across the servant's face that jarred his head to the side.

"Get out!" she screamed. "Out! Get out of my sight!"

The youth ran from the room, cowering as he went in an effort to avoid the lashing cane that stung at his body.

Arabella stood now like a circus trainer, the long cane poised ready to strike should her charge not comply with her wishes.

"Walk!" she commanded.

She took a first hesitant step, ungainly and clumsy it may have been but she succeeded and the more steps she took the easier it became and the better it felt, her body erect and proud.

"Chin up," Arabella's harsh voice coaxed and she tapped at Claire's backside with the cane.

For a whole hour she walked, turned and posed in the high heels and by the end of that time her whole body felt leaner, more poised and elegant. Her soft pale skin was crisscrossed with thin red stripes to bear testament to Madam's harsh coaxing and teaching.

"Enough for today," Arabella called a halt. "Take the shoes home with you after the weekend and practice, at least two hours a day.

"Yes, Madam," Claire responded pleasantly.

"See that you do girl or suffer my wrath."

***

Being tied was something that Claire was now becoming accustomed to, it seemed to form a great part of Arabella's training of her. To be restricted and helpless was certainly thrilling, the unknown and the inability to be able to defend oneself was exciting in the extreme. It was the first time however that she had been strapped down and found this many times more stimulating.

Claire was naked and laid back on a padded couch that stood about waist height. Her wrists and ankles were firmly strapped with wide leather cuffs that pulled her arms and legs wide apart. Heavily padded pillows beneath her backside forced her hips high to offer her mons and pussy in unhindered openness.

Arabella's deft hands used the thin scissors expertly to snip back Claire's dark thatch of pubic hair until only a rough stubble remained.

It thrilled Claire, not that Arabella had actually touched her sex but the very thought of it, the teasing thrill of the anticipation raised Claire's level of arousal to its highest state yet. She gasped as the warm shaving foam was brushed thoroughly all around her labia and mons; the bristles of the brush bringing delightful sensations rippling through her. A thousand little needles of caressing and teasing delight rubbing over her aroused sex. Claire drew breath as the sharp razor scraped at her flesh, so close, so dangerous and yet so bloody horny.

Tenderly Arabella worked, taking care to avoid either too hard a pressure or to create soreness with the blade. Once finished, Arabella patted the bare skin dry and dusted it liberally with sweet smelling talcum powder.

"That's better!" Madam announced proudly. "A bald pussy is such a delight both to see and to touch."

Claire shuddered at her words, a surge of nervous thrill shot through her. She gasped as Arabella's soft lips kissed tenderly just above her knee. Up her thigh the soft lips moved, planting a series of the lightest kisses on Claire's trembling

51

flesh as they moved towards their goal.

She cried out and tensed as the next anticipated kiss would land on her labia. Then she groaned her disappointment as the kiss landed on her other thigh just above the knee and began its slow journey back up. Madam's lips came close, almost touching her swollen and expectant labia before moving back to start once again at her knee.

"Please," Claire murmured in pleasure. "Please."

She gasped loudly, her back arching as the lips now changed to the tip of Arabella's tongue. Lightly, teasingly, it traced a line up toward her open pussy.

"Oh God!" Claire uttered as the soft worm of flesh reached close to her pussy.

She cried out in deep delight as the tongue flicked first at one side of her labia then the other. Teasingly it moved to thrill, circling now and threatening even to dip in between.

"Unnnh!" Claire grunted as the warm tongue delved in to taste her soft pink inner lips.

Her buttocks clenched tightly, her anus tensed in delight as the sensations of excitement and naughtiness rushed through her entire body. A woman's touch on her, so sensual and caring, so knowing and so very wonderful.

Claire screamed her delight as the soft lips now gripped around her hard bud of a clitoris. Her body shook in tingling little spasms as the pleasure washed over her. She screamed again and came as the soft tongue flicked across the very tip of her clitoris to bring her to her peak.

Without the chance to savour or recover from her racking orgasm, Claire felt two of Arabella's fingers pushing deep up inside her pussy.

"Grip them," Madam ordered. "Grip them with your internal muscles."

She tried but nothing happened.

"But I can't Madam, I don't know how," Claire moaned softly.

"Then we must assist you," Arabella giggled softly and

placed the finger of her left hand at the entrance to Claire's anus.

"No!" Claire protested loudly. "Please no! Not in there."

The long slim finger pressed against the tight circle of muscles surrounding Claire's most private of places.

Claire's body tensed, her inner muscles contracting to grip around the length of the fingers inside her. The sensations it produced caused the young woman to groan in delight before she relaxed her grip. Again the finger hovering at her anus pressed in slightly to repeat the process and to again grip her body around the fingers inside her.

Claire screamed loudly as, in one swift move, the long finger forced hard up into her anus. Her pussy muscles clamped tightly around the fingers inside her, she came to a thunderous orgasm that shook her whole body in violent shudders of deep pleasure.

"That's much better," Arabella praised and swiftly extracted her fingers.

Claire lay moaning and fully sated. The burning sensation in her backside mixed with her feelings of passionate delight at having experienced the using of her internal muscles. As she lay savouring the feelings she imagined a man's cock up inside her and of repeating the gripping around his shaft.

***

Arabella stood behind her using her knee to gain the extra purchase required, she buckled the strap and stepped back.

The training harness was of a strong leather construction it pulled her shoulders painfully back and together to force her chest out. Claire bore the pain gratefully as the trailing leash was pulled hard down to the thick belt that circled her hips. Uncomfortably erect, Claire's back arched to ease a little of the strain and she knelt passively whilst Arabella adjusted it further. Her wrists were then strapped tightly together behind her back and anchored to the wide hip-belt.

"Stand," Arabella commanded and stood watching as Claire struggled to her feet.

Claire was more used to the high heels now, her feet and body adjusting quickly to the sharp incline of the soles.

Once standing, Madam allowed herself a slow and lengthy feel of Claire's firm breasts, kissing the warm orbs and tweaking the nipple rings to further excite the girl.

Claire gasped and tensed as Madam twisted the rings cruelly, raw agony shooting through her breasts to feed through to her brain.

"You, bitch," Arabella breathed excitedly, "are now beginning to look like a woman in authority."

Back and forth Claire paced, adjusting her stride and the roll of her hips under Madam's guidance. Her chin up and head back, her shoulders forced further back still, Claire began to feel the very same herself. More poised and elegant, a sense of command and control simply by using her body in the correct way. The liberal use of the short cane stinging frequently at her body helped tremendously too.

"Excellent! Excellent!" Madam praised. "You progress well slut."

She took two thin straps, clipped them to the back of the hip-belt and passed them through Claire's legs. With a savage yank the thin straps were pulled harshly upward to squash Claire's labia tightly together. The pressure was immense with one strap on either side of her swollen lips. The ends were then secured to the front of the belt.

"Walk!" Arabella ordered.

At the very first step it hit her. The thumping surge of sensation racked Claire's body as her lips rubbed around and against her hard clitoris. The second step was more powerful in the charge it gave her and the third more intense still. It was moving masturbation, bringing herself to arousal and rubbing herself off as she walked. Claire moaned her delight as the feelings pumped through her. Each move of her thighs brought new and more powerful feelings, she felt light-headed and

54

distant, the electric sensations pumping her excitement to an all-time high.

Claire walked, turned and walked again as Madam barked the commands. All the time her body alive and seeming to urge her orgasm on. Claire moaned as the pre-ripples began to flutter through her, she steeled herself ready for the great surge of climax.

"Stop!" Madam snapped coldly.

The disappointment was all too clear on Claire's face. She was flushed and ready, so desperately in need of the sweet peak of sexual arousal.

Madam strapped a bar from one of Claire's ankles to the other to force her feet apart and to prevent further stimulation of her hard bud.

"Please, Madam," Claire whimpered softly.

Arabella smiled sardonically, her red lips moving so sensually as she gloated.

"Patience slut. You are far too eager."

Tiny pear-shaped weights that shimmered their silvery glint in the light were attached to threads and suspended from Claire's nipple rings. The incredible tearing sensations were painful but nice as the full weight pulled and stretched her nipples downward.

Arabella momentarily dipped a finger into Claire's pussy to test her wetness then sucked greedily on it to taste the sweet juices of the young woman.

"Mmmm, you are proving to be a most worthy student," Arabella complimented.

The door of the room opened and two servants entered; the big black youth Claude and the ever- faithful Jason. Together they sandwiched Madam's body between them; Claude at her back with his enormous cock pressing flat between the cheeks of her backside and his hands around her body cupping her breasts. Jason pressed against her stomach before shifting his hips to slip his cock up inside her pussy. As he slowly thrust into his mistress, his mouth sucked at her nipples whilst Claude's black hands kneaded them gently.

Arabella's head rested back on Claude's shoulders and she moaned her pleasure as the two youths attended her needs.

Claire was helpless, bound so securely that she could do nothing to ease the burning need within her. She wanted those cocks inside her own body, to experience those wonderful warm feelings as they fucked her. She silently cursed Arabella for having the fun and leaving her purely as a spectator. Her pussy tingled and ached, her nipples were stretched and sore but aroused nonetheless, Claire wished, hoped and prayed for her turn to come soon.

She gasped in shocked disbelief as Claude's huge cock began forcing its way up into Arabella's tight little anus. Claire experienced a dull thud low in her vulva, never would she have expected such a move. So wrong yet so thrilling, inwardly she delighted in Arabella's discomfort and pain. A perverse sense of arousal when seeing someone abused so coarsely. Those feelings increased as Madam screamed, Claude's huge cock was buried deep up inside her body and moving in tandem with Jason's.

Arabella went wild, her fingernails clawing frantically at Jason's bare back and buttocks in a fervent drive of high passion. She began grunting aloud, setting the rhythm to coincide with the men's inward thrusts.

"Unnh! Unnh! Unnh!," Arabella cried out in her urgency. She spurred the men on to an increasing pace, her voice raising in pitch with her excitement.

A low gurgle came from her throat and then she came, wailing animal-like as the two men battered hard against her slim body. As they withdrew, their sperm dripped copiously from both orifices of her sated body.

Claire was alive with anticipation, urging them to now see to her needs.

Both men lifted Madam as if in a chair, they linked arms, her own arms circling their necks and shoulders.

"Now bitch," Madam announced. "You will have several

hours alone in which to learn a little patience."

The three of them turned and left the room to Claire's desperate screams of pleading for sexual release.

***

Still Madam hadn't allowed her to come. Released but with her hands still tied firmly behind her back, Claire crossed her thighs instantly to rub her aching clitoris. Two stinging lashes of the cane stopped her frantic rubbing and she was led outside onto the veranda.

The servant who had previously come up inside Madam without permission was naked and kneeling on the grass. Across his shoulders was a long thick pole that his outstretched arms were bound securely to. As the women approached all of the servants formed two lines as was customary for punishment sessions and stood silently.

Claire eyed the rows of semi-erect cocks longingly, the burning need inside her was now almost unbearable. Those powerful male bodies simply oozing stamina and sexuality made her body throb its need in powerful surges of dull nagging ache.

Arabella reached the kneeling servant, placed her booted foot into his back and kicked forward to force him down onto his face. She released Claire's hands and handed her the thin cane.

"Punish the worthless shit!" she stated coldly.

A thumping surge of power shot through Claire, it tightened her chest and took her breath away. Raising the cane high above her shoulder she brought it down hard onto the man's presented buttocks to draw a grunt of pain from him.

"Harder!" Madam snapped.

Again Claire swung the cane and received a thunderous jolt in her vulva as the cane cracked harshly on the man's backside.

"Still harder!" Madam shrieked excitedly.

57

Three more lashes Claire laid on him before a wonderful warm wave of deep and satisfying pleasure washed over her. She increased the power of her strokes, lashing excitedly with all the force she could muster and delighting in his screams.

On and on the beating went, her whole body alive and pulsing. Several gasps of sympathy were heard from the watching men. Claire's head began to swim with the misty dullness of sheer pleasure. Her legs felt weak and her body trembled. She lashed at the man twice more then came to a wonderful climax that tore through her entire body.

The cane fell from her hand, her head threw back and her hips jerked forwards in reaction. Her knees buckled and she collapsed panting heavily onto the cool grass.

***

The weekend it seemed had passed so very quickly. It was Sunday evening and tomorrow Claire would once again return to her normal life for another week. The weekend here at the manor this time had been so much better and so much more thrilling than ever. She had learned a lot in two days about sexual delights and about herself.

The servants worked to strap her into the strong wooden framework, kneeling and with her arms outstretched in front of her. Strong leather straps secured her wrists and knees to hold her firmly against the crossbar beneath her stomach. Heavier weights were attached to her nipple rings to stretch her nipples down harshly beneath her body.

Madam approached and stood close, her pussy only inches from Claire's face.

"You have pleased me with your progress to date slut. Now you will be rewarded. A little gift to maintain you through the coming week until you return here."

Arabella moved close in to press her pussy against Claire's face.

"The servants will now use your delightful little pussy to

58

sate their sexual desires - all eleven of them."

Claire gave a low groan of deep excitement in response.

"You may also lick my pussy whilst you enjoy your rewards."

Claire's whole body shook as the servant's big hand slapped hard on her buttocks; a numbing and thumping slap of such power that the breath was knocked from her. Two more heavy slaps of his hand stung her pale flesh before he positioned himself behind her and pushed his cock in.

It felt wonderful to have a lovely thick cock up inside her again. All the waiting had not been in vain. He gripped her hips and lunged hard into her, brutal and uncaring in his quest for satisfaction. The big black boy, Claude was a veritable stallion, he rutted with a frantic energy of wild desire and battered into her slight body.

Claire found difficulty in holding her head still as she worked her tongue, the ramming of the man against her buttocks was so violent. The thick musky juices of Arabella's pussy were delightful, and teasing even as Claire tried desperately to work her tongue inside.

Claude came, his thick seed squirting deep up inside her soft interior. Once again, three thumping slaps of the next servant's hand on her buttocks preceded his forcing up into her. Again a frantic rutting began and Claire mewed softly as her tongue lapped at Arabella's wet labia.

She came at the same time as he shot his seed, thrilling at the feel of the second wash of sperm inside her. The slaps from the next servant were spiteful and agonising, the metal rings on his fingers unforgiving on her flesh. The thrill, the sex and the quantity; eleven men, eleven different cocks and all for her. Claire grunted her acceptance of his hard lunges into her and tongued Madam excitedly as the sensations pulsed through her. She felt a deep and loving devotion toward her mistress and licked to please, to repay a little of the pleasure she herself was receiving.

Four times Claire had come during the session; four intense and wonderful orgasms that had further confirmed what would now be her way in life. No more the infrequent missionary style sex that Robert offered, she needed far more, was getting far more and intended to increase that yet again. Claire felt proud too that she had made Madam come. Clumsy and inexperienced though it may have been and Madam had said this was the case, but she was learning. Claire had been prepared to learn, wanted to learn but now she had a greater and more fervent hunger to acquire the knowledge.

She sat now in the tepid water of the bath soothing her sore pussy lips. Uncomfortable but so satisfying, it felt good to have conquered them all. Each and every servant had had her but the better part really came afterwards when Madam had promised that Claire would soon control them all herself. That thought thrilled her immensely.

The parcel that had been left in her room intrigued her; it had written instructions for her to open it at her own home and not before. Impatient and excited she had thought of peeking but reconsidered; every instruction Madam gave was for a good reason. The parcel could wait and so would she; the continuation of her training depended on it.

***

It was the blue eyed chauffeur who drove Claire home. She couldn't remember his name or when he had taken his turn in fucking her but she liked him. He was so smart in his uniform and his thick blond hair made his tanned skin seem even darker and more attractive. Her pussy ached both from want and from the many cocks she had had in it. And as they sped along the lanes Claire could contain herself no longer. That burning ache and the need to exercise her new-found authority came to the fore.

"Stop the car," she ordered.

Instantly the car slowed and pulled to the side of the road. The chauffeur applied the handbrake and turned around in question.

"Find a quiet spot," Claire said firmly, her heart pounding fast in excitement.

"Yes, Madam," he said simply and moved the car off again.

Within minutes he stopped in the gateway of a field, and switched off the engine.

"Get out and drop your trousers," Claire ordered in a thick husky voice. Her mouth was dry and her nipples erect, the power she felt simply pulsed within her.

She watched as he complied, in smooth confident movements he stood next to the car window and dropped his trousers. Both his hands held his shirt and jacket up around his waist to expose his erect cock.

A casual wave of Claire's hand brought him shuffling closer, she wound down the window, reached out and gripped his throbbing member. So warm and firm, it pulsed its excitement in her hand, the huge head purple in colour and the shaft dark with pumping blood.

Claire brought her glossy painted lips close to the tip, delighting in his groan of anticipation. Her tongue flicked across the tip to send little involuntary jerks of pleasure tugging at his bloated cock. She covered the head with her mouth, holding her lips loosely and circling her tongue around the big bulbous head. Her hand squeezed his thick shaft, her fingertips caressing and kneading.

To her mingled delight and disappointment he came instantly, his thick salty seed gushing into her mouth and throat in powerful spurts. Claire licked and sucked, drinking the creamy liquid with much relish until he was finished.

She dabbed at her mouth with her handkerchief.

"Dear me," she stated coldly. "That deserves punishment."

A bolt of sensation ripped through her as he replied obediently.

"Yes of course, Madam."

Her hand slid beneath his balls to cup them, her long fingernails poised threateningly to press hard into the flesh. Her hand clutched claw-like and menacing.

"Apologise to Madam."

"Madam, I am sorry, please forgive me," he said earnestly and gasped as she gripped him.

His face contorted in a mask of pain as her nails dug harshly into his soft tender ball-sac. Harder she squeezed, her body thrilling in the pain she was giving him. Claire released her grip and then pinched again, delighting in his pained grunts of deep suffering. Every nerve end in her body cried out for sexual release, the pounding excitement was bringing her close. Patience, she told herself, be patient for that was what Madam would expect of her.

He sighed loudly in relief as she at last released him and withdrew her hand.

"Next weekend," she sneered menacingly. "I shall complete your punishment."

He panted his reply, glad that the pain in his balls was now subsiding.

"Thank you, Madam," he said dutifully. "Thank you."

***

It was delightful! The contents of the parcel has been accompanied by a handwritten note from Arabella. The message was short but it contained everything in the few words that Claire could wish for. 'To a most responsive student' it had said.

The suit was made of thin black latex that clung to her body so very tightly. Claire posed before the full-length mirror in her bedroom to admire the effect, she seemed taller, erect and authoritative. The glossy material pulled over and under her breasts to lift and to separate them into desirable peaks of firmness. It clung to her buttocks to hug every contour and to leave nothing whatsoever to the imagination. It stretched across her slim waist and stomach but best of all, it emphasised the mound of her mons so nicely.

The long sleeves of the suit gave her arms a sleek yet powerful appearance and the way it clung to her slender thighs delighted her even more. In the high heeled boots and with her hair styled harshly she had a wicked and menacing look about her. Tall, elegant and so firmly honed in all the right places she turned to admire herself, the blood red lipstick, darker than her usual at Madam's suggestion added to the devastatingly stunning look.

"Aren't you ready yet?" Natalie's voice called through from the guest bedroom.

"Patience slut or you will incur my wrath," Claire shouted back to her excited friend.

"Over half an hour I've been waiting to see this new outfit of yours - I'm losing any patience I might have had."

Claire smiled at her reflection. "You'll soon learn to maintain it," Claire said softly to herself.

She turned smartly and strode confidently out of the bedroom.

Natalie sat motionless on the bed, staring wide-eyed in shocked amazement, her mouth hanging open.

"Like it?" Claire asked brightly as she entered the guest room.

She turned and strutted, delighting in her friend's reaction, a wonderful tugging sensation in her vulva resulted from Natalie's deep shock.

Natalie blinked several times, her mouth closed at last and she tried to speak but no words came from her. She cleared her throat and came back to the present.

"Good God!" she gasped. "Is that really you Claire?"

Claire moved close, standing before the woman, her feet set wide in an arrogant stance. She loved the way Natalie's eyes flicked over her breasts then down to the tight mound at her crotch and back up again. Claire turned, offering her taut buttocks for her friend's approval.

"Is that," Natalie asked hesitantly, "what you wear at the manor?"

Claire ran her delicate hands down to smoothe sensually over the curve of her buttocks, her pale skin contrasting harshly against the jet black material. She caressed herself slowly for Natalie's benefit.

"Haven't yet but I will from now on."

"Incredible," Natalie sighed enviously. "I always admired your body....er....your beauty, but this...."

"Tell me!" Claire said firmly and turned back to face her. "Tell me what you see and what you like."

Natalie flushed and shifted a little uncomfortably.

"Do it!" Claire demanded.

"Well, your neat waist and hips, the way your breasts are emphasised....you look so very attractive."

Claire began striding back and forth, pacing the room to show herself to her friend.

"More!" Claire urged firmly. "Tell me what you imagine underneath the suit."

Natalie swallowed, her face was flushed, her expression simply radiated sexual arousal and excitement.

"A slim, neat body, firm and warm. Your slender thighs and tight buttocks."

"Yes!" Claire moaned aloud in deep satisfaction.

She moved again to stand close to and in front of the trembling Natalie, towering over her in a commanding and controlling manner.

Natalie cleared her throat, she continued not through obligation but through genuine delight.

"Your nipples," her squeaky voice blurted slightly hesitantly. "So long and firm, so thrilling and inviting."

Claire moved in closer, her mons now only inches from her friend's face, her voice low and excited.

"More bitch," she demanded. "Tell me more."

Natalie was having difficulty now, her eyes roamed the tightly clad body before her, thoughts distracted her to muddle her words and she fought to construct them into a coherent sentence.

"Your body excites me...."

"Pussy!" Claire demanded. "Tell me about my pussy."

"Hairy," Natalie moaned absently. "I think it would be so hairy and soft, wet and so...."

"Bitch," Claire hissed. "Dirty little bitch! Tell me bitch what you are."

Natalie's voice was now thick and excited, low and husky as she complied.

"I'm a bitch."

"Mistress!" Claire snapped harshly. "Call me mistress!"

A low whimper of delight came from Natalie's throat then a deep groan of extreme excitement. In one move she leaned forward to grip Claire's hips in both hands and pressed her cheek against the firm mound of Claire's pussy. She clung to her suited friend hugging her admiringly.

"Mistress," she breathed lovingly and came to a thunderous orgasm that shook her body violently.

***

Arabella took the lead, pulling a naked servant along with a cord around his cock. Long and thin the cord was looped tightly around the shaft of his cock just below the head and his hands were bound tightly behind him.

She led him through the house, walking fast and giving no thought to his discomfort as he struggled to keep pace with her. As she pushed through the swing doors of the small gym the servant yelped when the heavy doors swung back to hit at his shoulders; he cried out again as Arabella tugged impatiently on his leash. Without slowing she pulled him across the gym to face the wall bars and hoisted the cord over one of the high spars. As she tied the cord off securely he was raised onto his toes, his hips forward to try to ease the strain on his cock. Silently Arabella raised his bound wrists high up his back and secured those also to clear his buttocks.; a rope around his neck pulling hard against his wrists.

His position was most uncomfortable and painful for each time he lowered slightly on his toes the cord stretched his cock cruelly. The precarious position threatened to unbalance him at any time and etched fear into his already pained face.

Arabella wore simply a strap that circled her waist then dipped down and between her legs to pull up harshly against her pussy and buttocks. The front of the strap was split, divided in its length to allow her hard clitoris to peek out tantalisingly. It not only allowed unrestricted access to her hard bud, but the sides of the straps rubbed and massaged it with each step or body move she made. Her nipple rings were joined by a thin chain, tautly it pulled her breasts inward and together as it stretched the rings toward each other. As was normal she wore her high heeled boots in deep shiny black that added to her height and stature.

"Tell me!" she demanded. "Tell me your failing this time."

The servant grunted his reply, clenching his teeth to try to bear the excruciating pain in his member.

"I broke a glass Madam."

Arabella walked back and forth behind him, her heels striking the wooden floor noisily and threateningly, echoing in the room.

"You did indeed," she stated firmly. "And what is the punishment for failure?"

"Six lashes Madam," came the grunted reply.

He screamed loudly as the crop stung his bare buttocks; a savage lash that almost tipped his balance, and he murmured his agony as the stripe of red hot pain burned deep into his soft flesh.

"Not six!" Arabella screeched angrily. "I tire of your constant mishaps - twelve! Twelve lashes and I hope you will learn from it this time."

"Oh God," the servant mumbled and braced himself.

Arabella's voice was soft and mocking, she bent close to

his ear to say the words.

"He can't help you now, you will suffer for your clumsiness."

She stepped back away from him, raised the crop high above her shoulder and brought it down hard on his buttocks. Scream after scream reverberated around the gym as Madam laid the lashes on him. In a furious assault of sheer anger she swung the crop again and again. Arabella grunted with pleasure at each stroke she gave him, the satisfying smack of leather on his bare body and the pulling of the strap between her legs. It drove her to higher and higher planes of arousal that brought her close to the brink of orgasm itself. She paused, panting hard and composing herself to allow her rising orgasm to subside.

His white flesh was stained; with wide red welts on his backside, deeply coloured bruising that bore testament to the savagery of the beating. He was murmuring incoherently in his agony, struggling now to maintain his upright stance and in imminent danger of falling.

Madam released the cord attached to his cock, a great and grateful sigh of relief came from him as she did so. She freed his hands too, allowing the numbed limbs to fall uselessly to his sides.

"Down!" she barked in command. "Down on all fours."

The man was confused and dazed, the stinging pain still rushing through his body and mind. Another hard lash of the crop across his back helped urge him into the required position.

Madam straddled him, sitting astride his back in a riding position; her erect clitoris located against the hard bone of his spine. She began jerking her hips, rubbing herself against him, his warm body gripped between her thighs and her wet, open pussy pressing down on his skin. Arabella rode him frantically, gripping his hair as reins for purchase as she took her pleasure. Her back was arched, her chest out, her head fell back and she grunted with each urgent thrust of her body.

Faster and faster she spurred him with her hips, her hard clitoris sensing the wonderful feel of him on her intimate parts.

She dug her long heels back painfully into his thighs as her passion mounted. She was lost in a world of frantic pounding desire as her hips jerked wildly to bring herself off. Rubbing herself violently on his skin she came to her peak.

His head was yanked back cruelly as she came, her mouth opening to emit a low and long wailing of deep satisfaction. Arabella's thighs gripped vice-like around his body to crush the breath from him. She rode on, savouring every last blissful sensation before dismounting to lie on the floor murmuring softly in pleasure.

***

Natalie was laid back on the bed murmuring softly in the blissful state of post orgasm. From where she had sat on the edge of the bed during her climax she had simply fallen back sated and had remained there since.

"Fantastic," she moaned softly. "The best orgasm ever."

"Just the beginning bitch," Claire purred in satisfaction.

Natalie roused herself, lifting to support her upper body on her elbows.

"My God!" Natalie enthused. "It was so thrilling - so naughty - and so very nice."

"Glad you enjoyed it. Ready for another?" Claire asked smiling.

Natalie looked at her in amazement.

"What? Two straight off?"

Claire beamed a smile back at her.

"Why not bitch?"

The girl moaned and sighed deeply. Her voice was thick with arousal when she replied.

"I love it when you call me that. 'Bitch' it's so....well....demeaning and insulting but at the same time so very horny."

"Mistress," Claire prompted gently. "You will call me Mistress."

Natalie nodded her agreement.

"Okay then," Claire said firmly. "Stand up and strip ready to come again."

Natalie quickly sat upright.

"What? Take my clothes of in front of you!?"

Claire's hand shot rapidly our from her side to grasp a handful of Natalie's hair; she twisted it cruelly to bring a gasp of pain from her friend.

"Do as I tell you slut!"

Natalie whimpered in delight at the name Claire used to address her and the force she was using on her. She immediately began unbuttoning her blouse whilst the hold on her hair remained firm.

Claire towered over the trembling girl, looking down at the firm swell of breasts as the blouse parted. Her friend's soft orbs were firm and inviting, pushed together and upward by her bra to create a deep and tantalising cleavage. Claire's pussy throbbed its need as she commanded her friend, giving pain and having her under control was so exciting. Those feelings increased as Natalie's breasts were bared, her rosy pink nipples sticking out firmly in erection.

Pulling on her friend's hair Claire hoisted Natalie to her feet and released her grip.

"Now the trousers slut."

Natalie was trembling with high excitement and just a little apprehension as she complied, opening her trousers and slipping them down to the floor. She hesitated as her hands held the sides of her panties and then she slipped those down also to reveal a dark brown thatch of pubic hair. She stood naked and a little ashamed before her latex-clad friend.

Claire made much of inspecting her friend's body, her gaze lingering first on her nipples and then moving slowly and methodically down to her pussy.

"Turn," Claire ordered.

Natalie couldn't contain a gasp, the surge that washed through her as she was commanded so curtly thrilled her tremendously. Silently she turned and stood, aware that Claire was behind her but not knowing what would come next. It all seemed so exciting and wrong yet simply too thrilling to want to stop. Her friend's eyes would be roaming her naked buttocks and back, inspecting her thighs and legs. She felt pounding waves of deep sensation flooding through her at the thought.

"Part your legs," Claire's velvety coaxing voice said.

Natalie complied, shifting her feet to adopt a wide stance. When instructed, she bent over and placed her hands on the bed, her whole pussy exposed so wantonly between the backs of her thighs. Her heart beat fast, her breathing was laboured as the sexual thrill rushed through her entire body. Claire was aroused, highly so, her voice betrayed the fact.

"Lift your head and arch your back bitch."

She almost came at the terrific jolt she received, the position and the sheer naughtiness of the situation bringing her closer and closer toward her peak. She felt every bit a slut as she did as she was bid; arching to raise and offer her buttocks high in a base and unashamed fashion. She tensed slightly and let out a stifled gasp as she felt just the tip of Claire's fingernails touch between her shoulder blades. She sighed in deep pleasure and wild throbbing anticipation and uncertainty as the nail traced a slow line down her back and toward her private parts.

"Closer bitch," Claire breathed excitedly as her finger dipped over the small of Natalie's back and paused at the crease of her buttocks. "I'm moving closer to your secret passage."

"Oh God!" Natalie murmured softly as the nail began to move slowly down the crease of her buttocks. It passed the tight little ring of her anus, pausing, threatening before continuing downward.

"Almost at your pussy," Claire purred sexily. "Should I?"

Natalie nodded, her breathing fast and urgent.

"Yes," she whispered almost inaudibly.

Claire's tone became harsh and demanding.

"I asked you a question you cock-sucking little slut!"

"Oooh!" Natalie gasped and then added more loudly. "Yes! Yes! Do it - please do it!"

Claire's fingernail was teasing between the open lips of her pussy, probing lightly at the soft, pink inner lips.

"You want me to touch you?" Claire teased. "You want my finger inside you?"

Natalie's head nodded rapidly in agreement.

"God yes! Please yes just do it!"

Claire moved around to Natalie's side, her finger still poised teasing at the entrance to her friend's pussy, her left hand gripping her hair. She lifted Natalie's head, pulling back to arch the girl's back and to open her pussy fully. In one move she stiffened her finger and pushed fully home up inside the soft interior.

"Nnnnh!" Natalie breathed in pleasure as the long digit entered.

Her body shook uncontrollably as Claire's other delicate fingers teased at the girl's hard clitoris.

"Move it around - please move it," Natalie pleaded in a low and desperate voice.

Claire pressed her latex covered mons against the side of her friend's hip.

"I need to punish you first slut. Do you accept my punishment?"

Natalie nodded her head several times in quick succession without realising what had actually been said.

"Yes! Anything, but just do it!"

Her Mistress withdrew the finger and landed a stinging slap with the flat of her hand across Natalie's left buttock. She received a thunderous jolt in her pussy as the slap landed.

She was shocked, her body tensed and her head snapped around in surprise only to be wrenched back by the restraining hand. Another hard slap stung her and she cried out, wave

71

after wave of mixed pain and high pleasure pulsing through her body and mind.

"Dirty bitch," she heard Claire's voice spitting in disgust. "Filthy little whore!"

The incredible feelings became more intense, each slap that stung her seemed to jar right through to her hard clitoris. She began moving her body in time with the spanking, forcing her buttocks back to receive each one of them.

Faster the pain and pleasure came to her, pounding waves of extreme sensation fogged her mind and pleased her body. Natalie cried out, three of Claire's fingers pushed roughly up inside her and began moving within her moist interior. She came instantly, her internal muscles clamping hard around her friend's fingers to bring even sweeter and more powerful pounding pleasure.

Natalie collapsed forward onto the bed and whimpered softy as the after tremors of sweet pleasure rippled through her. The soft caressing hand that roamed over her reddened buttocks simply added to the wonderful warm sensations that she experienced.

***

Robert was naked in the lounge, standing with his cock only semi-erect; he was fearful of his wife's severe tone and attitude.

"Pathetic!" Claire snapped angrily. "You are a pathetic little wimp!"

"Yes, Mistress," he mumbled obediently in reply.

She circled him menacingly, dressed in just a pair of little panties and a tight bra both in black, she had a commanding and menacing manner about her. The high heeled shoes that she wore raised her height to a powerful and commanding level that equalled that of her husband. They added too to the overall sense of control that she felt flowing through her.

"Your licking techniques have not improved at all," she

said in a severe tone. "Fumbled and displeasing to me - not at all acceptable. My pussy is a prized possession and yet you lick it like an ice cream. I am most dissatisfied with your efforts."

"Sorry," he muttered and quickly added. "Mistress."

"Your silly little cock," she continued to mock him, "it doesn't even get hard, just hangs there uselessly like yourself."

Her tone changed to a taunting, low purr.

"Perhaps it's time for me to find a real cock to fuck me."

Robert gasped, his cock jerked in an involuntary spasm of delight and began to stiffen and rise.

Claire nodded and changed her voice to a low and coaxing sensual tone. Her manner softened too, she adopted a sexy gliding motion that simply oozed sexual teasing.

"Mmmm, I see the thought of me having another man's cock excites you Robert."

He shook his head slowly in denial, his face etched with a serious frown.

Claire moved close, cupping his stiffening cock in her hand to hold it gently with her warm fingers encircling the shaft.

"I think it does," she sang playfully.

Robert tensed at her delicate touch and again shook his head.

Claire's voice was now soft, low and very sensual, her face close to his and her red painted lips opening slowly.

"A nice firm cock Robert," she breathed huskily. "Another man's cock is what I need up me."

He whimpered and then groaned as she caressed him tenderly.

"Shall I get one?" she teased, "and have it up inside my wet little pussy?"

His cock was throbbing in response, the blood pumping fast and hard into it in his excitement. It pulsed its delight and high arousal at her teasing.

Claire released him and stood back, delighting in his loud

groan of disappointment. It was so thrilling to tease him, to see the way that he became instantly excited, his usually reluctant cock responding readily.

She slipped off her bra and cupped her breasts as he watched her. Her slim fingers kneading and caressing her soft orbs lovingly for his benefit.

Claire drew breath to add emphasis to her next taunting words.

"Would another man like to see these do you think? To play with them, feel them and to....kiss them?"

Robert groaned deep from his throat, his cock now at full erection twitched in delighted little jerks. His face was flushed red in excitement, his eyes closely following the movements of her fingers as they teased at her nipple rings. Her red painted nails pulling and twisting in her excitement.

Claire slipped down her panties and kicked them casually aside. She stood before him offering herself for his inspection and delighting in his obvious discomfort.

"He'd like to see me like this I'll bet, totally naked and ready for him. His cock would be hard, Robert. Hard and wanting for me."

She turned and bent over, paused then got down onto all fours on the carpet.

"Perhaps I'd let him have me like this, from the back."

Claire moaned softly as though imagining the very act.

"Would you like to watch me being fucked Robert?" she asked lightly.

"No," he muttered, cleared his throat and repeated the word louder and more forcefully.

"No! Never!"

Claire shifted her presented buttocks sexily.

"Yes," she teased. "Yes, I can imagine him now pushing it up inside me, mmm! So thick and so long."

"Bitch!" Robert spat angrily.

Claire was delighted by his angry response, her clitoris ached and her whole body was crying out in need but she wanted to delay and to savour the moment a little longer.

"Can you imagine it Robert?" her husky voice intoned. "His big thick cock sliding in and out of my warm, wet pussy, giving me what you can't - a nice hard fucking."

"Enough!" he shouted. "I've heard enough."

Claire giggled.

"Like to come Robert?" she asked teasingly. "Is your pathetic little cock ready to come?"

"Yes," he panted urgently. "Yes!"

"Come and kneel behind me then Robert but don't put your cock in me yet."

He was there in an instant, she could hear his excited breathing behind her but it pleased her to make him wait. For several moments she waited there knowing that he would be ogling her body, her open pussy and just longing to get his aching cock inside her.

"Just the very head now," she said firmly. "Any more than that and I stop immediately."

He complied, guiding the head of his excited cock just into the entrance of her pussy, resting it against the warm, wet inner lips. Robert paused there and then at her command pushed fully in and waited as he had been told to.

"Please," he whimpered pathetically. "Please Mistress."

"Please what Robert?" Claire teased.

"Let me move - to fuck you - please!"

The pounding excitement was almost too much to bear, she wanted to relent but was enjoying his agony too much. She squeezed her internal muscles around his length inside her several times to bring low groans of approval from her husband.

"I wonder," she posed the question almost absently, "what another man's cock would really feel like?"

She felt his cock jerk inside her.

"Bigger though," she stated raising her voice. "It would need to be much bigger than your silly little willy. A proper cock, with a proper man to fuck me as I need fucking."

His cock was pulsing rapidly in excitement, each little spasm transmitting its delight to her soft insides.

Her voice changed to a mischievous and taunting tone.

"Perhaps I have Robert."

"Have what?" he grunted almost in disinterest.

She giggled lightly.

"Had another man's cock up me."

No reply came, Robert remained stationary and silent; stunned at the very suggestion that she could have.

"Perhaps," Claire taunted further, "I have already been fucked by another. Possibly more than one."

She laughed aloud as she felt his cock jerking inside her, the little excited spurts of his sperm jetting deep within her interior. Then she came, a gripping series of intense and satisfying surges of deep sensation fed by flashing images of the servants at the manor.

CHAPTER SIX

Crestfallen, hurt and deeply disappointed was how Claire felt. She had even worn the suit into the lane as she awaited the car which was to collect her, albeit covered with an overcoat. She had so wanted to please Madam, to show herself to her in the tight covering that she had come to love, and Madam had spurned her. Cold and hurtfully Madam had told her to 'get that thing off instantly' and those scathing words Claire recalled now in her discomfort.

She was naked and standing, bent over at the waist with her wrists tied securely to her ankles and her forehead touching her knees. An uncomfortable position that she had been left alone in for over an hour now; but Madam would have known that when she tied her there. The high heeled shoes that she wore made even the slightest of movement a most dangerous prospect as she struggled to maintain her balance.

Claire started in surprise as the door was suddenly flung open and crashed back hard and noisily against the wall. Madam strode in, her spike-heeled boots striking noisily and menacingly on the wooden floorboards.

"Well bitch," Madam said loudly, "have you had time now to experience coping with a little disappointment and humility?"

"Yes, Madam," Claire grunted, speaking was a most difficult operation in her discomfort.

Madam grunted her disbelief.

"We shall see."

Claire gasped and held her balance as Madam's finger stroked down over her buttocks and pressed against her puffy labia. The long finger pushed in, exploring deep up inside her wet pussy. Claire could hear Madam giving little sighs of deep satisfaction as she fingered her. The thumb worked on her clitoris, rubbing and exciting the bud to full hardness. Claire moaned in pleasure and wished that she was free to arch her body to accept the wonderful feelings.

For several minutes the fondling continued, every part of her inside was explored thoroughly before the fingers withdrew. A terrific bolt of sensation shot through her as she heard Madam sucking and licking her pussy juices from her own fingers.

Claire almost lost balance as the thin cane cut harshly and without warning across her buttocks. A stinging and cruel cut that burned deep into her body. A second and then a third, each moving down toward her exposed labia.

A muffled scream came from the girl as the cane struck across her pussy lips, the agonising pain searing through and up into her pussy itself. A second stinging lash bit at her tender lips and then stopped. Claire tensed as the flicking tongue slid up and down the length of her labia, the tip resting between the swollen lips. Madam was kneeling behind her, that much Claire could see between her knees. The tongue drove in, wriggling delightfully to search her exposed interior. On

77

and on the licking went bringing wonderful sensations heightened by her inability to move.

Claire was close now, fear filled her as she thought of falling in her high state of arousal, the coming orgasm would surely topple her. Electric spears of sensations raced through her when the tongue slid out and moved down to her hard bud. She screamed a muffled cry as Madam's teeth gently gripped her erect clitoris. Her body began to tremble with the first flutters of approaching orgasm and then Madam withdrew.

"Another hour for you to contemplate your humiliation is in order I think."

"No! Please Madam. No!" Claire pleaded from her bent over imprisonment. "I'm almost there!"

Madam simply chuckled in response., she leaned down close to Claire's head, her voice low and taunting.

"Then that makes it all the better for you then slut. I'm going now to have Jason's lovely big cock up inside me, do enjoy the thought whilst you are alone won't you."

Madam stood, turned and walked out of the room.

Hatred filled Claire's heart and mind, the bitch was leaving her hovering after bringing her so very close. A ripple of excitement ran through Claire's body and then she began to laugh. Bitch, she thought, you wonderful, wonderful bitch.

***

It was two of the servants who had come for her, they had untied Claire and carried her between them ensuring to keep her legs apart. That action itself, the denial of being able to close her legs and squeeze her aching clitoris seemed wonderfully perverse. Their powerful young bodies pressing against her sides and their strong hands holding her were adding to her desperate need but once again, Madam would have been fully aware of that - the bitch.

Out of the front door they carried her and down the stone

steps. In one smooth action they lifted her over the back of the horse which stood at the bottom and dropped her carefully down on the hard leather saddle.

The girl cried out at the contact, her thighs stretched wide apart by the enormous girth of the horse's body. Both Claire's hands clutched the horn of the saddle as she pressed her pussy hard against the firm leather horn. Shifting her hips and sighing loudly Claire ground herself against the saddle to gain the blissful sensations it produced for her.

Madam sat astride a big stallion nearby, watching the girl's great relief.

"Worth the wait?" Madam smiled.

Claire could only sigh in response, she looked across at Madam, her eyes conveying all that was necessary to say.

At Madam's command the horse moved off, the servants led Claire's horse whilst Madam followed unaided. The great lurch and sense of power in the beast had an astounding effect on Claire. Her hips jerked sharply to crush her clitoris hard against the saddle and to jar her buttocks. With each step the horse took the effects became greater and sweeter, more intense and so very wonderfully welcome.

Claire's head hung down, chin on her chest as she took in the pounding sensations on her clitoris. Her hands now gripped the reins, her knuckles bled white in the power of her grip. Faster the feelings came to her, the rocking movement of her body on the horse as they moved across the lawns was hypnotic; pumping her headlong towards a tremendous orgasm. Back and forth she was jolted in the saddle, her open pussy lips pressing hard down on the brown leather. More powerfully and more frequently the spasms shook her body, building rapidly in a thumping crescendo of sheer bliss.

Claire's head threw back, her mouth opened and she screamed to the open air of the grounds as she came. A gurgling and then a sigh, her body locked rigid and she screamed aloud again as the orgasm tore through her. The girl slumped forward onto the neck of the horse and then slid around and down to the ground.

Her mind was a blur, a misty haze of detachment in the racking after tremors of the power of her climax. Rough hands grasped her, she was hoisted to her feet and pressed face first against the flanks of the horse. Her wrists were twisted cruelly behind her back and the head of a cock nudged between her firm buttocks. She cried out as the huge member pressed against the tight little entrance of her anus. The smell and feel of the horse against her face and body furthered her detached feeling.

Pain such as she had never before known burned cruelly in her backside as the tight little ring of muscles was forced apart and the great head of his cock pushed inside. Claire screamed, a pitiful and pained wailing as it pushed up inside her anus. The horse stood firm, hard and muscular, she was trapped, pressed against the beast with another defiling her most private of places. She began sobbing in deep humiliation as the man behind her began a frantic thrusting up inside her.

On and on the burning agony continued, raw pain and little excitement was all that Claire could sense. Harder and more brutally he rammed into her slight body, she could hear Madam's laughter as she watched Claire's deep shame.

He came, a powerful wash of sperm jetting deep up inside her rectum. Claire fought the pleasurable sensations, denying to herself that this could be at all enjoyable. She gasped loudly in relief as he withdrew, the sore and stretched muscles of her backside stinging painfully long after his extraction. Her hair was grasped by a firm hand, her head swung around so roughly that she lost balance and fell to her knees. Different hands now of the other servant held her wrists and pushed her forwards to press her face down onto the cooling grass. Claire simply sobbed her misery as his cock too then forced its way up inside her tender anus.

"Ride her!" Madam screeched in delight, her voice high and excited.

Claire's whole body shook with each forceful thrust of the servant's hips. He crashed hard against her, driving his thick rod painfully into her. Several horrible moments passed and then a warm and comforting wash came over Claire. Her mind imagined his thick cock pumping in and out of her secret place. The way her little body had stretched to accommodate its great girth and the sheer brutality with which be was abusing her. Her clitoris jolted, she found herself grunting in time with his pumping hips.

"The bitch is coming!" Arabella squealed. "The little slut is coming!"

Those words, the deep humiliation and the forced rape of her backside all combined to bring her off. Claire felt one great surge of sensation and then she came, her body shuddering in wild spasm as the feelings tore at her insides. A second wash of sperm inside her body drew even sweeter sensations and the servant's excited grunting simply added to her pleasure.

Finished with, Claire was shoved roughly to the grass to lay discarded and used to murmur and shiver before the watching audience. Like a rag doll thrown aside by a child that had lost interest in it, Claire was left alone as she lay, bruised and sore but satisfied.

***

The burning soreness remained but Claire felt strangely complete in a way; now that her last orifice had been violated by a man. It was as though nothing else could shock her and there was nowhere else in her body that a cock could be inserted for the first time. Reflecting back on it, the session on the horse, the awful agony of the long wait and then her brutal rape were so very exciting and horny. Not rape in the true sense of the word of course but certainly against her will - at first anyway. That rough and unexpected taking of her had simply heightened the experience; the second better still than the first time. Claire felt now that she was learning, but more than that she was beginning to understand herself better and her growing sexual needs and desires. Madam had introduced her to humiliation and pain, sexual practices that previously Claire would have considered utterly revolting and unspeakable; but now - it was all so very different.

She walked with pride, her head up and shoulders back during the 'corrective posture session' as Madam called it.

"Clench those buttocks!" Madam urged and flicked the long training whip to bite harshly across them.

Claire winced as the very tip of the thin whip curled around her outer thigh to sting cruelly at her soft flesh. Taut and tensed she walked naked, her buttock muscles now firmed and shaped with the constant training.

"During the week," Madam called to her as Claire walked in a circle around her. "You will insert objects into your pussy, to hold them and to train those juicy little internal muscles of yours into vice-like clamps of pure delight."

Two more stinging flicks of the whip urged Claire to answer, she was deep in thought, imagining gripping around a long thick cock that was buried up inside her.

"Yes, Madam," Claire responded loudly as she walked.

For more than an hour she had been walking, posing and bending. Each move now more sensual and confident as the training had begun to take effect. Facial expressions, a turn of the head, the use of the eyes to lure and to stun; nothing was missed in these sessions.

"Halt now," Arabella commanded. "We will take a fifteen minute break and then do something about getting your awful make-up straightened out."

"Yes, Madam," Claire said slightly hurt at the remark for she had gone to much trouble to look good for Madam.

The whip stung her body, flicking agonisingly across her breasts.

"Tone, girl - tone!" Arabella barked. "Never use such a tone. Positive in thought and positive in action, men will expect it of you!"

"Yes Madam!" Claire responded loudly and forcefully. She felt her pussy moisten as the numbing pain seeped through her breasts and tingled in her ringed nipples.

***

To her surprise it was a male servant that was to apply the makeup. Claire sat on the velvet padded stool before the dressing table in her room, Madam as always, was standing close by. The naked servant busied himself preparing the items, Claire moved her gaze over his tight buttocks and his dangling cock whenever the opportunity presented itself. She sat naked and aroused, shivering in delight as he leaned over her to work on her eyeliner. His odour and his closeness; the occasional brush of his naked skin against her shoulder or leg sent thrilling shards of pleasure running through her.

Claire found herself rubbing her knee against his leg, transmitting her arousal and need, delighting in the way his thick cock stirred and began to harden. Her body pulsed as his cock rose, excited and twitching it grew to full erection. She gasped as the big head touched lightly against the side of her breast, his hands now applying eye shadow to her closed lids.

The situation and the need overcame her, Claire grasped his cock and dipped her head, taking his thick girth greedily into her mouth. She sat whilst he stood, sucking and mewing her pleasure as Madam looked on.

Her other hand roamed his strong muscular thigh and teased at his balls, her need so great now her lips worked in tandem with her tongue to devour the throbbing cock. Claire's head dipped and then withdrew, pumping steadily in a bobbing motion of sheer and urgent need.

It hit suddenly, a forceful spurt of his thick seed jetting to the back of her throat. Claire gagged at the sudden rush of liquid but swallowed hungrily, the surplus sperm oozing out from between her lips and his cock. Her tongue worked to clean his juices, lapping lovingly at the wet warm prize and

83

curling around and under the big head. Her other hand smeared the thick globules that had dribbled down onto her breasts; massaging them into her skin like a lotion.

"You are learning bitch!" Madam complimented. "Men are to be used as and when you feel the need, I am pleased with your continuing progress."

Claire sat back delighted, not only with her accomplishment but more so with Madam's praise.

"There is however," Madam's stern voice announced loudly, "a matter of courtesy which you have not observed. When I am present you must ask - and you did not."

"But Madam...."

"Silence!" Arabella snapped. "Stand and turn, seat yourself against the dressing table facing me."

Feeling dejected Claire complied, resting her buttocks on the very edge of the dressing table and supporting herself with her hands to the sides. With her legs spread wide, her mons was pushed out and presented open, a flutter of excitement ran through the girl.

Madam knelt close and between her thighs, she held out her hand casually to receive the stick from the servant. Ultra thin and only about a foot long the stick was rigid and unbending in its length.

A blast of colour flashed in Claire's brain, her whole body seemed to be hit with a powerful electric shock. She drew breath at the intensity of the feelings as Madam struck with the stick. Arabella had held it upright and in line with the slit of Claire's labia; a sudden and hard tap had struck harshly on the girl's rigidly erect clitoris.

Again and then again the stick hit home, tapping like a drumstick in a steady and delightful rhythm. Claire's body tensed, the sensations were simply too wonderful to describe. It took only ten more taps to bring her off, her whole body shaking violently with the intensity of the orgasm. She slumped and then slid down to the floor murmuring her gratitude to her instructress.

Natalie was alone and naked, the burning need in her pussy had been eating away in her since the wonderful events with Claire. She had tried rubbing herself and inserting her own fingers into her pussy but to little effect, it had simply served to make the gnawing ache worse. She wanted those powerful orgasms again; the thrill and naughtiness of being with another woman and of experiencing the horny way Claire had seemed to control her. She felt secure and warm in Claire's company and so very excited under her control.

She straddled the arm of the settee, her hands resting on and gripping the high back; she groaned at the feel of the rough material on her open pussy. Natalie began to jerk her hips, the coarse covering of the wide arm rubbing her clitoris and soft inner lips delightfully. She moaned aloud at the relief it brought to her.

She moved her body and hips faster, riding the arm like a horse and building steadily to a full gallop. Her hands gripped hard on the back, her knees gripped around the sides of the arm as she rode headlong forward in her pleasure. Frantically she rode the arm, forcing hard to bring more pressure onto her private parts, her whole body bucking in a terrific crescendo of rising pleasure.

"Claire!" she cried aloud at the height of her pleasure. "Mistress," her excited voice cried again as she ground her pussy hard down on the firm arm.

It was a rapid and fervent jolting of her slim body now as she rubbed herself toward orgasm. The feelings so strong, the sensations so wonderful and the visions of Claire so sweet. Natalie screamed as she came, her head nodding in acceptance as the surges of pleasure washed through and over her. Her mouth was open and gaping in a silent pleading for the final surge. Her body locked, her head threw back and she shuddered with the force of the sensations. She slumped forward sated, her panting body coated in a fine film of perspiration, her eyes closed and ripples of after-pleasure twitching at her body.

"Mistress," she mumbled softly. "My wonderful Mistress."

***

The list was long indeed, an excited flutter shot through Claire's body to grip deep in her vulva at the very thought. Madam had compiled the list, ornate handwriting on stiff and very expensive paper in perfect keeping with Arabella's status.

The objects Claire should practice with throughout that coming week, to insert into her pussy and to begin to train her internal muscles. Twice already Claire had read the list and now she read it again - it excited her to do so. The instructions were clear and precise as always. 'Not before twelve thirty on Monday morning are you to begin.' Claire smiled at Madam's knowing ways, the bitch was making her wait again and she knew she would obey Madam's instructions.

A pencil, a hairbrush handle, carrot, banana and a cucumber; they were just the beginning of the list and Claire read on. A broom handle, a candle and many other objects all to be found around the home but best of all was the last item on the list, 'The contents of the parcel'. Gift-wrapped and tied with a bow of gold ribbon the gift sat on the bed teasing with Claire's impatience to open it. All other items had to be tried first and in the order of the list, only then could the parcel be opened and the contents used.

Claire looked again at the clock on her bedside table, eleven twenty, over an hour to wait and the need to experiment was growing. A momentary thought of starting early and of defying Arabella was pushed aside, Claire sat on her hands so as to help resist the urge to touch herself. She smiled and thought of Madam, the rotten bitch knew all and would be revelling in her forced wait.

She started sharply, brought instantly back to the present

by the shrill ring of the phone.

"Claire, I need you," Natalie's thick voice said as Claire answered.

"Not now, Natalie I'm a little busy at present."

"I don't think you understand, what we did the other day - I need it again and soon."

Claire couldn't contain a smile and the throbbing in her pussy had been made worse still by the thought of her friend in such desperate sexual need.

"Later."

"But when later?"

Claire felt a tinge of irritation, she wanted so desperately to try Madam's list of items. Not that Natalie was preventing her but it felt good to blame her friend for the nagging ache in her vulva.

"Er....this afternoon....about four."

"Not before?" came the urgent plea.

"Patience bitch, patience."

Claire felt a thrill much as she imagined Arabella would be getting by making her subject wait. The control and manipulation of other people sexually in need felt so very good.

"Four thirty now for your insistence slut."

A slight pause and then.

"Okay Claire, four thirty it is then."

"Mistress," Claire reminded lightly.

Natalie's voice lowered.

"Mistress."

"Oh and slut. You will come to me naked with only an overcoat to cover you."

"What!? Drive you your place naked!? It's hot sunshine outside and....well, I might be seen."

Claire chuckled at the thought of her friend, driving with one hand as the other gripped her coat tightly across her neck to cover herself.

"Do it slut," Claire said firmly.

There followed a short silence and then:

87

"Yes Mistress."

The line went dead and Claire sat back laughing. She looked again at the clock and only a few minutes had passed. She lay back and sighed deeply, imagining the servants thick cocks and all that had happened at the manor. The throbbing ache in her pussy was becoming unbearable, she wished now that she had asked Natalie to come over straight away.

Her fingers toyed with the pencil, there was still half an hour to go and her pussy was moist in anticipation. Claire slipped it through one of her nipple rings and turned it clockwise. The sharp pain that shot through her was wonderful, she twisted the pencil again to savour the teasing sensation that it produced for her.

Absently her other hand strayed down over her stomach and had almost reached and cupped her mons before she checked herself and sat up.

"Damn you Arabella!" Claire said aloud. "Damn you, damn you!"

Claire began to giggle, her thoughts turned then to Natalie's coming visit and the lovely sleek body of her friend.

She had slumbered, deep and distant in her thoughts, she came awake with a start and cursed herself. Twelve forty two the clock read, over ten minutes past the deadline.

Claire immediately raised her knees and parted them, holding the long pencil by the sharpened end and hovering the blunt end at the entrance to her pussy. She pushed it carefully in and relaxed. It was so exciting, a pencil wasn't thick but the act itself, the inserting of an unusual object into her body held a thrill all of its own.

She tensed her internal muscles as tightly as she could but to no effect. Again and again she tried, and then tried it standing up again with little success, the pencil simply stayed there held in place by Claire's wet pussy juices. The hairbrush handle seemed a better prospect, positioning herself in front of the long wardrobe mirror Claire shifted her legs apart and prepared herself. The handle was cool and rigid as it pushed up inside, she watched its progress carefully in her reflection. Up and up it went until only the bristles were visible projecting from her pussy then Claire tried tensing. It worked in part, she felt a momentary gripping and then her muscles relaxed. Still holding the brush into her Claire tried again using several different methods of coaxing her muscles to respond. More frequently she felt the delightful sensations, her muscles closing around the whole length of the handle inside her.

She rested a moment, took a deep breath and tried again, she could now release her hold on the bristles and delighted in the way her body held the brush firmly if only for fleeting seconds at a time. Gradually as the technique became clear Claire was able to grip and hold for longer and longer periods. The rhythmic pulsing grips were pushing her state of arousal higher by the moment. It was so exciting, fucking herself with her own body and method, the object not even moving to aid her pleasure.

With hands on her hips now, she watched in the mirror as the bristles of the brush jerked slightly in time with her gripping and relaxing. She could hold it in her at last! Claire imagined one of the servants up her, imagined squeezing his cock whilst staring directly into his eyes, teasing him, bringing him to the very brink of climax and then stopping to watch his disappointment. During her thoughts the rhythm had increased in pace to a regular jolting of her muscles. The handle served as the medium and she fucked vigorously as she moved closer to her peak.

Claire tensed her whole body, the throbbing sensations now pumping through her unstoppably. One hand moved down to cup her mons, her fingers pressing hard against her erect clitoris. She rubbed and gripped in tandem to send her arousal to the very brink. She hovered there, panting hard in excitement. She opened her eyes, looked at herself in the mirror, blew a sensual kiss at her reflection and came to orgasm.

With one hand extended and placed on the mirror to steady herself, Claire bucked and shook as the orgasm tore through

89

her. She watched her own expression, the way her face contorted in a mask of pained pleasure as she sank slowly down to her knees. Moaning her pleasure she rested there as her slim body shivered in the blissful aftershocks of climax.

As the wonderful sensations began to subside, Claire wondered what size the carrots in her vegetable rack were.

CHAPTER SEVEN

The back door was open as she arrived and Natalie was about to step in.

"Stop," Claire's voice commanded loudly. "Take your coat off outside."

Stunned Natalie looked hesitantly around her.

"But your neighbours!" she protested, "I'm totally naked underneath."

Natalie stared in disbelief at Claire's nipple rings as she stepped into the doorway.

"I said," Claire hissed sternly, "take your coat off outside."

Natalie complied, slipping the thick overcoat off to stand naked on the doorstep. Claire moved back to allow her entry and closed the door slowly behind her. She circled Natalie silently, walking slowly around her, both naked women pulsing with sexual expectation.

Claire took in the firm neat breasts of her friend, the slim waist and narrow hips and those slender thighs sculptured by much fitness training.

"Do you feel horny, bitch?" Claire's low husky voice asked in the stillness of the kitchen.

Natalie stood erect and motionless, her stare straight ahead of her.

"Yes, very....Mistress."

Claire moved to her front, aware that her friend's eyes were now searching between her thighs and inspecting the shaven mound of her mons.

"Squat bitch and part your thighs, I want to see your pussy."

Natalie gasped at the surge of excitement she felt and lowered her body as she had been instructed to.

Claire gazed at the wonderful open thighs and the very hairy pussy of her friend. The sense of command that she felt was a terrific high for her and her pussy contracted in delightful little spasms.

"Do you need to come bitch?"

"Oh yes Mistress! I need it so badly it almost hurts."

Claire nodded her acceptance.

"Touch yourself, your pussy..... touch it!"

Hesitantly Natalie's hand moved down between her thighs to rest on her dark thatch of hair

"I've never actually...."

"Do it!" Claire hissed menacingly and then watched as her friend's slim fingers moved slowly on her labia.

"Oh God," Natalie muttered, she flushed bright red at the humiliation and raw sexual excitement of the situation.

"Two fingers, put two fingers up inside."

Natalie complied, the look of disgust on her face made Claire shiver in delight. The girl fingered herself slowly and with the utmost reluctance.

"Enough slut. Now to the bedroom and run!"

Claire delighted in her friend's haste, watching her withdraw her fingers and get to her feet before scurrying through to the hall.

She moved the opened parcel and wrappings from the bed and Natalie climbed on to kneel on all fours as was required of her. She knelt there silently and obediently waiting for her next instructions. Natalie shivered in delight and let out a little gasp as Claire's hand began stroking lovingly over her presented buttocks; the long delicate fingers caressing and feelings the firm young flesh. Natalie tensed as the fingers slipped slowly down over the curve of her backside edging ever closer to her open sex.

"Punishment bitch," Claire breathed excitedly. "You must be punished first."

"Yes," Natalie agreed in a low voice thick with pounding sexual arousal. She would have agreed to almost anything in her desperate longing for fulfilment.

She yelped as the flat of Claire's hand slapped hard down on her buttocks but she remained as she was. Again the hand stung her to send a warming glow moving over her buttocks and between her legs. Slap after slap struck home, the naughtiness and sheer excitement making Natalie's pussy grip and her clitoris jolt in response. Fifteen in all, hard slaps and yet so sensual, her pussy was afire with burning need. She muttered and groaned as the stinging spanking continued and then groaned her disappointment when Claire stopped.

"Turn over bitch and lay on your back."

Natalie complied, snuggling herself deeply into the thick quilt.

"What? Oh my God!" Natalie uttered as Claire took her wrist and began tying the cord around it.

Once secured Claire pulled her arm up and out and tied it securely to the head of the bed. Both her wrists and both her ankles were similarly tightly tied, each to a corner of the bed to spreadeagle Natalie immovably.

Claire surveyed her handiwork on the stretched slim body of her friend before getting onto the bed and straddling Natalie's stomach. She lowered her open pussy to rest it down on Natalie's bare stomach and to drink in the warm feel of her flesh against her inner lips. The sense of power that Claire felt as she towered over her tethered and helpless friend pushed her level of arousal higher still. Her hands reached out to cover both Natalie's breasts and to begin caressing them lovingly.

Natalie whimpered softly, forcing her hard stomach upward to savour the wet warmth of Claire's pussy on her. The wonderful feel of those hands; another woman's hands, touching her so intimately, so passionately and knowingly. She gasped at the sudden shot of pain as Claire gripped both her nipples and squeezed hard; she cried out as the long finger-nails bit deeply into her tender little buds. All the time she was being caressed Claire's smiling face looked down at her in her torment.

Her face lowered to bring her succulent red lips close to Natalie's and hovered there expectantly.

"No!" Natalie uttered. "Not kissing, please not kissing."

She turned her head to the side in avoidance.

Both of Claire's hands gripped the sides of Natalie's head to jerk her face firmly back to look up at her. They held her head securely as Claire lowered her mouth and kissed her full on the lips.

The tethered girl whimpered and bucked her body but the soft warm feel of the lips, the hot and meaningful passion with which the kiss was delivered made her relent. Natalie responded, opening her mouth to accept the warm probing tongue into her own mouth. For several moments the kiss lasted, her bucking of protest changed to a wriggling of delight, her own tongue feeding into Claire's mouth in a desperate and heated search for sexual pleasure.

Claire sat back smiling then dismounted and walked around to the foot of the bed. She took two pillows and pushed them under Natalie's buttocks to force her hips upward. Her mons was offered invitingly, her pussy open and exposed between the parted slender thighs.

"Lovely kiss," Claire said casually as she worked.

"Mmmm," Natalie responded and wriggled her body in contentment. She pulled against her bonds as the excitement pulsed through her.

"Now your other lips need kissing," Claire stated and climbed on the bed to kneel between Natalie's open thighs.

It took a moment for the words and their meaning to register in Natalie's brain. A look of total dread and horror came over her face; she raised her head and shoulders to strain hard against the ropes holding her.

"You can't! Not what I think you mean!" she protested in

revulsion.

She cried out and half-screamed as Claire's head dipped downward.

"No! No! Please don't"

She gurgled and bucked her hips against the touch of the lips on her labia; sobbing lightly in defeat and her helplessness to prevent the unwanted violation. Natalie froze as the soft lips planted feather-light kisses up and down her labia. The feelings were simply too wonderful for words and Natalie began to relax her body and to welcome the sensual mouth against her sex.

Her body tensed again, a loud sigh and moan came from her as Claire's tongue slid up the length of her labia slit to taste the flowing juices. Natalie struggled against the ropes, not to gain release from her bonds but to cope with the powerful sensations that were ripping through her body.

"Oh God," she whimpered softly.

As the thick tongue pressed in and up inside her pussy Natalie came. Her thighs twitched in involuntary spasm, her head nodded wildly to urge the teasing tongue and her orgasm onward and inward. Her slight body quivered her delight, a loud sigh signalled the end and she slumped sated back onto the bed.

"Good bitch?" Claire's soft voice enquired from somewhere far off. " Not finished yet you horny little slut."

Natalie raised her head and shoulders; the smile left her face instantly and her eyes opened wide in horror. What the smiling Claire was holding in her hand filled Natalie with dread; and the knowledge that Claire would actually use the object on her simply turned that dread into a very real fear.

***

It was more a sedan chair than a throne that the servants carried out of the manor and onto the wide terrace. It looked like a throne but had two long bearers either side that the naked menservants used to carry Arabella to the designated spot before the arena. Once on the grass the chair and Arabella were lowered, the servants standing dutifully at attention by her sides.

The arena was a roped off area of grass and the two combatants stood ready, one in each opposing corner. Both servants were totally naked, their muscular bodies gleaming with the covering of baby oil. Their expressions were set and their stances defensive.

"You will," Arabella's voice announced formally, "engage in combat for five rounds each of two minutes, the winner - and only the winner - will share my bed tonight. No biting, kicking or punching allowed but otherwise - anything goes."

Arabella raised her hand.

"Let the contest begin."

Her arm snapped smartly down in signal and she settled herself to watch the fray.

Both men were at each other instantly, grappling and grunting, they used all the power in their strong bodies to try to defeat the other and to gain the offered prize.

Arabella gasped as the jolt in her pussy drew thrilling sensation to heighten her arousal. To watch two fit young men battling for her body and favours was so very exciting. The way they went at each other, headlocks and wrist grabs, the oil on their bodies making the contest even more exciting. She jumped to her feet in heated excitement as Jason threw the other servant to the ground and straddled his chest. To see the young men's bodies pressed hard against one another was so sexually thrilling; that Jason now had a partial erection simply added to that.

Suddenly Jason was thrown off, Clive rolled quickly to reverse the situation. He gripped hard around Jason's waist, his cock pressed hard against the other man's buttocks. Arabella groaned at the sight and thought of it and pinched her hard nipples. The two men grunted and cursed as they struggled, Jason broke free and twisted Clive's arm painfully up his back, his other arm pinned as Jason's powerful grip twisted it cruelly.

Clive cried out in submission as Jason's strong hands moved then to wrench his head to the side and the contest was over.

Arabella stood panting, her whole body alive with sexual pounding and need. Pulsing waves of tingling excitement tore at her inside to fire her level of sexual longing. Her pussy literally oozed its juices and her clitoris throbbed in desperate wanting.

"Jason," she said aloud, her voice thick and hoarse, "is declared the winner and comes to my room tonight. Clive - you go to the punishment wing and wait for me there."

***

"No!" Natalie protested urgently as her eyes fixed on the big black dildo.

The enormous phallus that Claire held up was truly huge; sculptured like a man's cock it was bigger and thicker than any man could ever be. The big bulbous head alone was the size of a small tomato and the veiny shaft was wide and solid.

Claire held the huge member up by the thick hand grip and smeared the lubricating jelly slowly up and down the shaft in mimicry of wanking it. The ebony shaft glistened menacingly in the reflected light to show clearly the enormous proportions of the member.

"Delights to come for you bitch," she taunted and moved to kneel next to Natalie on the bed.

"Please!" Natalie whimpered. "It will damage me - please don't!"

Claire ignored her, she used two fingers of her left hand to hold Natalie's labia wider apart and locate the huge head of the dildo at the entrance to her friend's pussy.

Natalie began to sob softly, the cold feel and the great size of the phallus made her tense in fear.

96

"Relax bitch and all will be well."

Natalie drew breath as the big head pushed in, stretching her soft inner lips wide to accept the bulbous head. She cried out as the head pushed in to pause and rest just inside the entrance of her pussy.

Claire looked down, amazed at the way her friend's pink inner lips gripped tightly and closely around the thick girth. Black against pink, it seemed an erotic sight in itself.

"Ahhh!" Natalie cried out as the long cock-like dildo began to push slowly up inside her.

Her head was forward, her shoulders straining and her face screwed up in a pained and fearful expression.

Up and up it travelled, seemingly never ending until the whole of it was inside her. Claire rested it there to allow her body to accommodate its huge size.

Natalie was panting, puffing and breathing as though in labour.

"Good?" Claire asked brightly and began to slowly withdraw the big dildo.

Natalie simply grunted her response, her eyes fixed firmly on the mound of her mons as she looked down over her own stomach.

Just the head was inside now, Claire paused there teasingly and then began to push back up into her friend's pussy.

"Oh God!" Natalie muttered and slumped back in defeat to accept the huge invader into her body.

Faster the rhythm built, each outward stroke leaving the head inside before the great length pushed fully back inside.

"Unnnh!" Natalie grunted as Claire began thrusting harder. With each powerful inward thrust Natalie grunted aloud. Her body was now relaxing and her hips moving to meet each inward push of the big cock. Her mouth fell open and her eyes closed as the wonderful sensation came to her.

"Little bitch!" Claire breathed in awe as her friend began to enjoy the feelings.

Faster and harder Claire pumped the dildo into Natalie's

pussy, her hand crushing hard against her erect clitoris on each inward push.

Natalie's hands gripped her restraining ropes and pulled at them urgently. Her stomach began to undulate and her hips rose to meet the thrusts.

"Yes!" she pleaded softly. "Yes!"

Claire's arm was almost a blur now as the pace had built to a frantic fucking of her friend. Her breathing was fast and laboured as she worked the big cock in and out.

"Harder!" Natalie pleaded and then became more demanding in her urgency. "Harder - do it harder!"

A rattle gurgled in her throat, her eyes locked wide open and rush of air came from her lungs. Her whole body locked rigid and she came to a thunderous orgasm.

She screamed. Her head nodding and her body trembling as the waves of sensation tore at her insides. She sighed loudly and slumped back onto the bed panting loudly.

***

Clive was suspended from the ceiling of the cellar in the punishment block. Thin cords secured only his thumbs but they imprisoned him painfully on tip-toe, he was naked and stretched uncomfortably awaiting Madam's arrival.

The door opened and Arabella strode purposefully in, a riding crop dangling from her wrist. She wore tight black leggings and boots, the high heels clicking noisily on the stone slab floor. Her top half was naked except for the tight lacy bra in black that squeezed her breasts tantalisingly up and together.

"You failed me," she said casually.

Clive cleared his throat.

"Madam, I am sorry," he croaked nervously. When Madam was angry she was a force indeed to contend with, all the servants knew this and to a man they both feared and yet loved her.

Madam positioned herself at his side, her body close and

pressing lightly against his side. Her voice was low and sensual as she sought to arouse him.

"So big! Your cock is mmm!..... so very nice."

He groaned, not in pleasure but in the knowledge of what was to come. Only once had he ever suffered the expected punishment and never again did he want to. Clive fought hard to stem his rising erection.

"My pussy," Arabella breathed, "is wet and in need of your cock."

He groaned loudly as his cock stirred into life and began to harden; the feel of her warm body against his, the heady smell of her perfume and the sensuality of her manner all combined to bring it up.

His head threw back and he screamed as she cut down hard on it with the crop. A savage and meaningful lash that jarred his whole cock downward and against his angle of erection.

"Failure," she purred sexily, "I simply do not accept."

A second stinging lash bit fiercely down onto his cock and again he wailed his pain to the cold stone walls. Arabella paused, one hand cupping his balls tenderly and the other using a finger to tease between his tensed buttocks.

"Get hard again my little man," she taunted.

Clive shook his head in denial, fighting desperately to avoid a second erection in his aching cock. The burning stinging had now turned to a dull and numbing throb that made any control difficult.

He whimpered as his cock began to rise, the teasing hand and fingers working to excite him despite the pain. Once again he was erect, her hand moved to grip the swollen shaft and to hold it tenderly.

"What does Madam not accept?" she asked in a singing and mocking tone.

"Failure!" he blurted. "Failure Madam."

"Yes!" she cooed sarcastically. "That's right and you did fail me Clive."

His screaming was renewed as two more cruel lashes of the crop struck hard down on his cock before Arabella again paused.

"Enough of that now," she reassured softly.

He groaned his relief and uttered gratefully, "thank you. Thank you Madam."

Arabella straightened her body, pushing her chest out for his benefit and to add emphasis to her words.

"Your internal tube will now be bruised and the passage of any liquids down it will be painful in the extreme."

Clive nodded mournfully his acknowledgement of the facts stated.

Arabella's voice again changed to a low and sensual tone.

"I will now insert my finger into your anus and locate your prostrate gland."

The servant looked up at her quizzically.

"The stroking of your little gland makes you come uncontrollably and unstoppably."

Several seconds passed as Clive absorbed the full implications of her words then he began to cry. Great heaving sobs racked his body as Madam knelt before him and slipped a hand between his legs and located the entrance to his anus.

He wailed pitifully as the middle finger of her hand pushed inside, forcing his little muscles wide in her exploration. Just a moment passed before his body began to twitch in involuntary spasm.

"You won't be able to stop it," she teased. "The gland reacts to stimulation that you simply can't control."

His cock jerked and rose to emit a long stream of this sperm that jetted forcefully out of the end. He screamed a long and pained wailing that echoed around the otherwise silent room. On and on the stream of sperm jetted in a seemingly never ending flow.

Arabella closed her eyes and moaned her delight as his warm sticky come splashed all over her face and breasts. She paused, moving the finger inside him off his gland.

"Good boy," she mocked. "Scream well my little man for I simply love it when you wail."

As the finger located once again his body stiffened, his mouth open and eyes locked wide. Arabella tensed herself as she squatted there and came to orgasm as his warm juices again spurted over her face and shoulders.

"Mmmm," she moaned sexily and licked at the thick globules on her lips. Several more times should do for today."

***

Claire was straddled over Natalie's face, her open pussy pressing down on Natalie's mouth.

"Lick me bitch," she demanded for the third time.

A muffled refusal came from between her thighs and Claire pressed down harder. She revelled in her friend's disgust and revulsion at being expected to perform such an act.

Claire leaned forwards, her hands placed one on each of Natalie's parted thighs, her head dipped down to kiss lightly on Natalie's erect clitoris.

"Do it bitch," Claire growled and closed her lips around the hard bud.

Natalie's body tensed, her mouth opened in reaction and her tongue pushed out.

Claire tensed and moaned in delight as the thick worm of Natalie's tongue slipped up into her open pussy. Her own mouth sucked and her teeth clenched lightly to trap her friend's hard clitoris. A series of quivering spasms gripped Natalie's body making it shiver as the grip on her bud increased. Her tongue pushed fully out and up inside to curl around in exploration. Thick musky juices filled Natalie's senses of smell and taste, her sense of feel simply tuned to a high pitch as the exciting sensations pounded through her.

Claire's hands stroked and caressed, moving ever closer toward Natalie's open pussy. Two fingers of each of her hands pushed inside the gaping tunnel to probe and search in a fervent hunger for release. Her mouth worked, the tongue flicking lightly across he very tip of Natalie's hard bud. The two women licking and sucking now in a passionate kissing of deep sexual pleasure.

Claire came first, her thighs clamping hard around Natalie's head as a terrific surge of sensation shot through her. Her teeth bit hard in her excitement and her fingers delved deep in her orgasm.

Natalie followed shortly after, sensing and feeling her friend's body as she came had a profound effect on her and brought her off instantly. She bucked and writhed as the waves of ecstasy tore through her body.

***

It was with a most casual ease that the two women now sat at the kitchen table drinking coffee. Both were fully dressed and fully sexually gratified following their session together. There was an easiness between them, one that had never existed prior to today and both women were appreciative of it and glad to be able to talk freely about it.

"Those!" Natalie said empathetically, "were the very best - and the most orgasms - I have ever had."

Claire smiled back and set down her coffee cup.

"Glad you liked it. You really were a bitch devouring that big dildo the way that you did. Much more though to come at the manor and with Arabella's servants."

Natalie's eyes widened in interest, she shivered in delight as the thoughts came to her.

"What do it with other men you mean?"

Claire nodded.

"Not just men, but strapping young and fit men with bodies straight from heaven and cocks like small cucumbers. Two or three at a time if you want."

"No!" Natalie squealed in disbelief but her eyes seeking confirmation.

"True I assure you. I had two blokes at once there."

"Two?" Natalie asked looking a little bemused.

"Claire leaned forward across the table and lowered her voice secretively.

"One cock in my mouth and another up my pussy."

Natalie swallowed hard and sipped at her coffee, when she spoke her voice was trembling with excitement but the tone was more serious.

"My turn to visit the manor next week and I must admit I am beginning to feel a little nervous about it."

Claire sat back and crossed her legs.

"Excited too - bitch?"

Natalie looked up mischievously.

"And that - Mistress."

The two women giggled and enjoyed the light-heartedness before the tone turned back to being serious again.

"Haven't told the others anything have you, wouldn't want to ruin the surprise for Amey and Louise."

Natalie shook her head as she sipped from her mug.

"Nope! Licking and doing things with another woman is not the sort of thing that one wishes to discuss with friends."

Claire laughed aloud.

"You utter snob! Happy to get your pussy licked by a woman but not to talk of it."

Natalie flushed at the mickey-taking and responded equally light-heartedly.

"I will need to cultivate my speech," she mimicked in a polished accent. "If I am to serve at the manor."

Claire fell silent and said softly.

"And at the manor you will do exactly that - serve the Madam Arabella."

"Oh God," Natalie mumbled. "The very thought makes me all horny again."

Claire covered Natalie's hand lovingly and stroked it tenderly.

"You serve me bitch. Arabella at weekends perhaps but

103

during the week you are mine."

Natalie leaned close, her mouth just inches from Claire's pouting lips.

"Happy to serve you Mistress."

Claire's hand slipped around Natalie's head to draw her on to a passionate and hungry kiss. Tongues entwined the women kissed passionately as two lovers would, then as the kiss ended:

"I'm in need again," Claire breathed in a thick voice.

Natalie stared back.

"Your turn with the dildo I think, my pussy is still recovering."

Claire smiled back.

"Do it bitch!" she hissed.

Natalie hissed back sexily.

"Yes, Mistress."

CHAPTER EIGHT

Claire was totally naked, she wore just her favourite high heeled boots and bright-red lipstick. She strode confidently into her lounge and halted with her hands on her hips, two lengths of strong cord clutched in one hand.

"Stand when I enter the room you little shit!" she snapped.

Her husband Robert simply put his newspaper aside and stood up meekly.

"Kneel!" Claire ordered and stepped forward.

The sense of command was total, the pounding excitement accentuated by his hungry looks at her naked body. She moved in close, her right hand with fingers spread, stroked lovingly through his hair. Her fingers gripped and clenched, she twisted her hand cruelly to bring a cry of pain from her grovelling husband.

Both his hands clamped over hers in an attempt to ease

the tearing pain. Back and to the side his head was pulled arching his spine to a painful angle. Her knee snapped up hard into his chest to knock him backward onto the carpet.

"You are going to fuck me Robert," Claire breathed excitedly then hardened her tone to a menacing hiss. "And it had better be good."

She moved forward, raised her foot and pressed the thin heel of her boot hard down into the side of his thigh.

"Aren't you?" She demanded a response.

Robert's hand went instantly to her foot, trying with all his might to ease the penetrating pressure that was digging into his flesh.

"Yes Madam....Mistress," he blurted quickly.

Claire paused a moment before lifting her foot and standing back.

Robert clutched at his thigh with both hands, rubbing the affected area to ease the throbbing pain. He slowly rose to his knees, his head down and gaze downcast.

"Are you hard wimp?"

He shook his head solemnly and answered in a low and pathetic voice.

"No Mistress."

Claire snorted in derision.

"Thought so! Your silly little cock is becoming totally useless to me." She sighed heavily to show her displeasure. "Once again I must do something to assist you."

Claire walked to the dining room table, swaying her hips and buttocks sensually. She leaned over and spread her long legs, wriggling her backside to taunt him.

"Oh God!" she gasped loudly. "I need a cock! Get me a cock Robert, a nice thick one that can satisfy me as you can't."

A terrific surge shot through her as she heard his little whimper. Her right hand moved down to cup her pussy, the red painted fingernails teasing at her open slit.

He would be watching; looking between her thighs at her pussy and imagining a cock being pushed up her from behind, the thought thrilled her so very much. Claire's fingers pushed in, two side-by-side to force her labia apart.

"Another cock Robert," she breathed huskily. "I need some-one else's cock."

Claire began to move her hips in a crude mimicry of being fucked. Her taut thighs and buttocks jarring in a make-be-lieve rutting motion, her fingers delving deep inside her own body.

"He could fuck me like this Robert," she breathed between little gasps of delight.

Robert's voce cracked as he shouted back at her.

"No! Never!"

Claire laughed aloud.

"Yes Robert! Yes!" she called out as her fingers pumped urgently in and out of her.

He simply mumbled in defeat.

She stopped, stood upright and turned, her fingers slip-ping out easily over her copious juices. He was hard, his cock jutting out and pushing his trousers into a tent at the front. His face was flushed and his eyes roamed his wife's body longingly. She stood silently, teasing him and offering herself so blatantly whilst he virtually dribbled for her touch. Her tone changed to almost matter-of-fact as she stated.

"I had a lovely cock up me earlier today Robert."

He looked up her, his pathetic eyes searching her face hopefully for signs of jest.

"Not sure are you?" she mocked. "I might have been fucked but then you wouldn't know for sure would you."

His cock jerked in response, the material of his trousers shifting to portray his excitement. Claire noted the movement and lowered her voice sensually, her hand stroke idly at her shaven pussy.

"A nice hard cock Robert," she purred, her red lips mov-ing in mimicry of oral sex.

He grunted and tensed, a wet stain spread out through his light grey trousers to announce his climax. Claire was at him instantly, her eyes blazing and her lips curled back in anger. She slapped hard across the side of his face to knock him sideways back onto the floor. Her booted foot landed a hefty kick into his side then another that crashed hard against his buttocks.

"Bastard!" she screeched furiously. "Bastard! I'll see that you suffer for that."

Seething, Claire stalked from the room to leave him cowering fearfully on the hearthrug.

***

Madam treated her differently this Friday. She greeted Claire on the front steps of the house and linked her arm as she guided her through to the breakfast room.

"First we eat and then," Arabella paused, "the fun begins."

Both women wore identical body suits in shimmering black latex that fastened tightly around the collar to leave just their faces and hands showing as flesh. Tight, so very tight and clinging the suits looked fantastic, portraying clearly the shape of their bodies beneath. High heeled boots and made up faces; the two women looked harsh and yet sensual, they settled themselves at the long table and chatted idly.

Two naked servants served the breakfast and stood back attentively but discreetly as the women ate.

Mid-way through their meal Arabella paused and posed the question.

"Would you like some little distraction fellow Mistress?"

Claire was eating and her mouth was full but she nodded her ready agreement. Arabella had used the term 'fellow Mistress' and Claire noted this, a certain pride filling her.

Madam turned to the servants and gave an order.

"One of you, up on the table now and lie back."

The man complied, Paul, the blond servant that Claire particularly liked, mounted the table and lay back along its length between the two women.

"Wank yourself off then!" Arabella's harsh voice commanded.

Claire almost choked but watched in fascination as he gripped his cock and began coaxing it to arousal. A moment or two passed before his cock began to harden and stand upright. It thrilled Claire to watch him, her eyes flicked rapidly over his thighs and chest, then to his face and quickly back to his cock lest she should miss some small part of the action. She watched spellbound as his great fist pumped fast up and down his thick rod.

It was so erotic, to have this gorgeous naked man only inches in front of her and playing with himself so unashamedly.

Her pussy gripped in excitement as the man rubbed harder and faster in growing arousal, his hand almost a blur as he pumped his cock furiously.

Arabella ate on almost disinterestedly with only an occasional glance up at the servant. He groaned and Claire sighed, she squeezed her thighs together as he approached his climax.

"Ahh!" Claire gasped aloud as he came. A thick stream of his sperm jetted out high into the air and landing in thick globules on his stomach and chest. She felt a terrific surge pass through her and wished that she could have had the privilege of doing it for him.

Arabella rose from her chair, leaned over and covered the end of his cock with her mouth. Her head bobbed and loud sucking noises were heard as she cleaned the servant's cock with her mouth.

Several moments passed before she straightened, licking at her lips in satisfaction. Not a hint of embarrassment or excitement showed on her face, it was as though she had just eaten a cream cake and nothing more.

"Come," she said casually to Claire. "Let's walk in the grounds, I have something to tell you."

***

Claire stood on the front steps in her suit and boots, her legs set wide in a confident and arrogant stance. In her hand she held a riding crop and on her finger a huge gold ring. 'The symbol of acceptance' Arabella had called it when she had presented it to Claire. She glowed, recalling Madam's words as they had walked in the grounds.

"You, Claire," Madam had said, "have proved to be a most worthy student. Whilst your education is not yet complete you have shown rapid and willing acceptance and compliance. You now hold the title of 'Mistress'. The ring will ensure that all servants will obey you without question. Today you have a special task, for this weekend we have two house guests, they will arrive shortly and be completely under your command. See to it Claire," Arabella had emphasised, "that they suffer - most miserably."

Claire glanced again at her watch and slapped the crop hard down on her other palm in impatience. The guests were late, not a good start for them, she thought. The time on the steps had given the opportunity for her to plan their demise, she would certainly make them suffer and that suffering would certainly be miserable indeed.

At last the black limousine swept up the driveway and pulled to a halt at the foot of the steps. The polished body-work looking regal and so important, the black-tinted windows hiding the occupants from view.

The chauffeur acted dutifully and opened the back door whilst the two suited men got out. They stood in awe, looking up at Claire from the base of the steps, their greedy eyes roaming her body hungrily.

Claire felt pulsing snags of excitement grabbing deep in her vulva, her nipples were hard and pressing against the tight material of her suit; her clitoris too formed a neat little bump at her vulva.

The chauffeur turned to Claire to offer his apologies for the late arrival.

"Madam, the delay was my fault and not...."

"Silence!" Claire snapped angrily from the steps above the three men. "I will deal with you later, now leave us."

She moved to the retaining rail and looked down, her arm pointed the crop distastefully at the two visitors.

"Remove your shoes and socks," she commanded. "And be quick about it."

Both men hesitated and then complied, to stand barefoot on the hard stones of the gravelled driveway.

Claire was aware of the men's frequent glances up at her, between her thighs to where the tight suit pulled into the shape of her pussy. Those leering looks pleased her much and her pussy responded by flowing its juices readily within the tight covering.

"Jackets and shirts now - take them off," she ordered coldly. "And walk around as you strip."

She watched them hobbling gingerly over the hard uneven stones, grunting their discomfort as they stripped to the waist.

One was older, in his early fifties she guessed, the other much younger, a son perhaps. Both men were well dressed and fairly fit with good lean bodies. The younger of the two was extremely good looking but that would pull no favours in softening his punishment.

They stood now like two pathetic little puppies waiting for their Master to command them. At the casual wave of the crop in instruction they loosed their trousers and underpants to drop them to the floor.

Claire laughed aloud, enjoying herself greatly as she inspected the naked men and their cocks.

"Small and inadequate," she chuckled. "Your tiny little cocks that you offer offend me."

Her tone then lowered to a menacing growl.

"And for that, you will both suffer."

In long loping strides Claire moved along the terrace and down the steps, aware of the lusting gazes that followed her every movement. At the bottom step she paused.

"Come here both of you."

They began to move but were halted instantly by Claire's cutting voice.

"Crawl you worthless shits, crawl on your hands and knees."

Their pain and great discomfort pleased her much as she watched them scrabbling toward her. "Nothing though," she said softly to herself, "compared with what is in store for you both."

***

Natalie's heart pounded in her chest, her hands trembled and her body felt alive with pulsing pleasure as she slowly parted her knees.

He sat opposite her on the tube train as it rattled toward Oxford Circus station, his frequent glances at her legs hadn't gone unnoticed by her. The man's eyes widened in delighted surprise as his gaze fixed beneath her skirt. His face flushed excitedly and he shifted in his seat, his big hands held the folded newspaper firmly across his lap.

Natalie received a terrific jolt in her pussy as she displayed herself for him. So secretive and naughty, the few other passengers further down the carriage blissfully unaware of her flashing. He would be able to see her inner thighs, the creamy white flesh above her socking tops and the tight white triangle of her panties. The thumping sensations in her body simply got stronger and more delightful. She slid forward slightly, opening her knees further as her confidence and excitement grew. She looked at him with wide moon-like eyes and smiled knowingly, parting her lips sensually. Natalie's fingers toyed idly at the buttons of her blouse, slipping one open to show the very beginning of her tight cleavage.

She slowly closed her knees, watching his expression change to one of disappointment before parting them wide again. Slowly back and forth she moved her knees teasing him with alternating glimpses of her hidden secrets. Natalie delighted in his obvious excitement, he was perspiring, his face red and stare fixed.

She stood slowly, towering over him and adjusting her skirt casually. As she moved toward the doors she turned and winked before stepping out onto the platform and walking away. Once in the exit tunnel, she stopped, leaned back again the wall and sighed heavily.

She was excited, her whole body crying out with the aching need and the sheer thrill of showing herself. It had been so good and so powerful, horny and simply wonderfully exciting. The pulling sensations deep in her vulva cried out for more, her nipples throbbed in agreement and her hard clitoris ached a dull nagging to further her need. She straightened herself, pushed out her chest and arched her back, undoing another button on her blouse before walking happily towards the exit and the main street above.

She bathed in the many admiring glances as she made her way through the crowds, stopping often at some of the many small stalls that lined the main streets; leaning forward more than necessary to give the stallholders ample glimpses of her cleavage. It maintained her high, the pumping need and thrill of the show. Her blouse was open down to the join of her bra, her breasts were swelled by the restricting cups to offer her firm orbs in a tight cleft of temptation. Her pussy literally throbbed its delight at the sensations that were pumping through her.

She lingered on stairways; close to the edge to afford unhindered sight up her skirt to the many interested men who passed beneath. She squatted and bent over often; all in seeming innocent actions like looking at goods on sale but each movement sexually loaded. She posed and moved to excite and delight, positioning herself so as to give the best sights of her body. For hours she moved along the various streets and locations, savouring the feelings and arousal of her secretive

112

offerings.

At last she could hold out no longer, it was in the toilet of a small cafÈ that she bolted the door and was at last alone. Her hand slipped urgently down inside her panties to cup her mons and pussy. She pressed and rubbed on her excited bud and came almost instantly to orgasm.

***

It was to the back of the house that Claire had herded the two men, lashing out with the crop often to guide them in the desired direction. They now knelt on the hard cobblestones of the back yard, their hands tied firmly behind their backs.

Claire stood before the elder man, her mons only an inch or so away from his face.

"Can you imagine my pussy beneath the suit?" she asked huskily.

"Oh Yes," the man answered longingly.

She struck swiftly, cutting the crop hard down across the shoulder of the younger man.

"Your friend here will suffer each time you fail to use my title," she stated casually and then snapped harshly. "Madam! You will call me Madam!"

"Yes Madam, sorry Madam."

She moved close to press her latex covered mons against his face.

"Would like to have me?" she asked in a teasing little voice, "to fuck me and to get your silly little cock up inside me?"

"Yes," he muttered in excited response.

She directed her speech to the younger man and tapped at his arm with the crop.

"And you? Would you like to fuck me, perhaps from behind?"

His face broke a huge smile.

"Yes please Madam!"

Claire paused as though considering the possibility. She

113

leaned down close to their faces and used an even tone of voice.

"Well," she teased. "You can't"

Claire laughed loudly, enjoying the crestfallen expressions on their faces and the twitching spasms of expectation in their cocks. She mocked the helpless men in their dejection and flaunted her slim body for their pitiful pleading gazes.

"Now. To begin the proceedings of your weekend at the manor we will have some exercise. You will both run around the full outside of the main house and buildings." Claire paused. "To meet with me back on the front steps of the main house. The first one of you to arrive will receive ten less lashes than the second of you." she paused again.

"Well? Off you go!" she snapped impatiently.

Both men struggled to their feet, both shouldering each other aside in their haste as they ran fast towards and around the potting sheds.

Claire was aware of someone moving up behind her, she moaned in delight as Arabella's hand cupped her buttocks from the back.

"You are progressing well with our guests young Mistress, don't however be too easy on them will you now."

"The weekend is yet young," Claire giggled back.

"Would the new Mistress care to share Madam's bed to-night?" Arabella's silky soft voice purred.

Claire closed her eyes to savour the caressing fingers on her body and murmured.

"It would be my pleasure Madam."

***

The waiter had the advantage and Natalie helped him to make the most of it as she hunched her shoulders. He placed the coffee down on the table and lingered looking straight down her open blouse. She sat at the pavement table outside the small cafe basking in the sun and the admiring glances. Again

114

and again he had returned to her table to clear, wipe it over and to wipe it again, his obvious interest pleased her greatly.

The rubbing of herself in the toilets earlier had helped ease the ache but it hadn't satisfied her; only one thing could do that, a man's warm and hard cock. She needed that now so desperately, the morning's teasing had maintained her wonderful high level of arousal but had not allowed it to subside.

She smiled up him, a knowing and encouraging smile. Words were unnecessary between them as he returned her gaze and smiled back. She rose to her feet, standing close to him, her chest pushed out invitingly.

"Are the toilets free do you know?" she asked sexily.

He led off, almost running in his urgency to lead her through the back of the cafe and into the corridor beyond. Natalie was almost dragged into the small cubicle as he pulled excitedly on her wrist. Once the door closed she was shoved roughly face against the door, one of his hands groping coarsely at her breasts the other lifting the back of her skirt. For several minutes he fondled and groped, his hands running over her firm buttocks and little panties.

Natalie gasped as her panties were pulled roughly down to her ankles and she stepped out of them, instinctively shifting her legs apart, the pumping excitement bringing her closer to her peak. She gratefully prepared to receive the stranger's cock up inside her.

He was against her in an instant, his hard cock pressing into the cleft of her buttocks, one strong hand clamping on the back of her neck to press her face to the door. She was trapped, squashed hard between the door and his excited body. It happened suddenly, he simply grunted once and shot his sperm up over the top of her buttocks and clothing.

Natalie was livid in her disappointment, she turned in fury and brought her knee sharply into his groin. He fell back onto the seat with both hand clamped between his legs to ease the excruciating pain.

Her pussy had been ready to be sated, her mind too had

welcomed the promised sex and now it was for nothing. The anger within her tuned her senses, adding to her level of arousal, she breathed deeply several times to maintain control. She gripped the man's hair roughly and pulled his head up to look at her. She was amazed at her own calmness in her actions, she leaned back against the door, parted her legs and lifted her skirt.

"Lick me you bastard," she hissed. "Lick me."

***

Claire stood waiting on the lawn in front of the house, a naked male servant by her side and her hand caressing his buttocks.

It was the younger of the two visitors that arrived first, panting, his face eagerly seeking acknowledgement he halted in front of Claire.

"I lied," she giggled. "You now get ten extra lashes."

He was deflated, his devastation and his exhaustion combined to lower his spirits admirably. They waited until the second and older visitor finally came along struggling hard to complete the course.

"Right!" Claire announced loudly. "Now a picnic for you my little teddy bears - off to the woods we go!"

With liberal use of the crop on their naked bodies Claire herded them across the wide expanse of grass and into the wooded area. At a point about two hundred yards into the wood she halted them and turned to the servant.

"Tie them as instructed," she told him.

The servant busied himself, selecting the necessary ropes from the small holdall that he carried. Both men were each tied to a tree either side of the small path and facing one another. With their backs against the trees, their arms were pulled harshly backward and securely bound; likewise their ankles were firmly roped to the trees. Claire watched intently as the servant looped a thin cord and attached a small weight then

116

slipped it over the head of the younger man's cock. The resulting downward pull of the weight on his cock made an erection a fearful prospect indeed. The older man was treated to the same and grunted as the weight was released to hang free.

Claire moved close, positioning herself to the side of the older man. She smiled sweetly at him as she raised the crop high above her shoulder.

"Sing loud my sweet for there are only the trees to hear your pain."

She cut down harshly with the crop to land a stinging blow to the top of his thigh.

He screamed, a pained wailing that portrayed his intense agony. Again she struck, the crop slicing through the air to sting savagely on his other thigh. Eight lashes in all she laid on him, on his legs, stomach and chest before she paused.

The pounding excitement she felt flooded through her, his muttering and suffering adding to her now high state of arousal. She moved to stand close by the younger man and raised the crop.

"No!" he wailed fearfully, "release me - I want to leave!"

Claire paused and looked a him questioningly.

"Leave? Did you say leave?"

She laughed aloud and then lashed savagely at his shins. Claire continued to laugh as she beat his thighs and lower belly, his chest and shoulder with sixteen hard and brutal lashes. She at last halted, her chest rising and falling with her excited breathing. Claire leaned close to his face, her expression stern and threatening.

"You came here for the weekend and you will stay for every last minute of that time. Your disobedience will only add to the suffering that I will inflict upon you during that time."

The man groaned mournfully through clenched teeth as he fought to cope with the searing pain in his body.

Claire moved back, discarded the crop and stood with legs set apart. Her hands went to the zipper of her tight outfit and slid it down past her breasts almost to her mons.

"Help me out of this," she called to the servant.

It was a struggle, the tight suit and her body moisture had created a tight vacuum that resisted efforts to remove it. Slowly and with the servant's help her glistening nude body began to appear. Claire was wet, her whole body coated in a heavy covering of perspiration that gleamed in the bright daylight. She stood proud and naked with just her long boots remaining on her slim body.

With a wave of her hand she beckoned the man around to her front.

"Lick my breasts," she instructed casually.

Claire stood erect as the big servant ran his tongue over her soft orbs, lapping eagerly at the moisture on her skin. Down between her breasts his searching tongue moved, then to her nipples and rings and onto her lower stomach. Many minutes passed before she called a halt, dropped her body to squat and gripped the servants cock. Her mouth cover the end and she feed the whole length of it deep into her throat. A surge shot through her as she heard the older visitor gasp in envious wonder at her actions.

For several minutes she sucked and licked the great cock, tickling at his firm ball-sac with one delicate hand. Her head bobbed in slow and sensual movements with her lips gripped tightly around its girth. A length she withdrew, stood upright and addressed the two visitors.

"You could have experienced the feel of my mouth on your cocks you stupid little men but you have displeased me. If your performance improves tomorrow I might - just might - allow you to touch me."

Claire knelt on all fours, side-on to the two watching visitors to give them a clear view of her.

"Fuck me," she ordered the servant.

Claire gasped as his great hands gripped her hips and the big bulbous head of his cock located at the entrance to her pussy. She cried out as he pushed fully home up inside her

118

and began a frantic thrusting with his hips. Her whole body shook as the man pounded hard into her, his whole strength pinioning her and crashing against her.

The thrill of the situation heightened Claire's pleasure. The two watching men were spellbound in envy, wishing that it could them having her in the servant's place. Their cocks began to stiffen, pulling painfully against the weighted cords attached to them. The men's faces screwed up in a grimace of tortured agony yet they continued to watch Claire in her pleasure.

She moaned and grunted as she was so violently fucked, it was not only for her benefit but for both of the visitors also. Claire cried out as she felt the servant begin to tense, his pace quickened and he grunted loudly. She screamed as he came, his hot sperm washing her insides in exciting little jerks. She came to orgasm instantly, her mouth open and her head nodding acceptance of the wonderful sensations. She slumped forwards murmuring her pleasure to the leaf-coated ground.

Several minutes passed in silence as she bathed in the after ripples of her climax before she at last roused herself and stood up.

"Mmmm, that was so good," she breathed sexily. "Tonight I will be sharing Madam's bed and we will enjoy all manner of delightful sex together. Think of us won't you, think of us in our pleasure as you stand here."

It took a few seconds for her words to register in their brains.

"I will," Claire said easily. "send someone to release you - but not until morning."

She walked away toward the house laughing loudly with the desperate pleading shouts of the two visitors becoming more distant by the moment.

CHAPTER NINE

Natalie trembled as she picked up the letter from the door mat, it was from Arabella, she simply knew it even before she had opened it. Carefully, she opened the envelope as she moved into the lounge and sat slowly down on the settee.

Her interest was total, Natalie read slowly so as to fully absorb each and every ornately written word on the thick cartridge paper. She gasped in excited pleasure as her instructions were issued, her pussy contracting in response. She was to go to the main park at midnight on Friday, at the point where the paths crossed near the main gates she was to wait there naked and alone.

She flushed with pounding excitement, her body throbbing in anticipation of her compliance. Natalie laid the letter carefully aside, next Friday simply couldn't come too quickly for her.

***

Claire entered Madam's bedroom totally naked; she hung her head and her hands were clasped behind her back as she had been instructed. Madam's firm hand guided her to straddle the low framework.

About four inches wide and two feet high the thin frame was about three feet long with two foot stirrups fixed to the base flanges at either side. A thick latex dildo stuck up from the centre of the frame and it was to this point that Claire was guided. She stood now with the framework slotted between her knees whilst Arabella strapped her feet securely into the stirrups. Her wrists were firmly roped together behind her back and her elbows pulled painfully in together and bound securely. Arabella stood before the tethered girl, a huge smile creasing her face and her eyes filled with dancing excitement.

"I call this contraption my 'Iron Maiden' and its delights

you will soon taste for yourself."

At the press of an electric switch the framework began to rise up slowly, Arabella guided the head of the thick dildo to locate in the entrance to Claire's pussy. Up and up the framework rose, pushing the full length of the dildo up inside her and then the motor stopped.

Claire's body was forced upward, her legs stretched by the upward pressure of the framework and dildo. The cock-like phallus inside her felt huge and firm, welcome but not really sexual.

Arabella approached and sprung open the little nipple clamp, holding it up for Claire's benefit.

"These my little bitch," she breathed excitedly. "Will help tune your senses - and your pussy."

Claire grunted as the sharp metal teeth bit spitefully into the very tip of her nipple; burning agony shot through her whole body but her inner muscles gripped in reaction. These sensations were repeated as the second clamp was attached to her other nipple and her body shook in pained tension. It felt so very wonderful, to be bound so uncomfortably, a dildo up inside her and now the introduction of raw and agonising pain. Her clitoris jutted out from her body in excitement, Claire just wished she were able to touch and to stroke her throbbing bud. She bit her bottom lip to stifle her rising emotions but remained silent.

Arabella moved onto the huge double bed and settled her naked body comfortably. She raised her knees and parted her long slender thighs to show her shaven pussy in all its glory. A huge black dildo was worked fully up inside her, forcing her swollen labia apart and stretching the pink inner lips tightly around its thickness. Madam rested there, one hand holding the handgrip of the dildo in her right hand, the left holding the control switch for the framework.

"I simply love this part," Arabella purred sexily. "I find it so very,.....well exciting."

It crashed against Claire's body suddenly, a brilliant flash

121

of confusion filled her mind. The framework suddenly dropped about six inches and instantly rammed hard back upward to jar Claire's frail body violently.

"Unnnh!" Claire uttered as the rapid ramming dildo was smashed into her. Pinioned as she was she could do nothing whatsoever but stand and accept the heavy pounding of her body. Fast and hard, the framework moved, jerking Claire's body harshly with the force of the upward move. Cruel and rough, hard and uncaring the rapid fucking went.

Madam purred her contentment and began to use the long dildo on herself, sliding it slowly in and out of her pussy as she watched the young girl in her demise. Faster Arabella moved her hand, her excitement growing as she watched Claire being battered so brutally. The girl's mouth hung open and her eyes wide in fearful uncertainty as she was jerked like a rag doll.

Madam snuggled deeper into the quilt, raised her hips and began pumping the dildo furiously into her open pussy. During her pleasure never once did her eyes leave the wonderful sight of the girl in pained ecstasy.

Claire was helpless and her mind felt distant, it was difficult to even think during the rapid upward pounding of the dildo. She had come once already, the sight of Arabella fucking herself so fervently with the long dildo, writhing and moaning her delight as she had brought herself off. She now felt herself building toward her second and seemingly equally powerful orgasm. And she did, as Madam's hips bucked high in a final surge of pleasure and she screamed, Claire came too.

***

Claire wore little suede ankles boots and black hold-up stockings. A tight uplift bra in lacy black and a tiny pair of panties that barely covered her pussy. Around her throat she wore a velvet choker and her hair styled to cling against the sides of

122

her head and face.

She stood in the large study, the morning sun beaming brightly through the high Edwardian windows to bathe the room with warmth.

The two visitors knelt naked before her, their hands tied behind their backs and ankles bound together with coarse rope. Their heads were forward and touching the carpet in a humble and subservient fashion.

"Did you enjoy your night in the woods?" she asked coldly. "I'm told that it rained hard at one point during the early hours."

"Yes Mistress," the two men answered as one. Their voices were low and defeated, all fight and resistance long removed from their spirit.

Claire grunted her approval but sought further confirmation of their commitment.

"You are then I take it, both now ready to comply with my instructions?"

"Yes Mistress," both voices answered solemnly.

Claire placed the sole of one of her feet down on the back of the younger man's neck to hold him firm.

"Excellent! Then we will start the day as we mean to go on- with a little pain."

In an overhead swing of the thin cane, she cut down hard to sting agonisingly down the crease of his presented buttocks and on the tender entrance of his anus.

The man screamed loudly. And then it changed to a pitiful pleading wail that bore testament to the excruciating agony that he felt. Twice more she lashed down on him, expert deftness aiming the blows precisely. She then moved to the second man and repeated three savage lashes also on his tender orifice.

It felt so good, the command she had, the way these pathetic men cringed at her feet in fear of her. Wave after wave of terrific excitement flooded through to pulse hard in her pussy.

"Madam tells me that you are here to learn the delights

123

that pain can bring. You will during this weekend learn a great deal my worthless little shits," she gloated.

One with each hand, she gripped their hair and hoisted them unceremoniously to their feet. Cries of pain filled the room as they struggled to gain their feet and to ease the tearing pain in their scalps. Claire manoeuvred them close and facing one another, their bodies just inches apart. Using her delicate fingers in a sensual and stroking fashion she coaxed their flaccid cocks to erection. Moaning and gasping softly for added effect, Claire fondled and teased until both were fully hard. She tied the two erect members securely together with thin cord, both the hard cocks pressed upright and against each other,.

Claire circled the two men, strutting confidently and proudly around them.

"I shall now beat you soundly. The first of you to come will reap the rewards of my pleasure - the other? Well let's just say - what a shame for him."

They screamed as one when she struck, one in pain and the other in fearful reaction. Stinging lashes that bit cruelly into the soft backs of their thighs. Lash after savage lash stung at them in turn as she moved around them. Their buttocks and shoulders, the soft flesh of their upper arms and the outsides of their thighs all warmed to the taste of the cane.

On and on the beating went, brutal and uncaring as Claire's excitement rose. She felt alive with control and the pain she was inflicting was bringing her close to her peak. The younger man grunted and tensed, his cock spat little jerks of sperm out to splatter over his friend's belly and stomach. The older man gagged in disgusted revulsion and that pleased Claire tremendously.

The sight of the two men, pressed cock to cock and in arousal was so electrifying, she was almost at her peak when the older man shot his seed to a loud groan of disgust from his younger partner. It was simply too much for Claire, she relaxed, allowing the pounding waves to fill and wash her body. Her knees tensed to brace herself, her head threw back and she came to a tearing and delightful orgasm.

*****

Arabella had lunched on the patio in the bright sunshine. The huge ham salad and a bottle of chilled white wine had been most agreeable and she sat back feeling relaxed and full.

Three naked servants stood in line and moved closer, their thick cocks jutting out from their bodies expectantly in erection.

"Now!" Arabella said softly. "Which one of you today I wonder."

She gripped the black servant's long cock, her fingers circling and her thumb teasing at the sensitive joint below the head. Her head dipped forward; her red lips kissing lightly on the very tip to draw a low moan of approval from the man. She licked the pinkish head for several moments before repeating the same on the next man.

"Decisions," she said as she withdrew and gripped the third servant's cock. "So very difficult to chose."

Arabella closed her mouth over his cock and fed the whole length into her soft mouth, her head bobbing as she savoured his stiff rod.

He came instantly, shooting his hot cream deep into the back of her throat and grunting aloud as his body jerked in pleasure.

"Mmmm," she murmured sexily. "All three of you I think."

Again she sucked and licked to bring the second servant to climax, slipping her head back as he came so as to receive his warm seed over her face. With the black servant, she simply placed her lips against the tip of his cock, parted slightly over the eyehole and teased at his balls. When he came it was with terrific force. The sperm spurted out to dribble from her mouth in thick clinging globules.

125

Arabella sat back, cleaning her face with her napkin.

"Now," she purred sensually. "Each of you may lick me in turn."

She lay back, stretched her legs and parted them. Her hand pulled the gusset of her little panties aside to offer her shaven pussy ready for the eager tongues.

***

She wanted to be sure for next Friday, nothing could be - would be -allowed to go wrong. Natalie stood at the park gates mid-afternoon reading the closing times written on the fading wooden plaque. She had found the cross-paths easily and was now desperately trying to work out how to scale the high railings and in the dark too. It was a test, she realised that, not a simple task but one that she was determined to overcome and to comply with.

The park was crowded, the abnormally long spell of good weather had brought sun bathers flocking to the park in droves. Late lunch workers, mothers with children and men, lots and lots of men simply ogling the vast quantity of female flesh on offer. Natalie too had taken advantage of the sunshine with her skimpy clothing but not for the purpose of gaining a tan.

She wore a thin flowery skirt, so short that it barely covered her crotch, stopping just short of it when standing upright. It was delightful in its material and length, accentuating her long slender thighs. Her top was little more than a light grey vest; two thin straps hung it from her shoulders and it finished just beneath her bra-less breasts to leave her midriff bare. The thin material hugged her body and breasts tightly to clearly show the bumps of her excited nipples. Her hair was tied up showing her graceful long neck and adding more to her sparsely clothed appearance.

Her mission today was simple, to identify access to the park and then to show herself off and to gain those wonderful feelings and sensations that flashing brought with it. To gain once more the thrill and excitement of offering her body for men's hungry gazes.

A smile broke on her face as the solution of entry came to her, she felt a rush in her body and sighed heavily. The problem was solved, now the really good part of the day was about to begin. Walking confidently, aware of the many admiring and leering looks that she was receiving, Natalie moved deeper into the centre of the park.

Near the middle of the park the path curved round a gently sloping bank of lush green grass. It was here that she chose to wait. She lay back resting on her elbows one knee raised and the other outstretched. Her little skirt had pulled up her thighs almost to her hip, her tiny white panties and most of her upper thighs would be clearly visible to any passers-by on the path. The very thought of it brought a rush of those wonderful sensations bubbling through her.

Several minutes passed before a couple rounded the curve, arm in arm they giggled and hugged close in their obvious love for one another. As they came close, the man's gaze fixed on Natalie's upper thighs, his stare incredulous but delighted. His female partner, oblivious at first to the point of his interest, noted his deep fixation and scolded him bluntly as they passed the smiling Natalie.

Two youths were next, even from far off they could be seen nudging each other excitedly and nodding in Natalie's direction.

She responded, raising both knees and parting them idly. Her clitoris gripped in jerking spasms as the obviously delighted youths took full advantage of her offering. Their mouths hung open and eyes were wide in disbelief at their good fortune. Both heads held their stare between her legs as they ambled slowly past. Natalie almost came, it was such a high, a thrilling and ultimate high to have them staring at her lightly covered sex.

For an hour she savoured the admiring glances and lusting stares of various men, the two youths returning again and again to view the display. It was all so good but it simply wasn't enough to feed that gnawing ache deep inside her. Natalie stood, her tight little panties pulling harshly across her firm aroused clitoris to further her need.

She walked, casually and in no particular direction, positioning her route so as to gain the most from the male observers. In an impulsive move she strayed off the path and across the vast open grassed area to a remote part where a sleeping man lay on his back. Natalie stood close to his head, her legs slightly apart and coughed politely.

As his eyes opened sleepily, they locked wide, staring straight up under her little skirt to the firm mound of her pussy.

Natalie stood erect and silent allowing him to ogle her secret place so blatantly. The thrill that she received was tremendous, her whole body quivered with sexual excitement.

"I'm trying to find the toilets," she offered in a helpless little voice and squatted down beside him.

Her knees were parted, the whole of her thinly veiled pussy offered between her open thighs. The charge almost brought her off, a heavy thumping that made her head swim in distant and detached mistiness.

"I need to pee," she said softly, her voice thick and sensual.

The man had roused himself onto one elbow, his stare however had not moved from under her skirt. He tried to speak but no words came, one hand gripped the front of his trousers to ease the pressure on his erection.

Natalie slipped one hand down under her skirt and hooked her finger under the elastic of her panties. She paused there teasingly.

"Should I?" she asked sexily.

The man simply nodded his agreement, his face flushed with excitement.

Natalie lifted the elastic and pulled her panties aside to show her hair coated pussy stretched wide and open. It was perhaps a combination of the powerful tugging at her insides and the build up of the thrill and excitement over a long period that made it happen. Her bladder began to empty as she squatted before him, the steaming flow jetting powerfully out of her body onto the grass below. Spread and exposed her labia were pulled apart and her pulsing clitoris jutting out in erection.

Never before would she have believed it could be possible but she came to orgasm as she peed. A long and satisfying stream of golden liquid and an equally long and satisfying orgasm that tore through her body in delightful little shudders. She allowed herself frequent glances at the man's face and his amazed expression simply added to the thrill.

Natalie casually accepted his handkerchief and slowly wiped herself dry with it. She replaced her panties to cover her pussy and stood up.

"Thank you so much," she said brightly, turned and walked away.

***

The two visitors were tied seated and naked on high-backed dining chairs in the study. They had been there for nearly four hours since Claire had left them to brood and think.

She entered theatrically, slamming the door behind her noisily for effect. She was naked, just her ankles boots and black hold-up stockings to cover her bareness.

Both the men's leering gazes followed her progress as she walked toward them. Already their cocks were stirring to hardness, twitching into life and beginning to rise. She posed and pouted, waiting until the full erections were attained and delighting in the lusting looks at her naked body.

She straddled the elder man's thighs, hovering her pussy tantalisingly above the tip of his cock. Her hands rested now on her shoulders and she gradually lowered herself down onto him. Claire halted when the head of his cock was just inside her, she smiled down at his beaming face and pouted her red lips.

"Like me to take it all up me?"

He nodded and grunted his delight in response. His desperate need obvious in his puppy-like pleading eyes.

She simply hovered there as she was and began flexing her internal muscles to grip and relax around the head inside her.

The man groaned, a pained and urgent moaning from deep in his throat. He longed to feel all of his cock inside her, to savour her warm wet body around him. Her youthful and fresh body that could bring such wonderful sensations but he was denied them all. He watched her taut stomach undulating before his face, her firm mons and heavy breasts all moving sensually as her body gripped him.

Clench and relax, clench and relax was the pulsing rhythm that Claire took up. Her thigh muscles were tensed as were her buttock muscles to hold her steady above him.

The man cried out, he tried to shift his hips and raise himself to get more of his cock inside her but she countered his move. Just the head remained inside to tantalise him mercilessly.

"Please!" he pleaded pitifully. "Please!"

Claire ignored him and continued pumping her muscles around his cock and revelling in his discomfort.

The man grunted several times.

"Oh God!" he muttered and then tensed.

Claire felt his cock twitch inside her and then a warm coating of his sperm as it spurted up inside her stretched pussy. She grunted loudly in satisfaction and moved back and away from him. Sperm trickled down the inside of her thigh as she moved around to the younger man. Claire straddled him and lowered herself fully down on his stiff cock until his pubic bone pressed against her clitoris. She kissed him full on the lips and then started working her inner muscles once again.

He cried out in pleasure, his voice faltering as he groaned his deep satisfaction.

Her hands gripped his head, her fingers entwining spite-fully in his hair and she began to chuckle. She screwed her hands around to bring a sharp yelp of pain from the cringing man. Again and again she twisted and her body pulsed its delight at her sadism.

"Like me to move on you wouldn't you?" she teased. "But I won't."

"Bitch!" he spat angrily in frustration.

She laughed and then gripped her internal muscles tightly around him and held him like that. He tensed and grunted, his face contorted in a mask of pained pleasure until she released her grip.

"Is it nice," she mocked, "to feel your friend's come all around your cock? He shot his load up inside me remember and now his seed is coating your dick?"

She laughed aloud at his look of sheer revulsion and gripped him again. Claire increased the pace, pumping his cock to milk it of its sperm. Her wet warmth clamping hard around the whole length and girth of his throbbing cock. His revulsion forgotten in his pleasure the man's eyes closed and his body tensed ready to receive his orgasm. Claire sensed his approaching climax and stopped, she stood up, lifting herself off him and standing back.

"Fucking bitch!" the man's screamed at her. "You fucking teaser!"

Claire's expression became serious, she stepped forward and slapped his face so hard that his head was jarred to the side.

"That," she stated coldly, "was a very silly mistake in-deed."

CHAPTER TEN

The two women sat at the small table on the terrace taking breakfast. Arabella, finishing her boiled egg and toast looked down over the verdant green lawns to the small copse beyond.

"Our visitors?" she asked casually and began spreading butter on her third piece of toast.

Claire sipped at her Windsor tea from the enormous breakfast cup.

"Shall we just say I have left them in suspension."

Arabella nodded her understanding.

"You have done well Claire, I should like to make you an offer."

Claire giggled impishly and quipped:

"My pussy is still a little sore from that machine of yours but I'm sure we could find some other way of enjoying ourselves."

"That of course is always on the menu but my offer is a little more serious," Arabella said firmly. "I have watched your progress, the way you have adapted so readily. You are a natural Claire and I want you here."

"What to live here you mean?"

"If you wish, we can certainly accommodate you, although living here wouldn't be a requirement. My staff need a firm hand to control them, I have plans Claire for this place and those plans are rapidly coming to fruition, I need your assistance as part of those plans."

Claire felt both complimented and excited by the offer, she sat silently absorbing the ramifications.

"You are unsure," Arabella stated as she refilled their cups from the silver teapot.

"Not so much unsure as, well, wondering how it will affect my other life away from the manor."

"It need not, we could come to a part-time arrangement at first to ensure a smooth transition, weekends and perhaps two weekdays. I would of course supply a car for you to get here, a room of your own to be used when you visit and expenses on top of a mutually agreed salary."

Claire accepted the offered tea cup and sat back stirring idly with the spoon, her thoughts distant and filling.

Arabella continued. "Natalie is due here soon and from what you have told me she is already hooked. Amey, sweet little Amey I know to be not only shy and timid but a veritable furnace of burning desire beneath. Louise afterwards; and we both know her tremendous sexual needs."

Claire could only agree with all that had been said.

"Three more additions in as many months, you see now why I will need a strong and trusted assistant. Think on it Claire but let me have your answer soon."

"If I don't agree?" Claire asked.

"Nothing changes, you are still welcome here at any time you wish to visit - and I would hope that would be very often."

Claire stood up, using her hand to signal casually to the servant to follow her.

"Okay, I'll consider it and let you know by mid-week is that okay?"

"Marvellous," Arabella purred.

"Now, sadly, duty calls. Men to beat and all that," Claire giggled and strode off down the steps and across the lawns towards the copse.

***

The visitors were tilted forwards at an uncomfortable forty five degree angle, their arms pulled back behind them and upward. A rope attached to their wrists looped over a branch high above them to wrench their arms high and shoulders painfully against the joints. Their feet were spread wide and tied securely to a wooden pole that held their ankles agonisingly far apart. Ball gags were fitted into their mouths and rubber butt-plugs had been forced up inside their anuses. As an added discomfort Claire had attached small weights to the nipple clamps that bit cruelly into their tender buds.

"So my beauties!" Claire announced loudly as she reached them. "Are we enjoying ourselves?"

Not even a grunted reply came from the gagged men.

She paced slowly around them, her auburn hair shimmering a reddish hue in the sunshine. Her now bronzed skin a deep copper against the jet black of her bra and panties. The long black boots added to her air of authority as she regarded the imprisoned pair.

"Do I take it that you have learned not to defy me?"

Both men nodded rapidly.

Claire moved behind the younger man, slipped her hand around him and gripped his cock. She teased and coaxed him to erection before releasing her grip and moving away.

"Mmmh! We will see," she stated unconvinced. "You will remain here a little longer in the sunshine, call it my little reward for your obedience."

Deep muffled groans of despair were the response to her statement.

"Two things I shall leave you with though to help you through your pleasant morning. Firstly, the marks of my crop and secondly a liberal coating of jam on your cocks. We wouldn't want to deny the ants and wasps their lunches would we now?"

Both the men's heads raised, pitiful pleading eyes implored her to relent but she simply laughed aloud in answer.

"Unnh!" Claire grunted as she lashed at the younger man's outer thigh. The surge of sensation, the first of the morning felt so sweet and powerful as it rushed through her entire body. A bolt of excitement gripped in her pussy as she lashed at his other leg. Each cruel lash she gave him brought more powerful and intense sensations. The way his body bucked and twisted against his bonds delighted her more and she gave him extra lashes in her wild state of arousal.

The older man received less lashes but those administered were equally harsh and unforgiving in the force that they were delivered with. At last she stopped, panting hard and trembling with excitement.

She watched as the servant knelt to apply the jam, an erotic sight to Claire seeing one man stroke the cock of another.

Claire slipped off her panties and leaned back against a tree, her legs splayed wide and her pussy offered.

"Fuck me," she told the servant.

He came to her, standing between her open legs and pushing his long cock up inside her. He began a rough thrusting that jarred Claire's body on each powerful inward stroke. The coarse bark of the tree scratched at her back, his hard pubic bone slammed against her clitoris to sent her to the highest plane of arousal.

Claire's hands gripped his shoulders, the long fingernails digging deeply into his firm flesh. Her body shook under the hard pounding of his body against her as she was slammed against the tree. She cried out as he rammed hard into her and then screamed as she came to orgasm. Flashing lights of blinding brilliance filled her brain, her body warmed and rippled in pleasure. He spurted up inside her to complete the act and her satisfaction. She knew then, at that very moment what her answer to Arabella would be.

***

"Are you mad?" Little Amey asked unable to disguise the excitement in her voice. "Showing yourself off to men in public!"

"It's great!" Natalie responded smiling and sat down at the small kitchen table opposite her friend. She leaned forward, her hands clasped on the table in front of her, her eyes wide in excitement and her voice full of enthusiasm.

"So horny and thrilling. The way they look and leer. They want me, to touch and to feel me but they can't, they can only look and long for me."

"Oh God," Amey muttered.

"They get hard, their cocks stiffen in their trousers, simply dying to get it up me or into my mouth."

"Your mouth!" Amey squealed in surprise. "Did you say your mouth?"

Natalie's face was flushed and excited.

"Mmmm, to taste a hard cock, to lick it and suck it is soÖwell, out of this world."

Amey sat silently staring, her face reddening and her hand resting between her legs beneath the table.

"You seem to know all - I could never - you know show myself off like that."

"But you could!" Natalie enthused. It's so easy," she voiced lowered to a sensual drawl. "And so very bloody exciting."

Amey swallowed and secretly pressed her hand against her clitoris.

"Show me!" she said excitedly.

Natalie smiled.

"What? Take you with me or show you what I do here and now?"

Amey uttered a little murmur when she replied. Her voice was thick and quavering, her little body trembling in excited anticipation and sexual pounding.

"Both."

Natalie paused, smiling, then her expression changed to a sensual look of deep sexual offering. Her hand moved to the neck of her blouse and began unfastening the buttons.

Amey watched fascinated and thrilled as the tight, firm swell of Natalie's breasts became exposed.

"Now you," Natalie probed gently.

"Me! But I couldn't! I really couldn't."

"Do it," Natalie growled in a low and firm voice.

The young brunette swallowed hard and then followed suit,

her movements clumsy and non sensual. Natalie pulled her blouse open and then watched as Amey's neat little bra and pert breasts came in to view.

"Feel good?" Natalie asked.

"Different, but yes, nice and well - sort of sexy."

"With a man watching you it would be more than just sexy, it's more orgasm inducing stuff."

"Huh!" Amey sighed wistfully. "Chance would be a fine thing."

Natalie stood up and turned, she bent down to touch her shoes fully aware that her little skirt would be pulled up over her buttocks. Amey gave a little gasp and took in the slender upper thighs of her friend, the way the tiny little panties pulled in between her firm rounded buttocks. But most of all the firm pouch created by the way the material hugged her pussy lips.

"Oh God Natalie, I see what you mean But do you really do that for men?"

Natalie stood and turned to face her.

"Definitely and much more too. Come with me she urged her friend. Come along with me this afternoon and try it for yourself."

The young girl sat silently for a moment, her thighs squeezing together rhythmically to crush her labia around her hardened clitoris.

"I will!" she stated firmly. "I bloody well will."

***

The cars were parked on the cobbled yard at the rear of the manor that had once seen ponies and traps as the transport of the day. The garage doors had been closed and the three of them were inside the oily smelling interior.

The younger visitor was hanging by his bound wrists, his feet swinging free just inches above the floor and his mouth firmly gagged. His body was crisscrossed with reddened welts

137

that bore testament to the severity of his beating. He hung there in discomfort, bearing his pain but his interest firmly centred on Claire and his companion.

His friend was strapped securely on top of a long narrow bench; his arms pulled down either side and tied tightly to the legs. Strong ropes pinioned his ankles and a wad of sacking had been pushed up under his buttocks to force his hips high. The older man whimpered fearfully as Claire prepared herself out of sight and below the bench.

Claire stood up at last, grinning wickedly and her eyes flashing deep malice and excitement. She wore just a little pair of panties in pure white, a thin chain connected her nipple rings to pull them in toward each other but otherwise she was naked.

She began a low moaning of deep sexual longing, her delicate hand stroking lightly over his tensed thigh. Circling and caressing her fingers inched ever closer to his flaccid cock that lay down between his legs.

"Hard," she murmured sexily. "I want you hard.

He gasped as her fingers brushed briefly against the firm bulge of his ball-sac, his cock twitching as it stirred into life.

"Mmmm," she moaned in a low appreciative growl and brought her head down. "Would you like to feel my warm mouth around your cock?"

The man groaned as his cock rose, stiffening steadily to firm upright. The foreskin rolled back to stretch tightly back against his pulsing shaft, the big velvety head exposed in all its glory. His hips pushed up a little expectantly to receive the soft lips on him.

"Ahhh!" he uttered as her soft hand closed around his cock, her fingers circling to grip lightly. "Oh God!" he cried out as Claire rubbed her thumb across the very tip of his cock.

"Good," she praised. "Very good, now we can begin."

She released him and reached under the bench. It was a thin stainless steel rod with a wire attached that she held up for his benefit. Claire smeared the hard pencil-like rod with lubricant and leaned over him.

He grunted and tensed his body as the cold rod was pushed up inside his anus, the little ring of muscles parted easily to accept the invader into his secret place.

"Now," Claire said in a mocking tone. "Your pleasure begins."

When the switch was flicked and the electric current flowed into the rod a bolt of sensation shot through Claire's body. Not that she received any of that charge but one of her own as she watched his body bucking in twisted agony.

His whole body locked rigid as the current flowed into him, his head raising to pull hard against his shoulders and his cock jerking in delightful little spasms. As the current was switched off he let out a great sigh of relief and slumped back onto the bench.

She gave him only a couple of seconds respite before flicking the switch again. Her whole body gripped in wonderful pleasurable sensation as she watched his cock throbbing and pulsing. Tingling shards of feeling flowed into her nipples and her clitoris pulsed its excitement. Deep within her vulva her internal muscles contracted involuntarily to bring a great tide of wonderful pounding thrill.

Again and again she first turned the current on and then off again in an alternating rhythm of exquisite sexual torture. Claire delighted in the little drops of lubricant that squeezed from the eyehole of his cock to show his state of arousal despite his pain. Sensing that he was close to his climax Claire gripped the base of his cock with finger and thumb, pressing hard to stem the flow. Time after time she switched the wrenching current on and off to build and hold his flow of climax. She held him there, hovering on the point of orgasm but never allowing him to tip over the edge to completion.

At last, the hot pulsing in her pussy became unbearable; she leaned close, her lips just an inch above the tip of his cock and opened her mouth wide. As she released the pressure of her thumb his cock exploded to jet a forceful stream of hot sperm up into her waiting mouth. Claire came instantly, pressing her throbbing clitoris against the edge of the table to urge stronger feelings to aid her torrent of orgasmic pulses.

For several moments she rested there, wallowing in the warm feelings of post orgasm before stirring herself with the utmost reluctance from the blissful state.

"Tonight you leave us," she said, her voice quavering and still filled with deep arousal. "I hope you both have enjoyed your stay and will return. As a little parting gift from me, I leave you now to be released later - but with one small addition."

Claire removed the rod from the man's backside and attached a tiny crocodile clip to the loose skin of his scrotum. She moved then to do the same to the suspended younger man. As she set the timer and clicked the switch, the first pulse of current shot into the small clips. Both their cocks jerked in a split second of contraction before relaxing again. About ten seconds passed before once again the current surged to jerk the flaccid cocks briefly before subsiding again.

"Every ten seconds you will receive a charge, not powerful but sufficient to ensure that you don't lose interest. During the coming hours you should climax many times."

Claire walked to the garage door and paused.

"If you return here again, you may thank me then for your pleasure to come."

She stepped out of the garage and closed the door firmly behind her.

***

The little coffee house near the main gates of the park was quiet, mid-week saw few visitors to it even in good weather. The two girls sat on the raised veranda next to the railings looking down on the passers-by.

Natalie shifted her chair closer to the railing, rested her elbows on the top rail and parted her knees wide.

"Watch this," she said excitedly and nodded in the direction of the tall middle aged man entering the park through the wide gates. He noticed the girls from a distance, glancing up at them frequently as he came near and nearer to them. His interest taken, his gaze dropped to the parted thighs of Natalie pressed as she was against the thin railings. Her little skirt had pulled high up her thighs hiding nothing from view. He walked, his head turned up and toward her as he slowed his pace and passed beneath them.

"Mmmm," Natalie groaned in pleasure. "Horny eh? Did you see his expression?"

Amey sat spellbound, she nodded excitedly, her eyes wide and nostrils flaring with sexual thrill.

"Could he have seen your knickers from down there?" her squeaky little voice asked excitedly.

"Doubt it," Natalie said in a thick low voice. "I'm not wearing any."

Amey gave a deep groan, her face was flushed and her whole body was trembling in excited anticipation.

"Your turn," Natalie stated casually and turned sideways closing her legs.

She watched as the petite Amey positioned herself, her little hands gripping the rail hard in front of her as though she might fall. Her knees parted and then parted wider as her confidence grew.

"Two of them," Natalie whispered hoarsely. "Two blokes heading this way."

Amey sat upright, her little thighs offered open beneath the mini skirt and her face etched with a pained expression of sheer excitement. As the men approached she braced herself, her teeth chewing nervously at her bottom lip.

"They've seen you," Natalie said urgently. "Look! They're nudging one another."

A little whimper came from Amey as the very interested men came closer, their heads upturned and staring beneath her skirt.

141

Natalie watched her friend, her hands gripping the rail were bled white in the power of her grip. Her eyes were wide and excited as she looked down on the gaping men. Her little body was twitching and trembling with the powerful sensations that were obviously pounding through her. As the men moved past and away Amey let out a deep sigh. Her body shook with little convulsions of pleasure and she groaned loudly before slumping forward onto the rail to twitch delightfully as her orgasm gripped her.

***

Arabella had gathered the servants on the front lawns. Firmly lush and green, well tended and bowling-green short the lawns were flat and large. She arranged the naked men in a single line and sat down on the upholstered sun chair provided.

"The race," she announced loudly and pointed into the distance. "Is twice around the copse and back here, the winner as usual will share my bed tonight. All the punches, elbow digs and kicks that these sessions seem to encourage in you all must be directed below the face."

Her tone became harsher.

"I want no repeat of the marking of Paul's pretty face as happened the last time."

She stood and raised her arm in signal.

"Ready!" her excited voice screeched. "Go!"

Her heart pounded wildly in her chest; the sight of so many naked young men tussling and shoving one another in a frantic race for her favours delighted her so very much. The naked buttocks and strong thighs all pumping furiously in an effort to gain first place. She lowered herself slowly into the chair and watched them running into the distance.

Arabella's fingers stroked idly at her shaven pussy lips and stiffened clitoris as she watched the struggling men battle each other. Two had fallen but only one regained his feet quickly and rejoined the race, that pleased her, it simply added to her excitement.

She rubbed furiously now at her sex in an increasing fervour of excitement as the running men reappeared from behind the copse. Her left hand squeezed her left nipple and pulled on the gold ring as she watched the sweating men rushing toward her. Arabella jumped to her feet, her hand rubbing fast on her excited pulsing clitoris. She could see their faces now, the set expressions and the flailing arms that sought to delay their opponents.

Another servant fell, sprawling headlong as he was tripped by the big black man. The fighting became more urgent and spiteful as the finishing line approached. Elbows dug savagely into ribs, feet kicked out at shins and thighs and hands gripped to pull and to punch wildly in their quest to gain the reward of Madam's body.

Arabella shifted her feet apart, two fingers now gripping her clitoris and rubbing hard on her mound. She stiffened and closed her eyes, the swearing and fighting excited her so and all to gain the delights her pussy offered.

As the panting servants gathered eagerly around her Arabella came to climax, she screamed aloud and slumped down onto the grass panting equally as hard as the men.

The servant Clive took command as he always did on these occasions, his instructions were deeply implanted in his brain. He uttered the commands, the wishes of his Mistress to stir the men to follow his lead.

"Rape the fucking bitch, all of us, we'll fuck the rich bitch rotten."

Many hands grabbed at her naked body, rolling her over onto her back. Her legs were pulled apart and an excited servant positioned himself between her thighs. Her hands and arms were pinned to the floor, her breasts crudely fondled by eager grabbing hands and a cock nudged expectantly at her mouth. Arabella grunted in delight as the first cock pushed up inside her wet pussy.

"My boys," she whimpered lovingly. "Take me my boys - all of you."

It was an unusual but thrilling step that Claire had taken. Her husband Robert was tied to a dining room chair in their lounge; his hands roped firmly behind him and his ankles secured to the front legs. He was naked and aroused, his cock stiff and jutting up from his lap as he ogled his wife longingly.

She stood confidently and arrogantly before him in a short pleated skirt and white blouse. Her legs covered by the sheer nylon of her black hold-up stockings and her high heeled shoes forcing her body erect. When she spoke her voice was thick with arousal, the thrill and excitement pumping hard through her.

"Something special for you today," she said with difficulty. Her pulsing body throbbed and her throat was dry as she prepared herself. She inched closer to the side of the spare dining chair next to her and called out one word.

"Paul."

Robert sat stunned as her favourite blond servant entered. Her husband gaped in silent awe as the big muscular servant walked slowly in to the room. His broad hairless chest and thick thighs, his handsome face and the long thick cock dangling semi-erect between his legs.

Paul moved as he had been instructed and sat himself on the chair next to Claire, his cock now standing up ready and excited to show his deep arousal.

"This is Paul," Claire said excitedly. "A very good friend of mine."

She gasped aloud as the servant's hand slipped up to touch the back of her thigh just below the hem of her short skirt.

"Oh God Robert!" she moaned in delight. "He's touching my leg."

Robert watched in silence as his wife's expression changed to a deep and longing smile of sheer bliss. His cock pulsed hard in response to her teasing and the fact that she was allowing another man to touch her. The bitch was loving it, her eyes half closing in ecstasy as the man's hand touched her.

"His hand is under my skirt now Robert, stroking so nicely at my buttocks."

She gave a soft gasp and whimpered sexily.

"His fingers are probing, slipping under the elastic of my....unnnh! Panties."

"My pussy!" her voice raised excitedly. "He's touching my pussy!"

Robert was shaking, not in anger but in pure pumping excitement, his eyes flicked greedily at the hem of her skirt in an effort to see the act itself.

Claire let out a deep groan of satisfaction.

"His fingers are up inside me now Robert," she teased sensually. "So thick and wonderful, moving around inside me to feel my warm pussy juices."

Claire gripped the hem of her skirt at the front and raised it to her waist. The moving bulge of the man's hand was clearly visible beneath his wife's panties, it made Robert groan aloud in deep excitement.

"You dirty little bitch," he uttered.

"Yes," she purred sexily in response. "I am, a very dirty bitch."

As the servant slipped her panties slowly down, Claire held her skirt up with one hand, her other tearing open her blouse buttons.

"He loves my breasts Robert, don't you Paul?"

"Yes Madam," came the dutiful response. "I love to feel them and to kiss them whilst I fuck you."

Robert grunted and tensed, trying desperately to stem his rising climax.

Claire shifted to hover with her back to the servant's lap, her pussy just above his erect cock. She lowered herself, moaning in delight as he slipped easily up inside her lubricated pussy. She moaned again as the huge cock filled her completely, both hands holding her skirt high to afford her husband sight of its entry.

"So good Robert," she breathed excitedly. "So good to have a proper cock up inside me."

As she began to ride the servant's cock Robert came, his sperm jetting out forcefully in a high arc of deep excitement. Claire plunged her body wildly down on the stiff rod of flesh to sate her own pounding thrill. She watched her husband in orgasm, revelling in the teasing of him that she had so wanted to prolong but had failed to do.

Paul's hands came around to cup her breasts and he began forcing his hips up to meet her descending buttocks. Faster and faster the couple pounded against one another until finally Claire screamed as she came. Slowly she rose to her feet, copious quantities of his thick seed dribbling from her sated pussy. She moved to kneel before her husband, she held his softened cock and smiled up at him.

"Lick me Paul," she said without turning around. "Lick my pussy clean."

Her head descended and she took her husband's soft, wet cock into her mouth. She moaned in contentment as the servant's tongue began probing into her moist pussy from behind.

CHAPTER ELEVEN

She had timed it so that she arrived inside the park just before nine o'clock that Friday night. Natalie slipped in under cover of darkness and staying close to the railings squatted down in the bushes to wait. The keeper's tuneless whistling kept Natalie informed of his whereabouts as the park gates were slammed shut and locked. Her heart beat fast and a slight shiver ran through her despite the thick overcoat that covered her naked body beneath. She waited in silence, frequent glances at her watch in the semi-darkness of the street lights saw thirty minutes pass before she moved.

It was a strange feeling, to be totally alone within the great park, the darkness simply added an extra thrill to it, a certain naughtiness that couldn't be described. As she found the path and strolled slowly, Natalie opened her coat and held the sides wide, it felt so exhilarating and wonderful to be naked in the night air. Her nipples hardened as did her clitoris, she felt alive with tingling sensation and expectation. In the stillness the only sounds were to be heard were the distant drone of traffic and the clicking of her heels on the tarmac path.

Her confidence grew despite the long wait until midnight, Natalie slipped off her coat and folded it neatly over her arm. She walked naked, an electric buzz fizzling through her at the excitement of her escapade. After a few minutes she sat, resting back on the cool soft grass that tickled teasingly at her enflamed pussy lips and thighs. Natalie turned over to lay face down on the soft blades of grass and stretched lazily. The surge that shot through her was intense, her whole body was caressed and stroked by the thin teasing blades.

Natalie pressed her mons onto the ground, her buttocks clenched tightly together as she began to rub herself on the hard turf. Feelings so delightful and powerful came to her, she raised herself on extended arms and increased the pace of her jerking hips. Thus raised, direct pressure was against her hard bud, she worked her legs and hips in tandem to grind her clitoris down onto the ground beneath her.

Faster and faster she rubbed her body, her eyes closed and her mouth hung open as she accepted the wonderful sensations it produced. She whimpered just once before tensing her whole body as it shook with the tearing tremors of orgasm. Natalie slumped down onto the ground, cradling her head on her arms as a pillow to savour the sensations that followed.

She woke with a start, fearful that she might have missed her rendezvous but her watch showed only eleven thirty and she sighed heavily in relief. So long she had waited for this

147

moment, and now she needed to be ready. She rose and walked slowly to the appointed place at the crossing paths. There, she folded her coat and placed it on the ground before her, clasped her hands behind her back and hung her head as she had been instructed to so. She closed her eyes and waited.

The sudden snap and the swift application of the hand-cuffs to her wrists were her first indication that anyone was behind her.

"Hello bitch," the velvety smooth female voice droned.

A blindfold was slipped over her head, extinguishing the last remnants of distant streetlights to plunge her into an eerie blackness.

Natalie gasped and shuddered as the hand came around her, cupping her right breast and weighing it lovingly. A shiver of thrill shot through her breast as the thumb of the hand rubbed against her erect nipple. She could smell the heady perfume of her molester, feel the soft warm breath on her neck and then a second hand cupping up under her buttocks. Shock waves of raw pleasure tore through her deep in her pussy as long fingernails teased at the entrance of her anus. Light kisses started, fluttering tenderly down the side of her neck to thrill further and to excite much more. The silence and the inability to see heightened her sense of being touched.

"I watched you slut," the mysterious voice purred close to her ear. "Watched you rub yourself off on the grass back there."

Natalie gasped, the thought of someone actually having seen her brought spears of stabbing pleasure rushing through her. A finger teased at her labia, delving between the backs of her thighs to stroke and caress the swollen lips.

Her molester moved around to Natalie's front, kisses touched lightly on her hard nipples in turn and then sucked the rosy buds into a welcome warm mouth. Moments later the mouth withdrew and then nothing but silence and still-ness again. Natalie called out nervously, fearful that she might have been left alone and handcuffed in the park. Slight trem-bling rippled through her body, her heart beating fast as panic rose within her.

She came to orgasm the instant that the mouth covered hers and the soft warm tongue slipped in between her teeth.

***

It was her reward Madam had told her, for devotion and service. Claire rested back over the big barrel in the stables her feet tied to steel rings set into the concrete. The strong ropes around her wrists were stretched painfully back and down to be similarly secured far behind her. Her body was forced into an arch, her mons offered high and pussy open, her head face up about three feet off the floor. She was stretched tightly as it on a rack but bent back and over the hard wooden barrel.

Arabella moved close to her head, parting her thighs to rest her shaven pussy over Claire's mouth. She lit the candle and rolled it around to melt the wax with the flame. Her hands working in a calm and unhurried fashion she reached out over Claire's naked body and tipped the candle. A muffled scream of raw agony came from the tethered girl as the hot candle wax dripped into her navel. Her mouth worked to scream but was hindered by the inflamed pussy lips of Madam pressing down on her.

Drip after drip of hot wax burned cruelly at her tender flesh, tracing a line up in between her breasts. Claire's slight body bucked against its bonds as the next drip fell on her left nipple to send searing pain tearing through her. The right nipple received the same treatment to send white hot pokers of raw agonising pain to her brain.

Claire found herself forcing her tongue eagerly up into Madam's wet pussy as the drips began a downward direction over her body. She whimpered and licked in a fervent mix of hunger and fear, the intended goal of the series of hot wax drips both excited and frightened her. Grunting hard and forcing her tongue far up inside Arabella, Claire sought to please and perhaps avoid the coming pain.

149

She cried out as a searing hot drip landed on her shaven mons. She steeled herself for the next white hot drip to land. Her mouth sucked with all the passion she could muster, her tongue roving rapidly around inside Arabella's warm interior in her effort to placate. A vivid explosion of brilliant colour flashed in her brain and eyes as the searing hot wax burned in her sensitive clitoris. Her slim body bucked and locked rigid, her toes curling and hands bunching into tight fists. As the second drip hit the side of her clitoris and part of her labia Claire came. A tearing torrent of intense sensation the like of which she had never known ripped through her. Every nerve end was wrenched and ripped to fuel her body's need and to feed the thirsty orgasm that drained her lithe body.

She slumped back, her body relaxing and the taste of Arabella's orgasmic juices filling her mouth.

***

Natalie had not the faintest clue as to her surroundings. Following her orgasm in the park she had been led, still blindfolded to a waiting car. Sound-deadening ear muffs had been placed over her ears to further add to her feelings of isolation. Both the deprivation of her sight and hearing had made each and any light touch against her bare flesh seem amplified many fold. The material of the car seat, the brush of cloth against her all now took on a very different feel indeed.

She had been guided and manoeuvred out of the car, up steps, along wooden and carpeted floors to the place she now was in. Her handcuffs had been removed only briefly to be secured once again around her wrists but this time in front of her. She had been stretched, still standing but her hands pulled up high above her head to raise her onto her toes. There she had been left alone in total darkness and silence for what seemed to her like hours.

She gasped as a hard cock suddenly pressed against her lower stomach. So long and thick it felt wonderful as its

150

warmth pulsed excitedly against her body. This, she thought, was her very reason for being here. To be fucked, to experience the delights of plentiful and varied sex in whatever form it might take.

She groaned her disappointment as the throbbing cock moved away from her and the dark, silent loneliness returned. Many minutes passed before she again felt the huge head of the cock nudging at the lips of her pussy. Natalie assisted eagerly by parting her thighs as much as she could but the cock simply withdrew once again.

"Oh please," Natalie moaned in frustration. "Please, whoever you are, just do it to me please."

Nothing, just the tantalising silence that filled each moment with the hope of the cock returning to tease at her willing body.

It hit her like a tornado, the shock stunned her to silence, her mouth gaped but no sound emerged. She felt the red hot searing pain across her buttocks burn deeply into her flesh. It took several seconds for it to register in her mind that she had been hit. At the second lash she screamed, a wailing of sheer pent-up frustration and pain combined. Her slight body shook with racking sobs of emotion as the third and forth lashes stung her. A whip or stick it must have been for the pain was concentrated into a thin stripe as it cut into her time and again.

Natalie felt so alone, she could not see and she could not hear, she could only scream her agony and need to the person who was torturing her so brutally teasingly.

A long period of nothing followed. Her mind played tricks on her, her body shrinking fearfully at the expected sting of the lash but it never came. Again and again she tensed and steeled herself only to realise that it was she who had conjured up the expected pain. Her body and mind were now tuned to expect pain, the senses too, multiplied the effects of that pain to make it a fearful thought.

For many minutes, perhaps longer the inactivity continued. It was a welcome relief to feel the big strong hands grip her hips from behind. Natalie couldn't stifle a little sob at the wave of emotion that swept over her. Visions filled her mind of that wonderful warm cock pushing up between her thighs to fill her grateful pussy. These were furthered as the whole length of his cock was pressed flat against and along the cleft of her buttocks. Her pussy contracted in involuntary little spasms, she wished and urged it silently to move down and to at last fill her wet pussy.

She tensed and held her breath as the head of the cock slid down and hovered threateningly, pressed lightly against the entrance of her anus. Natalie sucked in breath, her brain screaming its disbelief and revulsion as the pressure against her little ring of muscles increased. She cried out pleadingly as the burning pain came to her, the great head was forcing in and prizing her tight little entrance apart. The big hands slid down to hold her buttocks, the thumbs stretching them apart to gain unhindered access to her most secret of places.

"No! For pity's sake not in there please no!"

She screamed in deep despair as the head pushed hard and slipped inside her tight little tunnel. Her body shook in deep sobs of humiliation and pain, her head threw back and her screams renewed as the long cock pushed ever upward. On and on the agony went until his body was pressed against her buttocks and the whole length of his cock up inside her. The soothing laps of the tongue on her clitoris at first didn't register above the pain in her backside but after several moments it began to feel good. It was a weird sensation, the cock inside her anus remained stationary if painful, her body gripped around it in little spasms as the tongue on her pussy worked its magic.

Natalie found herself responding, her brain telling her that it was not possible but her body screaming its need in denial. She was becoming aroused, more aroused than she had ever known and it felt so very good. It was the abuse, the violation of her private entrance, the indignity and the sheer thrill of not being able to resist.

The cock in her backside began to twitch, her own body responded in excited little grips of pleasure around it. Natalie gurgled as he shot his thick cream deep up inside her rectum and teeth gently gripped around her clitoris. She came, the orgasm tearing through her like a steam train to hurtle her unstoppably toward her peak. She mumbled her pleasure, as her body jerked in spasms and she cried out as the cock slipped out of her. The burning pain in her backside remained, a fire that lingered long after the huge cock had left her body.

Drained and sore, Natalie hung there murmuring softly. A hand removed the ear muffs and then gripped her hair roughly behind her head. A mouth kissed hers, a woman's mouth, sensual and loving in its applied passion. The smell of her own pussy juices was thick on the covering mouth and that simply added to the thrilling excitement.

"Welcome to the manor Natalie," Claire's thick voice said as the kiss ended.

***

The three women sat around the small table on the terrace as was usual at the start of the day. It was Natalie's first real look at the vast estate and the house itself. She had arrived blindfolded and had slept if somewhat fitfully afterwards to wake this morning and to come down onto the terrace. She stared wide-eyed in disbelief at the naked man servant. Her hungry gaze roamed his big body and then fell between his legs as he carried out the tray of glasses and placed one on the table before each of the women. She flushed as Arabella casually extended a hand, gripped his cock and wanked it slowly as he served the table. Her actions were so natural and unashamed, it was as though he was simply there to use as his boss pleased. Instant stirring sensations rushed to Natalie's pussy, she felt herself instantly aroused at the erotic sight.

"Nice?" Arabella asked brightly. "Like him?"

Natalie swallowed hard and nodded, her voice cracked as

she tried to reply.

"Yes, very much."

"Nice cock don't you think?" she asked as she massaged his erection. She flicked her thumb across the tip to cause the man to draw breath.

Natalie shifted uncomfortably in her seat, her gaze held on the stiff member of the servant. Her throat dry and pulses racing, she felt embarrassed that her growing arousal might show. Her gaze however, would not move from the arousing hand of Arabella as her delicate slim fingers coaxed his big cock.

Arabella addressed her speech to the servant, her tone was playfully mocking.

"Your naughty cock invaded our guest's backside last night didn't it?"

Anger and hatred welled up instantly in Natalie, she stood and in one swift move slapped the servant hard across the face. The soreness in her backside remained as a reminder of a most unpleasant experience and a restless night. She grabbed at his hair, pulling and spitting pure venom and seeking revenge.

"Calm yourself!" Arabella snapped sharply. "I won't have you attacking my servants."

Natalie halted and turned to Arabella, she was shaking with emotion her fists clenched tightly and her face red with anger. "He attacked my backside last night didn't he?"

"On my instructions yes he did," Arabella retorted firmly. "And you came to orgasm as a result of it - now sit down!"

Natalie had no answer, she backed away slowly and lowered herself into her seat defeated.

"Later," Arabella's soothing voice calmed, "you will have the opportunity to repay his kindness."

"Kindness? Huh!" Natalie snorted in disgust.

"Oh dear," Arabella stated softly but firmly. "It appears that you need some of the fight knocked out of you my dear for we simply cannot tolerate personal vendettas here."

Natalie nodded her acceptance of the reprimand.

"I apologise to you Arabella, I've abused your hospitality and I'm very sorry."

Arabella smiled back, her voice low and serious.

"But of course you are my dear, more sorry than you realise, for I will be supervising your punishment."

Natalie cast a nervous glance at Claire and then to Arabella, the set expressions on their faces made her begin to tremble.

***

Little Amey was hooked, she still couldn't believe that she had actually come simply by opening her legs to man. Natalie had coaxed her and she was thankful to her for it. That day on the coffee shop veranda would remain in her mind for always. Never had she told her friends, nor anyone come to that, but it was her first orgasm ever. Okay she joined in the sexual banter and had always given the impression that she was man - mad but the truth was that she remained a virgin.

Desperate though she was to lose it, her virginity still remained intact. Men simply weren't attracted to tiny women she had told herself many times, but she hadn't convinced herself. That orgasm, the powerful and wonderful sensations that she had received she knew instinctively was merely a taste. What lay ahead, the delights that a cock actually inside her could bring would be so incredible, and she meant now to experience it.

The time was near, she trembled slightly, pulling her robe across her near nakedness as she stood at the lounge window looking eagerly out. She had read it somewhere but couldn't remember exactly where. The story of a bored housewife who phoned salesmen to give her quotes. Once they were in the privacy of her home they were seduced and frantic sex took place on each occasion. Amey doubted that it was reality but it was a God-given way of getting a man into her house and she had taken it.

She took a deep breath as the car pulled up outside, she rushed to the mirror, checking her hair and wishing the flushed redness on her cheeks would fade rapidly. Trembling fingers pulled the neck of her robe open to show a good amount of tight cleavage that her little black bra had created. She again dabbed drops of her favourite perfume on the sides of her neck, the heady scent adding to her arousal. Her heart missed a beat as the doorbell chimed, she straightened and steeled herself before walking through to the hall.

"Mason's carpets," the suited young man announced formally as she opened the door.

Her stomach gripped in little flutters and she fought to control her quavering voice as she stepped aside to allow him in. The feelings had started already, those wonderful pulling sensations deep inside her vulva. She noticed his furtive glance down the neck of her robe as she closed the door behind him. Her nipples were hard, pressing delightfully against the insides of her bra cups and a rhythmic pulsing in her clitoris nagged constantly. Her pussy was wet and she tingled all over with sexual anticipation and arousal.

Once in the lounge she sat on the settee, crossing her slim legs and allowing the silky robe to fall to the sides. Her legs and thighs were exposed indecently wonderfully she thought, stopping just short of her crotch but only just maintaining her modesty. It thrilled her to see him leering at them as he seated himself opposite.

He busied himself, laying out sample squares of carpet on the floor between them, looking up often to her exposed cleavage as she leaned forward to inspect them. The man thrilled her, he was blond and young, tall and so very good looking. She mentally undressed him, trying to imagine if his cock matched his bulky strong body. Mental images came to her; of him on top of her, his taut little backside pumping into her like a rabbit mating and her legs wrapped tightly around his waist.

He was talking but she didn't hear him, his voice seemed

distant and detached somehow as her interest lurked between his thick thighs.

Amey parted her knees seemingly absently to offer a glimpse of the tight white triangle of her panties for his searching blue eyes. A bolt of powerful sensation shot through her as his eyes flicked beneath her robe to accept the offered view. Casually she shifted and moved, feigning deep interest in the carpet samples but checking frequently the growing bulge in the front of his trousers. Little by little she allowed robe to slip to the sides, the silky material sliding easily against her smooth skin. Her whole thighs were now on show almost up to her hips, the little panties plainly on view including the side strings across her lower hip. The robe joined just around her waist and held precariously by the wrapping cord. Above it and below it her bare flesh was uncovered, soft pale skin that bore the aura of innocence.

Again and again she parted her knees, leaning forward and offering her body so blatantly. It was a heady pounding excitement that throbbed in her little body. Great waves of pure and exquisite pleasure rushed through her body to grip down in her pussy. Each series of waves became stronger, growing in frequency to signal her approaching climax.

"Fuck me," she breathed excitedly without looking up from the samples.

He choked, cleared his throat and sat back startled.

"What? What did you say?"

Little Amey looked up with an impish grin, she stood slowly but confidently. Her hand pulled at the cord around her waist to allow her robe to fall open.

"I said fuck me," she repeated sexily and dropped the robe to the floor.

He sat stunned, his eyes flicking first to her breasts and then to her pussy and back up to her face. He was flushed, very excited and nervous but he stood up self-consciously. The front of his trousers pushed out hard and tent-like in his arousal, he was trembling but delighted, it showed clearly in

157

his expression.

A little gasp slipped from Amey's lips as he stepped forward and took her in his arms. He kissed her passionately as his eager hands groped clumsily at her buttocks. In a heated frenzy of urgent need the two worked as one to remove her bra and panties. Amey's searching hand gripped his long cock as it was freed from his unzipped trousers.

She was alive with pumping excitement, the feel of it, warm and throbbing in her hand, so thick and yet so very nice. A flutter of apprehension was soon dissipated in her longing to feel it inside her.

He kissed her again, her legs raising to clamp around his waist, her arms locked tightly around the back of his neck. He lowered her slowly onto his stiff cock to bring great sighs of appreciation from Amey. In the big head slipped, pushing her sweet little labia apart and stretching her innocent pink inner lips tightly around his girth. Lower he moved her, paused and then pushed fully home up inside her little body.

A small sigh and whimper came from her before her mouth hungrily sought his again in a fiery passion of longing desire. The man backed her to the wall, crushing against her frail little body and trapping it, he began pumping hard into her in his excitement. It was a frantic and wild passion that drove them both in urgent need. Seconds only it lasted before he shot his seed deep up inside her and Amey came to climax. As he lowered her to the floor, she positively glowed, she felt now that she had become a complete woman at last.

CHAPTER TWELVE

Natalie was in Madam's study, naked and leaning forward on the desk. Her hands were planted firmly on the top and her legs spread wide apart. Her slender long legs and thighs were braced as were her arms. The smooth curve of her arched back flipped up to the rise of her taut buttocks and her head was held high.

"Six strokes today," Arabella said firmly. "A mere introduction to the cane for you and a little part of your punishment as a starter."

Arabella moved close, the fingers of her left hand eased the lips of Natalie's labia apart and she slipped the plastic vibrator fully up inside.

Natalie grunted at the stiff intrusion, her clitoris jolting in response to the warm fingers on her sex. Her body closed around the long probe inside her to gain delightful little ripples of exquisite pleasure.

"You will," Arabella stated, "hold this inside you with your internal muscles during the caning. Should you not - then we start all over again."

Arabella stepped back, raised the cane above her shoulder and paused.

"Count them bitch."

She swung hard down, the thin cane slicing through the air to land with a sickening crack on Natalie's backside.

She screamed, her body tensed and bucked, the vibrator plopped out and fell to the floor.

"Oh dear," Arabella said in a level tone. "I think we may be here for quite some time."

She picked up the vibrator and reinserted it inside Natalie's pussy, allowing herself a loving stroke of the girl's wonderful full buttocks.

The cane bit deep, stinging harshly at the firm rounded flesh. A deep burning sensation seeped through Natalie's buttocks, she gripped with all her might to hold the vibrator inside her. The combined clamping action and pain produced the most wonderful sense of pleasure in her. Hurt and sweetness mingled, to tease and then tear at her nerve ends. Her head threw back and she screamed loudly as the next lash stung at her lithe body. A cruel and devastating blow that cut across her buttocks just at the top of her thighs. The vibrator was propelled out of her body to thump heavily on the floor.

"Dear me," Arabella tutted mockingly and pushed the vibrator back in again. "Your pretty little backside will certainly suffer today."

Further caning saw the vibrator drop from Natalie's pussy on several more occasions. It seemed to happen all at once, Natalie felt her pussy grip but in a different way. The warming heat of her pain seemed spread over her buttocks and down between her thighs to excite her pussy. Her muscles gripped around the stiff rod inside her to envelope its whole length and to send the wildest of exquisite sensations pounding through her. The thwacking cane on her sore flesh was welcome now and her body pulsed in eager expectation of its cruel sting. Her head filled with sound-deadening mist that swirled around confusing her emotions further still.

Natalie jerked forwards, the force of the surge taking her breath from her. She braced her body and began to howl then screamed a long and high pitched wail of deep pleasure. Her body quivered, her head and arms slumped to rest on the desk top and she shook uncontrollably in orgasm.

From somewhere far off she heard voices, the words mumbled and mixed so as to be unintelligible to her. The after tremors racked her body sweetly and she rested there accepting them. Her hair was roughly grabbed, her head pulled back hard to raise her head up and to strain against her shoulders. The vibrator was pulled roughly from her sated body, slipping out easily over her orgasmic juices. She cried out as a huge and real cock pushed into her pussy in one easy move to fill her completely. Natalie grunted in tandem with the servant's hard thrusting as he slammed his hips hard against her firm buttocks.

The introduction of the cock into her pussy, so warm and pulsing after the hard feel of the vibrator was so wonderful. Her pussy, still sensitive following her orgasm was buzzed by a thousand little sparkles of sheer teasing delight. As Arabella's hand cupped her breast and pinched at her nipple Natalie came

160

again.

The room was obviously little used and Claire had found it purely by chance as she had wandered the upper floor. The single item that it contained however had taken her interest instantly. Obviously fairly old and coated in a layer of grey dust the wooden seat construction has been very specifically designed. It had a shaped, sloping seat that rose up and out to render the seated person inclined backward with their hips thrust forward. A back support also shaped to accept the rounded contours of a body and leg supports that would splay the seated person open. Two things about the chair were of more interest to Claire though; the thick straps attached that would secure the wrists and ankles and the sculptured wooden cock that stuck up from the seat. It was inclined backward at just the correct angle to slip up inside a woman's pussy.

Claire called out, holding the door open to shout excitedly along the corridor. It took only moments for a servant to respond to her bidding and to come running along to the room.

"Get me a duster and polish - now!" Claire demanded impatiently.

She stripped her clothes from her body as the servant rubbed hard to bring forth a deep reddish mahogany glow to the wooden structure. Her body pulsed in high sexual anticipation as she moved to the chair, placed her hands on the arms and began lowering herself down. At first she was seated with the tip of the wooden cock just an inch from her pussy. She fitted her legs into the supports and gently allowed herself to slip down onto the hard wooden phallus.

Hard and uncompromising the thick cock was but it held delight and mystique of its own as it moved up inside her. At last she was there, fully down on the hard phallus with her legs wide and body leaning back against the support. In any other circumstances her position would have been deemed as

161

crude and indecent but at the manor it suited admirably. Claire's legs were open, her hips forced up an her mons presented high, the mound of her pussy level with her throat and her shoulders in line with her thighs. A cunningly designed bump on the top side of the base of the wooden cock pressed against the underside of her hard clitoris.

"Strap me in," Claire told the servant urgently.

A thrill shot through her as she was secured immovably into the framework. The thick straps pinning her defencelessly and feeling so strong in their imprisoning grip. Her position was surprisingly comfortable and not just a little exciting as she relaxed to savour the feel of the rod inside her pussy. She found herself complimenting the designer of the chair as the servant knelt between the opened halves of the leg supports before her open pussy.

"Tongue me," Claire ordered, closed her eyes and laid her head back.

It was heaven! Pure heaven, the soft loving mouth kissing her enflamed labia, the snake-like tongue flicking out to taste her wetness and those strong hands caressing the insides of her thighs. Claire struggled weakly against the restraining straps and wriggled down onto the wooden dildo. His tongue moved, in long cat-like licks he scraped the flat of his rough tongue over the tip of her hard clitoris.

Claire bit her lip, she panted heavily with mouth open, gulping in air to feed the electric sensations that were rushing through her. She came, her pussy gripping hard around the wooden phallus and her whole body shaking in involuntary spasms of exquisite pleasure.

This chair she thought, would be a firm favourite with her from now on, she fully intended to sample its delights again.

***

Natalie was kneeling on top of the long dining table, she was naked and bound between her two Mistresses. Her elbows were pulled back harshly behind her back and tied tightly together. Her wrists were bound and secured to the ropes around her ankles behind her and she was gagged.

Arabella ate heartily, ignoring the tethered girl until Claire brought attention to her.

"Natalie seems to have adapted well and quickly," she observed.

Arabella picked up the long serving spoon and lashed it hard and spitefully across the tethered girl's upper thigh.

"You have haven't you, you little slut?"

Only a pained grunt came from behind the gag but Natalie's eyes widened as the numbing pain spread across her thigh. Immobilised, she tensed as much as she could within the restricting ropes but could do nothing to ease the dull ache.

"I credit the greater part to you Claire, your introduction of Natalie in to our womanly ways certainly helped."

"She received her punishment?" Claire sought confirmation.

Arabella sipped at her wine and then answered enthusiastically.

"She enjoyed it like the little sex-hungry slut that she is. Natalie warms to the taste of the cane as naturally as she receives a man's cock. I look forward to eating the little bitch's pussy. I like to think of it as one of those cream cakes that you keep in the fridge. You know it is there and the delights it can bring, but you resist and the waiting then adds to the final pleasure."

"Is she to get the opportunity of repaying the servant that abused her backside?"

Arabella laughed aloud.

"You young girls! The servants' stiff cocks are all that you are concerned with. Yes my dear she will and later, but for now he is in punishment preparation. Learning the error of his ways so to speak."

Claire nodded her approval.

"Your friend too must suffer of course, her punishment is

163

only partially complete."

"Naturally," Claire agreed firmly.

She cast a glance at Natalie who responded with the only part of her that was able, her eyes.

"When?" Claire persisted.

Arabella smiled.

"Anxious to taste your friend's pussy juices again perhaps?" she teased.

Claire smiled mischievously.

"Perhaps," she beamed back. "Amongst other things."

"This afternoon maybe but tell me first of this other friend Amey."

Claire thought for a moment.

"Small - tiny is the word, she is neat and petite and looks far younger than her true age."

"Mmmm," Arabella muttered. "I remember little Amey, the freckly little flat chested girl who used to annoy everyone."

"Not now," Claire corrected eagerly. "A full and attractive chest and body to match, the freckles are still there but faded. She is, we think, still sexually inexperienced."

Arabella stopped eating, her eyes staring up with a hint of devilment and salacious longing.

"Virgin?" she drooled hopefully.

"Almost certainly. She has gone to great pains to have us believe otherwise but, as you know, a woman can detect these things."

Arabella sat back, she reached out to the servant beside her and gripped his cock. Her delicate fingers teased as she talked and once he was erect she broke off to suck him.

Her soft mouth worked sensually, closing tightly around his thick shaft and drawing back up his length before plunging back down on it. For several minutes she worked on him, her other hand teasing at his balls. Arabella sucked greedily as he came, shooting his sperm deep into the back of her throat.

"Sorry, do continue," she said casually as she pushed the

servant away. "Can't go without my afters."

She wiped at her mouth with the napkin and stood up.

"Shall we take tea on the terrace? It's far too nice to sit in here on a day like this."

She turned to address the servant. "Bring the slut on the table and put her next to my seat on the terrace."

Claire and Arabella strolled together around to the side of the house. At the cobbled entrance to the yard beneath the great brick arch Madam showed Claire the servant in punishment. He was naked as usual, his feet forced apart by a stretching bar secured to his ankles. A thick leather belt around his waist had two side straps that pinioned his wrists. A harness around his shoulders held him leaning forwards at a forty five degree angle supported by a heavy chain attached to the wall. Around his cock a cord supported weights that swung free and pulled harshly downward on it. The servant was gagged, effectively and seemingly painfully for his mouth was forced wide by the ball inside it.

"Every half an hour he receives two buckets of cold water and six lashes of the cane," Arabella explained. "He has been here all night and the other servants have taken turns throughout the night to ensure that sleep has not come to him."

Claire was impressed. The man's body was crisscrossed with reddened welts, his hair sodden and stuck to his head. It pleased her to see his pleading eyes looking mournfully up at her.

Arabella moved close, she opened her tight blouse to exposed her little bra and her tight cleavage. Her hand gripped the hair at the back of his head and pulled his face down onto her soft breasts.

"I'll just get him a little excited," she explained. "It adds to the strain on his cock - and his discomfort of course."

The servant groaned aloud as his cock began to harden against the heavy weights.

"After tea," Madam stated loudly. "You will receive your punishment."

She stepped back and slapped his face twice before taking Claire's arm and guiding her back to the terrace.

"The attack on him by Natalie cannot go unpunished. I must make an example of her, you know that don't you?"

"Yes, Madam," she said.

Claire poured the tea whilst Arabella stripped off her panties, she sat with her knees parted wide and pushed her hips forward to the edge of the seat. At a wave of her hand a servant removed Natalie's gag, lifted her and placed her kneeling and still bound between Arabella's thighs.

"Lick me well slut for the degree of severity of your punishment depends on it."

Madam accepted the cup and saucer from Claire and moaned contentedly as Natalie's mouth made contact with her shaven pussy lips.

***

It had been Claire's suggestion but Natalie had loved the idea and had agreed immediately. Unused to wielding the crop or cane Natalie had refused a substitute saying that she would 'learn quickly.'

All were gathered on the front lawn, the servants in a formal line standing rigidly to attention but their cocks showing less enthusiasm. Madam was seated in her throne chair, totally naked save for the heavy gold bracelets and the velvet choker around her throat. Claire was standing dutifully to the side of Madam in just her boots and makeup, the light breeze teasing her nipples to hardness. Natalie, was in boots also, long and tight they came up over her knees to end mid-way up her slender thighs. She had chosen to wear a tight little Lycra skirt that stopped just short of her crotch and above her waist a tight uplift bra in black.

The servant to be punished was already in place, tied securely to the framework and looking not a little fearful. A low horizontal rail at about three feet off the ground was supported

166

on two thick uprights, he was bent forwards over this with his ankles bound securely to the upright posts. His arms were extended out in front of him, pulled forward by the thick ropes around his wrists and stretched to the thick post ahead of him.

The position was perfect Natalie felt, bent as he was, with legs spread wide, his buttocks were presented high and jutting out. She screamed aloud as she laid the first lash of the cane on him, a savage blow delivered with all the force she could muster. It sent a shock wave of raw delight rushing through her to push her wild excitement higher still.

"Vengeful little bitch isn't she?" Arabella commented easily to Claire as she watched the proceedings.

Seven more harsh lashes Natalie flailed him with, beating his buttocks with a burning anger. She paused only to get her breath and to allow her level of excitement to lessen a little before laying stripe after stripe across his back. So hard did she beat him that the cane snapped in two. Natalie ignored his desperate screams for mercy and used the crop as a replacement.

"Bastard!" she screamed excitedly as she thrashed the backs of his thighs. "You utter bastard!"

At length she stopped, panting hard from her exertions. Her expression was set and serious as she paced confidently up and down the line of watching servants.

"Anyone," she announced loudly, "who should consider defiling my backside in the future will know what to expect."

No one answered, their fearful eyes looked straight ahead of them, avoiding making contact lest she should direct her boiling anger at them.

"I like her," Arabella said firmly. "She's a natural commander."

Natalie turned, placed her left hand on the small of the servant's back to steady herself and positioned the huge black dildo at the entrance of his anus. A rippling murmur ran down the line of servants at the sight of her poised so.

The servant screamed as the dildo pushed in, the great

167

bulbous head forcing his tight ring of muscles easily apart.

"Now you know how it feels," Natalie yelled excitedly. She revelled in his discomfort and forced the whole length up his backside. Natalie straightened her body, her hand still holding the handgrip of the dildo, she began thrusting hard up inside him. His body shook with the force that she slammed into him with, his head shook rapidly in a wild denial that this could be happening to him. He wailed and sobbed as the brutalizing of his little tunnel continued. On and on she pounded into him, her whole body braced so as to gain purchase. She violated him with a fury that made even Claire wince.

"Enough!" Arabella shouted aloud. "Enough! The punishment is now over."

Natalie slowed, took a deep breath to calm herself a little and stepped back away from him. She turned and walked to stand before Arabella, her nostrils flaring, her eyes wide and flashing anger and excitement.

Arabella's hand was between her own thighs, her fingers stroking over the puffy lips of her labia. Her face was flushed in excitement and her nipples hard, she was trembling with deep arousal.

"Go to my bedroom and wait for me there," she said, her voice quavering as she spoke the words.

Claire had never seen Madam so excited, she felt a pang of jealousy at what the two of them would get up to. She hoped against hope that she wouldn't fall out of favour with Arabella now that Natalie was on the scene.

***

Little Amey stood at the top of the stairs pointing up in explanation to the decorator. She throbbed with excitement, her short skirt pulled up with her body as she stretched out her arm, her panties fully on show to man below her. She had rehearsed for his visit, posing and finding the best positions before he had arrived.

168

He was older, much, much older and not at all sexually attractive to her but he could provide good entertainment. He could give that thrill, the pumping heady thrill of showing herself, he would lust and want and that in itself excited her.

The man was sweating, his face flushed and his pencil poised uselessly over his notepad. From six steps down below her he could see right up her skirt, her firm little mound and her tight swelling buttocks. He was hard for her, his cock erect and pressing painfully against the inside of his trousers. The little bitch was fully aware of what she was doing to him and seemed to delight in it. She needed a damned good fucking and he could think of little else as he viewed the flesh of her upper thighs. In the bedroom it continued, she bent and stooped, squatting and reaching to further her teasing of him. In front of the low dressing table mirror she bent, fully aware of his stare into the reflection of the mirror that gave a back view up her skirt.

She stood deliberately silent for a few moments, feigning embarrassment and using a squeaky little voice filled with naive intonation.

"Oh dear, you must have been able to seen my knickers."

He croaked, his response stalled as he cleared his throat. Before he could reply Amey spoke again, this time in a low and sensual tone that jolted his cock in excitement.

"Like to see more of them?"

He swallowed hard and nodded, his eyes wide in excitement.

"Ask me," she breathed excitedly. "Ask me and I will."

"Show me more," he said in a thick voice.

"Please, you have to say please and tell me what you want."

"Please," he panted. "Please show me your knickers."

Her little hands were trembling as she gripped the hem of her skirt at the front and slowly pulled it up to her waist. She stood brazenly whilst his hungry eyes took in the slim upper thighs, the little hips and the way her panties pulled tightly across the mound of her pussy. Amey turned and lifted the

169

back to show her pert little bottom and the way the thin white material pulled across the firm flesh to follow every contour.

She turned back to face him and hooked her thumbs in the side strings of her panties. Amey paused there, the wild thumping in her chest and throat rendering her unable to speak. She looked at him, her smouldering eyes transmitting all her sexual need and longing. At the rapid nodding of his head she began to slide them down over her hips and thighs, the dark bush of her pubic hair standing out against her creamy white thighs. Amey dropped the panties to the floor and stepped out of them, tossing them casually onto the bed.

He moved instantly, grabbing them and putting them to his nose, he grunted in delight as he sniffed heavily. Both his hands crushed the flimsy material to his face as he muttered his delight.

A thunderous bolt of sensation shot through her at his act, to see a man sniffing her scent was so erotic. She moved, climbed on the bed and lay back parting her knees. Amey drew her knees up to offer herself open and exposed. It felt so good, to control him with just her body and a few words. To have him comply, willingly and desperately simply to be able to view her firm young flesh. The look of delight on his face and the hard bulge in his trousers simply added to her deep excitement. Her pussy was wet, this she knew, her coral pink inner lips would be glistening in her arousal and in turn arousing him further. He would be wanting, wishing and praying perhaps to be able to touch or sniff her sex. The feelings rushing through her became stronger and more wonderful by the second. She felt wanton and a slut but she didn't care one bit, the pulsing in her clitoris and pussy were simply too good to want to stop.

"You can watch but not touch," she said softly.

He stood at the end of the bed, his eyes fixed firmly between her open thighs. His look was hungry and longing, a film of perspiration coated his forehead and his face was flushed bright red.

"Show me yours," she said throatily and gripped her pussy with her right hand.

The man gasped aloud as she touched herself and watched her slim fingers stroking idly at her open pussy. He fumbled clumsily with his fly and with some difficulty eased his stiff cock out.

Amey held his stare as she rubbed herself.

"No touching," she murmured sexily. "Yourself yes, but not me."

She groaned in pleasure as he gripped his cock in his hand and watched in fascination as he began to slide his hand back and forth along his cock. Amey rubbed her clitoris as she watched his foreskin roll first over to cover the rounded head and then back along the shaft. In slow and deliberate movements he wanked himself as he in turn watched her.

Her hand rubbed fast, swirling her hard bud around in little circles of drumming pleasure. She was building fast, the pounding sensations coming to her faster and faster.

"Sniff it," she panted breathlessly. "Sniff my pussy.

He hesitated and then knelt on the bed, one hand supported himself and the other resumed the grip on his cock. His head lowered close to her open pussy and then he began sniffing loudly. It was such a high for that she almost came, she paused in her rubbing breathing deeply so as to delay the moment a little longer. Her body was afire with hot burning need, older he may be but she needed his cock - any cock up inside her.

"Now you can fuck me," she moaned softly.

She started in surprise as the thick globules of his sperm splashed against the undersides of her buttocks in warm little spurts.

He was groaning and wanking his cock to finish himself as he sniffed continually.

Deep disappointment filled her, she had been robbed of a stiff cock inside her and was livid at his premature ejaculation. Amey grasped his hair with both hands and forced his face down onto her wet pussy.

171

She ground her hips to press her pussy hard onto him and began to wail as his tongue slipped into her warm, wet interior. His top lip rested hard against her clitoris as he tried to get as much of his tongue up inside her as he could. It circled inside her, curling to explore and to taste her fresh young interior, brushing the sides and delving deep toward her cervix. One of his thick stubby fingers stroked at her anus and she tensed in delight. It hovered tantalisingly over the rosy little opening and then began to press inward.

Amey screamed loudly, her hips bucked up high, her hands pulled hard on his hair as the sensations ripped through her. Up the finger drove, spurred on by wild excitement and heated sexual passion to stretch her little tunnel. Her buttocks clenched and her body locked rigid in orgasm. She wailed her pleasure as she came and then slumped back onto the bed cooing softly in satisfaction.

CHAPTER THIRTEEN

Natalie was kneeling on Madam's bed her arms outstretched to the front and sides with soft red cords binding them to the bed-head. Her ankles were bound; the cords stretching back to the bottom legs of the huge bed and cords around one knee passed under the bed and up to the other to ensure her helplessness.

She screamed as the wide leather strap slapped hard across her raised buttocks to burn deeply into her soft flesh. The hand that administered the lash was obviously experienced in the use of the strap and wielded it with devastating effect. Five more hard lashes stung at the girl before Arabella paused.

"Quite a performance you put on today, slut."

Natalie grunted a reluctant "thank you Mistress" through gritted teeth.

"You are wrong on one very important point though you

172

little whore. Your body - and all of its orifices are there to be used as and when I wish."

"Not my backside," Natalie protested.

She screamed as the strap hit her buttock, the end whipping around the curve to sting cruelly at her open pussy.

"All orifices," Arabella restated firmly.

"No," was the simply answer.

Two more stinging lashes with the strap bit at her body to draw pained wailing from the trembling Natalie.

"Yes! Tell me yes."

Natalie shook her head and steeled herself. Her head threw back and she gulped in air as the strap lashed savagely across her back. The pain was incredible, a burning sting that seemed to seep down into her very soul.

"Yes."

"No!"

Thwack. The sequence went on, first demand and then refusal followed by the slap of the strap against flesh. Twenty three times the strap landed on Natalie's body before she at last relented and nodded her head sobbing loudly.

Arabella ran her hand over the curve of Natalie's buttocks, trailing her finger down the crease between them to rest threateningly over the entrance of her anus.

"You are a defiant little bitch Natalie, I remember you were at school too. You must however learn here that to defy me brings pain and you have defied me many times tonight - twenty three times to be precise."

Natalie gave a deep groan. From the corner of her eye she could see Madam exchanging the strap for a wickedly thin cane and began rapidly to mumble her apologies.

At first there was nothing, she waited, her body tensed to feel the lash of the cane but it didn't arrive.

The cold feel of the gel was her first indication, it touched against her anus to send little shivers of fear running through her. The thick rubber plug pushed in and up, squeeze her buttocks as she might Natalie couldn't prevent its intrusion. She

173

sobbed her misery as the plug pushed up and in, sliding over the gel to give her a feeling of fullness inside her. Thin little straps were secured around her upper thighs to hold the plug in place and she sobbed softly in humiliation and discomfort.

"Every orifice," Arabella said again mockingly. "You are mine to do with as I wish."

Natalie gasped as Arabella's tongue began probing at her labia, tracing the shape of first the right side and then the left. She cried out as the warm worm of flesh teased over her soft inner lips and then wriggled up inside her pussy. She came, a shuddering orgasm that shook her bruised body in delightful spasms. As her body tensed, it amplified the feel of the plug inside her anus to bring her off on a second and immediate orgasm that equalled the first in intensity.

Time was not given to savour the orgasms however, Madam raised her arm and struck with the cane across Natalie's outer thigh.

"Obedience!" Madam said firmly and struck again. "Obedience."

With each lash she gave, one for each time Natalie had defied her, Madam shouted the word over and over again above the girl's screaming.

"Obedience," she intoned and struck. "Obedience."

In the corridor outside the room Claire rested back against the wall. Her legs were spread and her hand was down inside her knickers rubbing frantically at her clitoris. A surge passed through her every time Natalie screamed to bring the sweetest of sensations rushing through her. Claire came, listening to her friend wail in agony at the hands of her Mistress. She sighed heavily and slid slowly down the wall to sit on the floor.

***

'Fun time' Claire liked to call it. One of those sessions where she had a free hand to do anything she pleased and with whom

174

she pleased. Today she had chosen Natalie so as to round off the weekend in a most satisfying of ways.

All were naked, Natalie, Claire and the two male servants that Claire had brought along, walking boots and thick white socks were all that covered their bodies. Natalie carried a heavy rucksack on her back, the shoulders straps pulling harshly into her arm pits and rubbing against her back. The collar around her neck secured the long leash that Claire led her by as they reached the far end of the estate grounds.

Two and a half miles they had walked, struck often with the cane, the servants and Natalie all bore the marks to bear testament to Claire's coaxing. They arrived at the grassy knoll that lay on the outer fringe of the grounds and stopped.

"Unpack the food and drink," Claire instructed the servants. "We eat first and then - enjoyment."

A full and formal picnic followed with a huge white tablecloth spread out on the grass. Salad, quiche and sparkling wine, all ate heartily with Natalie being hand- fed afterwards as she sat back and away from the others.

Once the cutlery, plates and remaining scraps had been packed away the big black servant was ordered to lay back on the tablecloth. Claire knelt by his side and fondled his cock to full erection, her other hand working on the other servant that stood close. Her delicate fingers stroked and caressed, her soft red lips planted light kisses on the swollen members in an unhurried period of extreme pleasure.

At length she stopped and guided Natalie with several pulls on the leash over to join them. The tall girl was made to straddle the black servant, to sink her pussy down over his huge cock and to sit there on him. Natalie moaned excitedly as the long, thick cock filled her insides, she began to move on him but was checked by Claire.

"Patience slut," she snapped. "Your hungry little pussy will get all the cock it needs."

Under Claire's direction Natalie was bent forwards, her breasts crushing down on the servant's chest and her buttocks raised. The second servant straddled his colleagues legs, placed his hands on Natalie's back and pushed his cock into her pussy also. She cried out, the one cock in her pussy felt great but the thought of two in the same hole at once drove her wild. She tensed slightly as her pussy was forced apart to accept the second thick girth into her. One cock sliding in against the other, she panted hard allowing her body to adjust to the enormous filling of her sex. So horny, so exciting, she rested there, her face on the big black chest as the strange sensations rushed through her.

Claire came around to her head, straddled the black servant's face and lowered herself to press her pussy over his mouth. Her hands lifted Natalie's head and held it lovingly to stare into her brown eyes.

"Nice change from your other hole being used eh?" Claire said softly.

At a nod from Claire the white servant began thrusting, slowly at first but building rapidly as his cock moved within her. Claire leaned forward and kissed Natalie on the lips, a passionate and hungry kiss that made Natalie come instantly. The kiss continued as the men thrust hard into her pussy, Claire's soft wet tongue entered her friend's mouth to search and probe. After only minutes had passed, Claire came, the tongue wriggling up inside her pussy and Natalie's sweet responsive kiss was too much to bear. She held her friend's head tightly and kissed her with a fervent passion as she came.

Natalie came for a second time, her body shuddering as the surges of pleasure racked her body. Then her third orgasm tore through her as first the white servant shot his seed inside her followed seconds later by the black servant. Both men's seed, spurted up into her moist interior and mixed in a horny and thrilling wash of sheer bliss.

The three of them disentangled themselves, Natalie was pushed back on the grass by Claire's guiding hands. With her knees raised and thighs parted wide, she waited as Claire positioned herself. Her soft probing tongue licking at the sperm dribbling from her pussy sent Natalie rushing headlong toward yet another powerful orgasm. She cried out and bucked her body as the tongue slipped inside to lap and to taste.

***

Amey had read the letter over and over, at first she had thought it some kind of joke and then it had begun to appeal to her. Her initial offence at the reference to her small stature had given way to that throbbing ache in her pussy. The more she thought about her instructions from Arabella the more it excited her. It was as though Arabella could read her mind and was telling her to do the very things that she had come to know well and to love so much.

The phone call to Natalie produced confirmation for her only that the activities at the manor were 'sexually inclined' more than that Natalie had refused to say. It was sufficient reassurance however, for Amey to comply and to follow the instructions to the letter.

The excitement had been building throughout the week and at last Friday had arrived. Amey stood naked before her wardrobe mirror, she pulled the little white panties up and smoothed them lovingly over her hips and buttocks. The little bra, under-wired and lacy white was fitted to her body with the same ritual reverence to give her a look of youth and innocence. The pigtails in her hair and the accentuated freckles did much to add to that effect.

Amey raised her foot to step into the skirt, the little white ankle socks and patent leather shoes looking so sweetly youthful. She pulled the pleated skirt up and secured it, short and in light grey the schoolgirl look began to grow. A crisp white blouse and a striped tie completed the authentic and convincing look. She seemed so young, so very naive and so devastatingly attractive. For one so apparently young her breasts pushed hard out to create a great swell in her blouse and to pull it tighter still across her body. Bright red lipstick gave her full lips a sensual and naughty glow, her freshness and wide eyes added a deep and simmering tinge of devilment and naughtiness.

All was ready, her little panties were wet at the gusset, her excited pussy juices soaking into the flimsy material as it flowed readily. Her nipples were hard and her clitoris throbbing its aching need, she checked herself one final time before slipping the satchel strap over her shoulder and walking to the door.

***

Natalie had responded well both in becoming accustomed to the high heeled shoes and to the posture training. Her look of sheer delight as Madam had handed her the suit was obvious to all. Claire felt a surge in her pussy as she imagined her friend clad in the same tight latex suit that she herself owned. Madam made much of praising Natalie and it wasn't without a tinge of jealousy that Claire added her congratulations to the beaming Natalie - now also to be known as Madam.

The three of them sat in the study, a formal meeting that had seen the routine matters dispensed with and now ready to move on to Arabella's announcement.

"I am planning to hold, once Amey and Louise are inducted, a grand ball. A celebration that will bring my friends and acquaintances from far and wide. You girls, you new Madams, will play a great role in that special occasion."

Both girls looked at one another, delight etched in their expressions.

"I make the same offer to you," Arabella continued. "As I made to Claire, that you become a staff member here at the manor and may move in here if you wish. Claire has given her acceptance already and I await yours."

"Yes!" Natalie said instantly.

Taken a little by surprise at her ready agreement Arabella cautioned softly.

178

"Take time to consider...."

"Nothing to consider," Natalie said firmly. "My answer is an emphatic yes."

Madam nodded her head in acceptance and continued.

"It is my hope, subject to their suitability naturally, that Amey and Louise will join us here also. I have brought Amey's invitation forward and arranged that Louise will follow almost immediately afterwards should she choose to accept."

"That dirty bitch will agree to anything sexual," Natalie quipped and gained giggled agreement from Claire.

A thrill rippled through the two girls, they beamed a smile at one another at the prospect of the friends being together.

"Now," Arabella announced loudly in a tone that signalled the end of her speech. "I can't wait to see Natalie in her suit and to stripe both of your lovely little bottoms for you. Claire, you may select the implement of your punishment whilst Natalie dresses.

***

Little Amey sat on the bus, her schoolgirl's uniform giving the impression that she was simply in the upper forms of secondary or comprehensive school. Her little grey skirt was pulled high up her thigh to show a good expanse of silky smooth thigh. Her tie had been loosened, the collar undone and her blouse open several buttons down her smooth neck to show a hint of her cleavage.

He had noticed, the man in the seat opposite, his frequent leering looks roamed her legs and breasts hungrily. About forty something Amey guessed him to be, clean and well presented but shifty in his furtive ogling.

She raised one knee, pressing it against the back of the seat in front of her, allowing her skirt to slide up further. Her body pounded with electric sensation as he increased his interest in her offered thighs. Only two other passengers remained on the bus now and they were both seated far down in front of Amey close to the doors. She looked across at the excited man and pouted sexily. Her fingers gripped the hem of her little skirt and pulled it up to her waist. His eyes widened, his mouth hung open in stunned amazement as he leered greedily at her little white knickers. He was hard, his cock pushing his trousers up into a straining bulge.

Amey stood, allowing her skirt to fall back and cover her thighs, she moved into the aisle and leant over, looking out of the window beyond the man. Her heart beat fast as she posed for him, aware that her breasts and cleavage were his main point of interest. She smiled broadly, blew him a kiss and walked away to the front of the bus swinging her hips.

As she alighted onto the pavement Amey took a deep breath and calmed herself, the thrill had been so very wonderful. She checked her watch, part two of her instructions had been completed, next was the tube and then to the park. She walked confidently, chest out and bathing in the many sexually loaded looks she received from passing men. At the entrance to the tube station she paused, composed herself once again and then walked in.

***

Robert, Claire's suffering husband was naked and bound, his hands behind his back and kneeling on the floor. His face was pressed hard down on the carpet where Claire's firm grip on his hair twisted his face painfully downward.

"Did you enjoy watching me get fucked?" she mocked.

"Yes," he muttered and winced in pain.

"He had a wonderful cock didn't he Robert? So big and thick, hard and powerful. So unlike your pathetic little offering."

He grunted in response.

Claire swung a leg over his head to straddle him, her thighs clamping around his head as she faced his body and her buttocks pressed his head down. Her open hand landed a sting-

180

ing slap on his backside.

"Tell me," she breathed excitedly. "What it was like to watch?"

"Horny," came the muffled reply as a second stinging slap landed on him. "The way his huge cock stretched your pussy wide around it."

"Unnnh" Claire gasped. Her fingernails dug into his back as the surge shot through her.

"The way you took his whole length up inside you, you bitch and loved every second of it."

She dragged her fingernails down his back, peeling the skin from him in her deep excitement. She ground her clitoris hard against the back of his head, her hips jerking in a rush to sate her need.

"You took his come up you and then made him lick it whilst you sucked me."

She moaned aloud in deep ecstasy and increased the pace of her jerking hips. Her head was back and eyes closed as her nails tore at his back in fervent excitement.

"And then," Robert stuttered as he coped with the raw pain in his back, "you rotten bitch, you got him to fuck you again whilst you kissed me."

Claire came, her whole body stiffening and her strong thighs gripping around his head. Her back arched, she let out a long deep sigh and slumped forwards onto her husband's back. Her knee was wet with thick globules of Robert's sperm that had jetted out in his great excitement.

***

Arabella was in the gym watching the servants exercise. A daily routine that she insisted upon so as to maintain their strong athletic bodies for her viewing and use. She sat as always astride a vaulting horse, her favourite place at this time of day with the added advantage of pressure against her pussy. The firmly padded suede top angled beautifully to press hard

181

against her clitoris. With so much wonderful sweaty male flesh on offer it helped to maintain the stimulation. She would fuck one of them, at least one, but it was so very hard to decide which. All of them posed and strained as they worked, conscious of her presence and jockeying for attention and the reward of her body. It was the prize she offered for bodily perfection and they all them responded willingly to the challenge.

Muscles strained and bulged, rippling stomachs and sculptured thighs simply labouring to please her whims. Best of all though for Arabella was the swinging cocks between the thighs, some in states of semi-erection and anticipation of her body. She sat with only her nipple rings on her otherwise naked body, she felt it added a little to their enthusiasm.

"Paul," she called and pointed. She paused....... "Not you!"

She laughed aloud. It was her little joke, to raise their hopes, and their cocks mostly, only to dash those hopes and the erections that they may have gained. Her eyes roamed the gleaming buttocks of the big black boy but she had had him yesterday. Her pussy was in need now, that wetness and the dull throbbing ache had started and it was time.

She lay back on the vaulting horse, her legs wide and her buttocks resting just on the edge.

"Clive can fuck me," she announced. "And Vincent, I will suck your cock."

Both men attended her readily, one cock slipping easily up into her pussy and the other offering its great head close to her mouth.

"Slow and sweet today I think," she murmured softly and closed her mouth over the glans of the erect cock.

Tantalisingly slowly the other cock moved back and forth in her pussy, Arabella sucked equally as slowly on the one in her mouth. With her free hand she motioned to the others and gripped yet another one as it positioned itself for her. She worked with the three cocks, fondling sucking and gripping with her internal muscles as she mewed contentedly.

Two men came almost at the same time, sperm jetting into her mouth and her pussy. Her other hand worked to wank the third man and she moaned aloud as his thick seed jetted onto her arm and wrist.

Arabella sat up slowly, addressed her comment to the servant who had shot his seed over her arm. Her tone was level and calm but the sinister meaning was all too apparent.

"For that my dear boy, you will suffer."

***

The short journey on the underground had been every bit as thrilling for Amey as that on the bus. She was deeply enjoying her schoolgirl role and had to admit that she felt good in the little uniform. She had squatted on the platform, pretending to search in her satchel. She had bent and sat whilst waiting for the train, showing her neat little body at every opportunity.

One thing was certain Amey felt, men liked schoolgirls. Young and old alike the men had leered at her, some furtively and others quite openly but it was a different type of ogling from the normal. The image and youth, innocence and naivety seemed to appeal to men in a very different way. Older girls and women received admiring and of course sexually loaded lusting gazes, but in her uniform she had drawn deeper, more hungry and wonderfully exciting wanting leers.

On the train itself they had continued, looking at her breasts, positioning themselves to stand over her as she had sat to look down her blouse. Seating themselves so as to try to look up her skirt. Amey giggled as she thought of the pouting little smiles that she had given them. Deliberate looks of blissful ignorance as to their sexual motives.

She sat in the park now, her legs crossed to show her slim thighs almost up to her sodden panties. She had become so excited during the journey that the whole of her gusset was not just damp but soaked through with her juices. The tall, elegant woman that walked toward her seemed to take as much interest in her as the men. The chauffeur by her side certainly had noticed but the woman's looks were doubly thrilling to Amey. A different kind of tingling sensations play in her pussy, a naughtier and more forbidden type of feeling.

"How simply divine!" The polished accent enthused as the two reached and stopped before Amey. "My dear! You look the picture of innocence itself."

Amey watched the woman's hungry expression, excitement flared in her eyes, it was an expression that equalled those of men, one of deep sexual longing. The lustful gaze roamed over her, slowly and deliberately so as to leave Amey in no doubt of her sexual longing for her.

"Don't you think, Clive," the woman sought confirmation from her chauffeur, "that the little slut is simply perfect?"

It took a few moments for it to register in Amey's brain.

"Arabella!"

"I thought for a moment that you might never recognise me. One thing is certain little Amey, that you are to sit on my lap in the car - all the way to the manor."

***

Claire and Natalie had been entrusted with the task of writing the many invitation cards in preparation for the coming ball. They sat opposite each other at the desk in the study of the manor, naked and giggling.

It had been Natalie's idea and a little competition agreed between them had resulted. Both were seated on the lap of a naked servant, one beneath each girl. The men sat unmoving with their cocks up inside the girls' pussies.

"You wriggled your backside you cheat!" Natalie accused giggling.

Claire feigned innocence.

"I did not! Anyway you are using your internal muscles to try to get your man to come first. That wasn't in the rules."

"I am not," Natalie sang in a childish tone.

"You were too!" Claire responded laughing. "I can see the expressions on your face."

Natalie shrugged.

"Well, perhaps just a bit," she said seriously and the two girls exploded in a fit of giggling.

The laughter stopped and the writing resumed, continuing for several minutes in complete silence. Natalie broke the quiet with her comment.

"My hand is shaking so much that they will never be able to read this."

Claire fell back against her servant, tears of laughter running down her cheeks, her slim body shaking as she enjoyed the quip. Her expression changed and she bit her bottom lip, her face flushed and her body tensing.

"You rotten bitch!" Natalie shouted laughing. "Yours has come hasn't he?"

Claire remained silent, her eyes widened and her expression changed again to one of deep satisfaction. Her voice rose to a high pitch and she smiled as she replied.

"Rather!"

They both laughed again, enjoying the light-hearted sex session before Natalie became silent. Her hands gripped the desk top and her eyes closed. She sat as though in meditation for a moment and then let out a long deep sigh.

"Mmmm," she moaned sensually. "So has mine now."

Claire watched her friend and allowed her to savour the wash of sperm being injected up inside her before speaking again.

"Mine came first though so I win."

"Did not! You cheated."

"So did you!"

A moment passed before Claire made the suggestion.

"I know, we'll have a second round to decide the winner. I'll cane your servant and you cane mine, the first of them to scream is the loser."

Natalie looked thoughtful.

"Tied up?"

"Naturally."

"Beaten hard and severely?"

"Is there any other way my dear Natalie?"

Again Natalie looked thoughtful and responded lightly.

"Okay, deal it is."

***

Madam had rushed Amey straight to her own bedroom, her excitement obvious to all including the male servant she had called in with them. Throughout the car journey Arabella's hands had roamed little Amey's body, feeling her breasts and stroking her thighs. Madam had sighed a low and meaningful groan of pleasure when her fingers had stroked Amey's sweet little pussy for the first time.

Amey now was bent over touching her toes, the short uniform skirt lifted and rested bunched up on her back. Her panties had been removed and her buttocks, so taut and firm offered themselves like fresh rounded peaches. The first lash of the cane stung hard but Amey was unmoved and remained silent. The second blow swished down hard to thwack noisily on the delicate little bottom. The girl simply grunted and remained as she was, the bright red stripes showing brightly on her pale skin.

"You take the cane well you little bitch," Arabella said in a thick excited voice.

She swung the cane down again and again, her pussy jolted in spasm as each cruel lash landed.

"You will be mine," Arabella panted breathlessly. "My own personal property and unavailable to others."

She paused in the beating to run her hand over the tiny buttocks, her finger slipping into the wetness of Amey's sex.

"All mine," she moaned softly as she moved her finger around inside the girl. "So long I have waited for someone like you little Amey. You have filed my desires and my fantasies, but now I have you in reality."

At the wave of her free hand, Arabella beckoned the servant around to the front of Amey. His erect cock jutting out hard and close to the girl's mouth. As Madam continued to finger the girl, Amey gripped the thick member and circled her fingers around it just below the head. Arabella let out a groan of approval. The tiny hand and fingers around the thick cock made it appear ever larger than it was. Impossibly long and thick, seemingly too huge to fit into Amey's tiny mouth.

"Suck it," Arabella commanded and increased the pace of her fingering.

She watched spellbound and excited as Amey's mouth stretched wide open to fit around the tip of the big bulbous head. The girl adjusted the angle of her head to accommodate the cock and slid slowly down on it. Arabella came, not a thunderous orgasm but a rippling and delightful one that was merely a prelude to a building torrent. Arabella withdrew her finger and sucked lovingly on the thick musky juices of the little girl, she watched the hungry mouth sliding up and down the huge shaft of the servant's cock.

"Fuck her" Arabella commanded excitedly. "I want to see you fuck her."

The servant withdrew with some reluctance, he moved around to Amey's rear and positioned himself with he head of his cock at her pussy.

Madam looked on lovingly, the pert little bottom of the girl against the great bulk of the man, his cock seemingly set to split the tiny little body in two. A thunderous surge passed through her as she nodded her consent.

Amey screamed a half-cry as the big cock pushed inside her. Her body lifted to try to straighten but a powerful male hand forced her back down. She sobbed in pained pleasure as he began thrusting up inside her. Amey's whole body was jarred and shaken as he lunged brutally into her, her frail little body battered by his great powerful one. She whimpered as the assault on her soft interior continued, her head jarred into nodding motion as the man battered against her little back-side.

Madam came where she stood, the delightful scene before her simply too much to resist. She shuddered in orgasm as she watched the servant tense and then shoot up inside the squealing Amey. Wave after wave of terrific sensation tore through her, Arabella's body shook violently as she accepted the racking orgasm. Her knees buckled and she sank to the floor murmuring softly.

"Amey, my very own little Amey."

CHAPTER FOURTEEN

The girls were gathered in the sun on the terrace and both Natalie and Claire had welcomed Amey with genuine affection and pleasure. The talk of the morning between them was the beautiful bodies and huge cocks that the male servants possessed. Amey had been relating the previous night's experience when she had first sucked and then been fucked by one such cock. She sat wide-eyed listening to some of the stories the others told her. Of using the servants as they wished, of getting good hot sex whenever they wanted it and of abusing the servants as they saw fit.

Amey had a childlike innocence about her; not only in her looks but in her speech and mannerisms, it was easy to see why Madam had insisted on the schoolgirl look for her.

Arabella strode out of the house, her expression serious and a frown on her forehead and in her hand a letter. She slapped Amey's backside playfully as she passed her and sat down to join the others.

"Good news and bad news this morning girls," she announced in a slightly agitated fashion so rare in the usually confident Madam.

Arabella smiled across at Amey, her genuine pleasure beaming out momentarily from her gloom.

"Amey has agreed to be my personal slave," she said and paused. "This means that she is off-limits unless I am present."

The tone of her voice contained a warning that Claire and Natalie noted.

"The bad news now," Arabella referred to the letter she held. "Louise has refused my invitation."

The three girls were stunned, the sex-hungry and laugh-a-minute Louise was a popular girl and good friend to them, this was news of the very worst kind.

"Why?" Natalie asked.

Arabella sighed.

"I won't read the whole letter but basically she feels that she and I never saw eye-to-eye at school and there is no reason, in her thinking, why that should have changed. She in essence tells me to go fuck myself."

Claire laughed.

"Straight talking Louise eh! Always to the point."

Arabella broke into a smile.

"If only she knew, that I have eleven male servants to do exactly that for me. But the fact remains that she has refused and...."

"Could I try, talking to her - to persuade her I mean," Claire asked.

Arabella looked pensive and then cautioned.

"She would have to come willingly."

"She normally does!" Natalie quipped.

Her comment brightened the conversation with a round of laughter before Arabella spoke again.

"Very well you may try but she must plead allegiance to me first and that, sadly, I cannot see Louise doing."

Several moments of gloomy silence passed and then Madam took the lead. She raised her voice and smiled, clapping her hands together for emphasis.

"On to other business then," Arabella stated firmly. "Amey

189

will come with me now to begin posture training, Claire I will see you in the study in two hours to discuss costumes for the coming ball. And Natalie," Arabella smiled broadly, "may amuse herself with the servants."

Delighted, Natalie punched the air triumphantly.

"Look out cocks for here I come."

Arabella scolded her gently.

"Please my dear, a little deportment and restraint please. Our guests at the ball will expect to see well trained and obedient girls under my care and such will not enhance my reputation one bit."

"Sorry," Natalie said as she stood, she hung her head in playful shame.

"Twenty lashes for you bitch," Arabella said sternly but her eyes portrayed her playfulness. "Later though."

"Oh goodie!" Natalie quipped and the meeting broke up on a light-hearted and positive note.

***

Long high heeled boots added to her height and shaped her slender thighs. Tight black panties stretched tautly across her mons and the back string pulled harshly into the crease of her buttocks. Natalie's unpierced nipples stood out proud in erection and she tapped the crop again the side of her boot.

All of the servants were lined up the lawn facing her; two had semi-erect cocks and the others hung flaccid between their thighs.

"Press-ups!" Natalie commanded loudly. "Exercises, begin."

It was an erotic sight, eleven muscular men, all naked and down on their stomachs before her. Their tight buttocks pumping up and down in a mimicry of sexual activity. Natalie thrilled as she towered over them, her body aching its need for their attentions. Arabella had told her to exercise patience; her own, staving off the burning desire to savour the moment until later on. Natalie began to see what she had meant by her words. The slow and unhurried way she could command them, knowing that at any time she could have any one or more of them in her. The waiting however, was better in a way, a teasing period of sheer sexual arousal and longing.

She halted them, their bodies pressed face down on the grass and buttocks sticking up tantalisingly. Natalie walked up and down the line strutting like a sergeant major inspecting his troops. Her pussy was wet and clitoris gripping in excited little spasms, her nipples were hard as the blood pounded into them. At the end of the line she turned and paused, then stepped up onto the first man's back.

He grunted and tensed with the weight of her on him, her thin heels digging deeply and painfully into his flesh. Natalie walked, stepping from one servant to the next in slow and unhurried strides. She received a jolt in her body with each cry of pain the men uttered and revelling in the cruelty she was exercising. As she stepped off the last man's back onto the grass once more she barked the command.

"On your hands and knees - now!"

Slowly she walked down the line of presented buttocks landing a savage lash of the crop on each man's buttocks in turn. When she reached the end of the line she turned and repeated the beating in the reverse order. Three times in all she walked back and forth lashing out to give pain to the bowed men.

Her body was trembling with excitement, her breathing hard and laboured as she fought to control the urge to simply get down and suck one of them. The waiting was great but it was becoming unbearable, Natalie paused until her pumping arousal subsided a little.

In front of them now, she stood arrogantly, her feet set wide in an authoritative stance.

"Up on to your knees, grasp your cocks and wait."

One hand teased at her left nipple, a mischievous grin came over her face.

191

"You will all now wank for me. The one that holds out the longest and is the last may stop and," she paused for effect, "he may fuck me afterwards - go!"

The men's hands rubbed up and down their cocks slowly, each man trying hard not to come and to be the one that could fuck the relatively new Mistress.

Natalie posed and pouted, winking and sighing sexily to add to their discomfort. Her hand stroked down over her body in slow and sensual caressing to tease them all the more. She gasped as the first man shot his seed, a great stream of thick white sperm jetting out excitedly from the hole on his cock. Natalie cupped her pussy, squeezing and gripping as she watched the horny spectacle. Each time a servant came it sent a buzz of raw sexual thrill tearing through her. They all wanted her, to get inside her and to touch and feel her body; that thought was nectar to her and her arousal built to a hovering peak just short of orgasm.

At last only one man remained, he released the grip on his cock smiling broadly at his accomplishment. At the wave of Natalie's hand he stood, his cock bouncing slightly as he moved toward her. She slipped off her panties and lay back on the grass with her knees raised and wide apart.

"Gather round and watch," she called excitedly.

The big servant hovered over her, his cock pushed up into her pussy to fill her completely.

"Hard," she whispered hoarsely. "Hard and fast."

He began a frantic thrusting that jarred her body and inched her along the grass with the power of his rutting. She cried out in deep pleasure enhanced greatly by her very envious audience. Natalie came almost straight away, the servant pulled out of her as he came to send thick blobs of his seed squirting over her belly. She moaned contentedly and rested back bathing in the envious and wishful looks of the other men around her.

**

It had been a brilliant idea Claire thought and slipped the video cassette into the player. She moved back to sit on the settee next to the tall blonde Louise.

"This is pointless Claire," Louise protested. "I didn't like her at school and I don't like her anymore now."

"Bear with me, this isn't about liking or disliking Arabella it's about sex; good hot sex and plenty of it."

Louise giggled.

"Then you have my undivided attention."

The screen flickered and the video began. Louise squealed in delight as the male servant was seen walking out of the house and onto the patio. His long cock dangled down lazily between his thighs and his muscular body moved so very sensually.

Louise moved forwards on her seat, her buttocks just resting on the edge and her full attention now on the television screen. Her mouth was open and drawing in little gasps, her eyes wide in disbelief at what she was seeing.

She watched Arabella stroke his buttocks as he served the table, her hand slipping under to cup his balls. She coaxed his cock to full hardness and sat casually as she turned her head to suck him.

"Good God!" Louise gasped.

"There are ten more just like him Louise," Claire prompted. "All much the same in looks and equipment.

"Mmmm, gimme, gimme some of that sausage," Louise sighed wistfully.

"And you can have all that you want," Claire soothed gently.

The blonde girl looked at Claire, her eyes searching for signs of jest but there were none. The scene changed to Arabella caning a servant who was bent over the back of a chair.

"When?" she asked excitedly. "When?"

Claire sat back and crossed her legs.

"You simply need to accept Arabella's invitation."

"I do! I do," Louise breathed excitedly, her gaze now back at the screen.

Arabella was on her hands and knees now, a servant thrusting his cock hard into her from behind.

"There is something else," Claire offered a little hesitantly. "You would need to swear allegiance to serve Arabella."

The screen now showed Natalie, hung by the wrists from a rafter, her body crisscrossed with red cane marks and Arabella licking at her pussy.

"In all sorts of ways," Claire added.

Her own excitement had reached fever pitch, the way that Louise was watching the action, her face flushed and her hand gripping absently between her thighs.

"If it got me into contact with just one of those servants I'd kiss her bloody feet if necessary," Louise breathed longingly.

"You probably will," Claire muttered softly and placed her hand gently on Louise's knee.

***

Natalie quivered nervously as the last of the knots was tied. She was standing, bent over at the waist with her wrists tied to her ankles.

"Twenty lashes for you my girl," Arabella reminded as she prepared to punish her. She raised the cane and mentally visualised which part of Natalie's bare buttocks it would stripe first. Little Amey was laid back on the bed watching, her knees raised and parted wide. The enormous latex dildo was up inside her pussy, the great girth stretching her pink inner lips tightly around it.

"Begin," Arabella ordered and swung the cane down hard.

Amey grunted as she began to work the dildo in and out of her pussy, the noisy thwack of the cane on her friend simply heightened her arousal. Her hand pumped fast to feed the

194

dildo in and out of her little body; great surges of sensation gripped her with each sound of the cane striking. Faster she rammed the huge phallus into herself as Natalie's cries of pain urged her on. Her hips raised and back arched so that she was supported on only on her shoulders and the soles of her feet. Her body was twitching and heaving in pleasure as she forced the big cock into herself in a frantic fucking motion.

She grunted and tensed, her hips bucked higher still one final time and she came to a crashing orgasm that tore through her like a tornado.

Madam was pleased; very excited and very pleased.

"Wait there Amey, only six more strokes and then I will lick your sweet little pussy whilst Natalie considers the error of her ways."

***

It was Claire's suggestion and Louise had seen the sense in it. As the two women got out of the car at the front of the manor Arabella was waiting. Dressed in her latex suit, Arabella looked tall and menacing flanked as she was by two beefy servants.

Louise walked up the steps and onto the veranda, she fell instantly to her knees and kissed Arabella's boots several times in a sincere and humble way.

"I apologise to you Arabella for the things I wrote and I ask you to invite me once again. I am so very sorry."

Arabella remained stationary, she looked down at the pleading face looking back up at her.

"Why of course you are sorry my dear Louise," she said softly. "More sorry than you could ever realise - take her to the basement!"

***

The basement room was of a heavy construction that was an obvious choice for its use as a prison. In its time the manor had been a fortified manor house, the civil war having left

195

evidence of its cruelty in the cell itself. The low curving ceiling was made of heavy brick arches, the dampened walls of heavy stone and a small grilled window sat high up the wall. The door was of a solid construction with a small grill for viewing the occupant a strong lock and two long bolts on the outside face.

It was here, in that cell that Louise now found herself. A thick post was set upright in the centre of the dingy room, about four feet high it had strong steel rings attached near the top and bottom. The blonde girl's ankles were shackled either side of the thick post, her buttocks pressed back hard against the ageing wooden stake. She was bent backwards so that the top of the post pressed into the small of her back and her wrists pulled down to be shackled to the steel rings at the top. It was a most uncomfortable position; one that allowed Louise's head either to hang back and stretch her throat and body unbearably or to suffer constant strain by keeping it raised. Her view of the cell from that position was the ceiling only, she could turn her head to either side but little else. Louise had been chained there for some time now, shivering in her nakedness and apprehension.

When the cell door finally opened it allowed entry to the full staff of Madam's manor. Claire, Natalie and Amey all moved to one wall to stand silently and obediently as instructed. From her upturned position Louise could see that all three of her friends were dressed identically to Arabella in tight figure-hugging latex suits.

Arabella tapped the thin cane menacingly across the front of Louise's thighs.

"Well bitch, have you had time to reflect on your errors?"

It was with not a little difficulty that Louise answered.

"Yes, and I am sorry Arabella., truly sorry."

Arabella again tapped the cane against the girl's naked thighs several times.

"Regret is a strange thing," Madam announced philosophically. "It seems so profound at the time but pain? Well pain is the teacher and cure-all of life, when we experience pain we remember so much better."

She leaned close to Louise's face and hissed venomously through gritted teeth.

"Today, Louise you will learn. That the stuck up bitch as you called me, the overbearing rich bitch that you think I am, will teach you the meaning of pain."

Louise whimpered fearfully and cringed as the cane raised high above Arabella's shoulder.

A swishing sound followed as it sliced through the air, it fell across Louise's full breasts to bite deeply and spitefully into the soft orbs. Madam moved around the girl, using the cane to cut down, from the side and from all angles to whip the bouncing orbs. Liberal lashes stung at the girl's breasts, each a savage blow designed to inflict maximum pain.

Louise's eyes locked wide, her mouth gaped open in a silent pleading for mercy. It was a several minutes before she could find the voice to scream; when she did so it was a loud and wailing of deep agony and suffering.

"Sing well my little bird," Arabella chuckled. "For your punishment has only just begun."

She swiped the cane down hard to sting across the front of Louise's thighs, then laid a lash across her bowed stomach. Thighs, stomach and breasts, the lashes tore at Louise's body in a repeating cycle that allowed the girl to anticipate where the next pain would land. Many minutes passed before Arabella paused, her breathing rapid with excitement.

"My staff and servants expect an example to be made and I demand it of myself."

Louise screamed louder as the cane then struck across the puffy lips of her labia. An indescribable bolt of red hot burning and numbness shot through her pussy. Six lashes made it glow with heat and raw pain of the very worst kind.

"Do you swear allegiance to me bitch?" Madam asked evenly.

"Yes! Yes!" Louise yelled loudly. "I'll serve you!"

Arabella rested the cane across Louise's nipples.

"You will do exactly that my insulting little bitch. You will serve me as no other has ever had to serve."

Madam turned to address the other girls.

"Retie her facing the post."

Claire offered a cautioning note.

"Don't you think she has had enough Madam?"

Arabella's nostrils flared and she screamed her answer in a wild fury.

"Don't you dare argue with me - do it!"

Louise was released and turned to face the post, her ankles and wrists secured once again. She stood sobbing, her buttocks now facing outward for the expected onslaught on them. It came instantly, seven stinging lashes that cut hard into her flesh to force her pussy and mons against the rough wooden post. Her back arched with lash of the cane to press her clitoris onto the cold wooden post.

Madam paused and again addressed her staff.

"The new bitch wants to come, she doesn't realise it though, pain is her only thought but her body is crying out for climax."

The three other girls were unconvinced, after such a ferocious whipping they felt that orgasm would be the furthest thing from their minds.

Two more lashes swished down, well aimed blows that caught across the round curve of her buttocks to jolt Louise's body. She tensed and cried out softly, her body began to shake and her head slumped forwards. Her hips ground against the wooden post and then she screamed as she came.

The three friends gaped in awe, the orgasm was thrilling, but that Madam had foretold it under such circumstances filled them with renewed respect.

Madam stood proudly, her expression one of knowing wisdom.

"You still have much to learn girls," she said casually. "But we have time enough to teach you. The bitch Louise is of a special breed, she loves - and welcomes - pain of the cruellest kind. Being abused and misused is her bag, I recognise it in her."

"Thank you," Louise muttered softly. "Thank you, thank you."

Two servants entered on cue, they threw the buckets of cold water over the naked girl and turned as one to leave the cell.

"We will leave the slut now, later you can all take a turn at leaving your mark on her body. She must learn that she serves us all, for we are - all of us now - her Madams."

CHAPTER FIFTEEN

It was the afternoon of the ball, the acceptances to the invitations had been coming in all week by post and by phone in a steady flow. Much to the girls' disappointment Madam had kept the servants busy with the preparations and strictly away from their female flesh. The girls too had been given their allotted tasks and these in turn furthered the separation from the men. During their frequent chats the girls moaned constantly about the deprivation of good stiff cocks and discussed their needs in great detail. It was almost as though Madam was deliberately starving them of sexual gratification they had decided.

Claire was busy in the study arranging the servants' costumes. She hadn't really liked Arabella's choice of outfit for the Madams but had said nothing. Natalie had duties in the centre of the wooded copse to the front of the house, her task was secret, Madam had told her, it would be the main event of the evening and was not to be discussed in any form with the others.

Little Amey had been allocated duties too; the first part of those now completed she was in the basement taking her turn to leave her mark on the tethered Louise, then to bathe and prepare her. She pressed her fingernail against Louise's buttocks and drew the side of her nail down to score a red line in her flesh.

"I leave my Mark as instructed," she announced formally.

Louise thanked her most gratefully for sparing her another caning, her body still bore the marks and pain of Madam's ministrations. She then steeled herself and closed her eyes as Amey made a further comment.

"I leave on your body a second Mark - but this time my lipstick."

Louise gave a great sigh of relief. She relaxed as Amey's soft sweet lips kissed at the back of her thighs, she leaned forwards to allow her friend's mouth access to her sex.

The little girl knelt there, her hands caressing the long slender thighs of the tall blonde. Her head moved in and her kisses then touched on Louise's labia, the tip of her nose pressing against the puckered ring of her anus. Her tongue flicked snake-like at the puffy lips and slid up and down the slit of her pussy before pushing in between them. Both girls moaned in contentment as Amey's tongue pushed deep up inside to circle around and to explore her friend's pussy. They came as one, both orgasms striking simultaneously in a passionate bucking and writhing of female flesh.

When released from her bonds Louise, grasped Amey to hold her body close to her own in a loving and silent embrace.

"I have to prepare you," Amey offered to break to silence. "And time is now short."

Louise's hand strayed down to cup little Amey's hairy pussy, her fingers resting down the length of the moist lips.

"There is time surely for me to do you now," Louise said in a thick excited voice.

When no protest came, she moved her mouth down and kissed Amey full on the lips, her middle finger easing up inside her friend's pussy.

***

All of the servants were lined up outside the front door, five either side to form a guard of honour. Their costumes consisted of inch wide leather strapping in black that pulled over their bare shoulders and clipped together in the centre of their chests. Around their wrists and forearms they wore shiny black leather cuffs that reached almost to their elbows. Thin leather formed the 'Arab straps' that were secured by little buckles around the base of their cocks and testicles. When pulled tight in constriction, the straps maintained a man at full erection for an indefinite period. They stood then at attention, both their bodies and their cocks rigid and expectant.

The girls stood in line behind the male servants, two of their costumes were identical with only little Amey dressed differently, Louise was not present.

Claire and Natalie wore little ankle boots with incredibly high heels and black hold-up stockings. Tight shiny Basques pinched their waists into impossibly thin proportions and velvet chokers nestled around their necks to frame their faces separately from their bodies. Heavy mascara, deep blue eye shadow and bright red lipstick contrasted strongly against the white face makeup that masked their faces. They too stood ready and silent, their breasts jutting out naked and their legs set in a wide stance.

Amey, the small figure at the end was naked. She wore little patent leather shoes with ankle straps and short white socks. Around her neck she wore a school tie, loosened to hang at an angle around her throat but still to dangle between her neat little breasts. Around her waist she wore a mockery of a gym slip; a navy blue pleated skirt so short that it didn't even reach down to her mons. Around her wrists she wore thick and ornately carved gold bracelets linked by a long golden chain to signify Madam's ownership of her.

The theme for the ball was Medieval/Victorian, the choice left to individual guest. Madam had dressed in accordance and drew gasps of surprise from the girls as she appeared in the doorway ready to greet her guests. Her hair was styled and piled on top of her head giving her an appearance of taller than usual elegance. Her face was made up with the same white face paint and scarlet lipstick. Her neck and breasts were bare, uplifted by the stays in her royal blue court dress of the period with only her nipple rings as decoration. The lower half of the dress hung to the floor, swept back behind her and cut up to her waist at the front to leave her pussy and thighs totally naked. Little ankle boots and black stockings with a red garter completed her outfit for the evening's celebrations.

The first of the cars swept down the driveway, six in the first batch and all in convoy. Mercedes, Rolls Royce and other various makes of limousines were to be seen pulling majestically to a halt at the foot of the steps. Madam's chauffeur, bare-chested but in his cap, breeches and boots opened the doors and assisted the passengers out.

The first couple strolled up the steps, the man dressed as a court jester from the middle ages but his cock protruding from the front of his tights. The woman, a blonde petite woman of about thirty was dressed as a serving wench with breasts bared. She moved along the line of servants, grasping each man's hard cock as she passed and giving it a squeeze. Like royalty shaking hands she was slow and deliberate in her movements. The man, a middle-aged but handsome fellow stood looking longingly at Amey before sighing heavily and moving on the Natalie. His hand cupped her pussy, his middle finger slipping up inside to feel her wetness. He planted a light kiss on each of her erect nipples before moving on to Claire and repeating the same procedure.

Whilst Madam greeted the couple with much hugging and delighted over-the-top gesturing the second couple were moving through the lines of staff and feeling their sex freely.

"My God!" Natalie whispered to Claire during a pause. "I could do with about another hour of being fingered like this."

"And a good fucking afterwards too!" Claire said back in a hushed tone, fearful of Madam seeing them talking.

The guests were many and varied in both age groups and sex. Some males arrived alone as did some females. All though took swift advantage of the bodily parts on offer to greet them and many compliments and comments were passed during the very long process. Claire and Natalie both were highly aroused, their breasts had been felt, their pussies fingered and their bottoms felt. It was made all the more difficult to bear for them by the rigid cocks of the servants only a couple of feet away. Both girls eyed the twitching members hungrily, Natalie pouted and winked at the blond servant Paul to further his obvious excitement.

Little Amey seemed to be the star of the show however; without exception all of the men and some of the women stopped to look her over, leering and lusting for her neat body.

In the main hall of the manor, music played and a party atmosphere abounded. It was a noisy affair, with all of the guests sipping at drinks, nibbling at the food on offer and screeching their conversations loudly so as to be heard above the rest. Groping of the servants was rife as they moved between the guests with trays of drinks. The girls too were felt and fondled plentifully as they held trays of sandwiches to pass around.

Natalie almost came at one point; a man slipped his arm around her waist from behind to pull her back onto him, his hard cock pressed into the cleft of her buttocks. She gasped and tensed ready as the tip of his cock slid down and then back up to locate in the entrance of her pussy. It was only Arabella's untimely intervention that made him stop and withdraw.

"Stephen! You naughty boy!" she scolded. "The bitches are for later, you must learn to control your urges."

The evening passed slowly for the girls, their pussies were wet and clitorises erect as their level of arousal grew. They danced with inviting male guests, the hard erections pressing against their stomachs did little to ease the nagging need. Arabella was aware of their hunger, often she could be seen watching, smiling and revelling in their sexless contact.

It was at eight thirty that Arabella stepped up on a small rostrum at the end of the hall, stopped the music and called the revellers to order. Her announcement was greeted with a thunderous cheer and clapping.

"Bottom warming time," she announced loudly.

Little Amey stood by her side silent and in awe of the many costumes, bathing at the same time in the many hungry eyes that roamed her body.

Madam extended her arms in front of her and moved them slightly outward in signal that the crowd should part. Amid much excited murmuring and chatter a huge central space was cleared, the crowd moving back to pack closely together along both sides of the long hall.

Arabella pointed down to two separate spots on the floor in front of her.

"Claire and Natalie, stand here."

The girls moved through the crowd to take their positions and to stand on the appointed spots facing Arabella.

"Part your legs my dears and touch your toes."

The girls complied, their open pussies and backsides displayed for all to see. Between their legs the girls could see two servants standing the other end of the hall ushering eager men into two lines.

"Oh God," Claire muttered as she saw the servants hand a cane to each of the first men in line.

At Arabella's command the two men began to run, positioning their route to come alongside of the girls; the canes raised and ready to strike as they ran past. The crowd went wild, loud cheering, clapping and stamping of feet urged the men onward.

A blinding explosion of pain flashed in Claire's head, the cane had landed with full force on her backside. A deep and cutting pain such that she had never before experienced. She heard Natalie gagging as she too received her lash. The burning pain was acute; nothing sexual just raw and penetrating agony.

They steeled themselves as two more men started their run, Claire closed her eyes and gritted her teeth in expectation, her hands gripping hard around her ankles. A loud roar of approval went up from the crowd at the sickening thwack of bamboo on flesh. The game continued and all the girls could do was to look down at the small puddles that their tears had made on the polished floor.

Six more runs were made before Natalie dropped forward onto her hands and knees; her head back and spine arched, she screamed and came; shuddering her body to wring every last drop of her orgasm from her body. Claire followed suit, dropping to her knees and faking the best and most realistic orgasm she could through her pain.

"The horny little sluts have been deprived," Arabella announced in explanation to the disgruntled crowd. "Otherwise they would have lasted longer."

Both girls retired to the back of the room, humiliated by the sniggering crowd of guests as they hobbled painfully to the rear of the hall.

"If I'd realised they were waiting for us to come I'd have faked it sooner," Claire said through her sobs.

Natalie nodded.

"It took me a while to realise - too bloody long actually."

They watched as two servants were given the same treatment by lady guests to the noisy roar of the watching audience. Claire closed her eyes and shuddered at each sound of the cane landing, that sound would remain in her mind, she felt, forever.

The entertainment continued, one or two men beat their partners before the baying crowd; one even fucked his afterwards to the shouted encouragement of the onlookers. Two women did a lesbian show that interested the girls far more than the caning before once again Arabella called the revellers to order.

"Ladies and gentlemen," she announced formally in her

polished accent. "One round more of champagne will be served on the terrace and then I ask you to all make your way to the copse at the front of the house. Please all be there by nine thirty when the main event of the evening will begin."

A low muttering swept through the guests, gasps of excitement and anticipation rippled amongst them.

"Any clues?" one voice shouted to Arabella.

In her element, Arabella stepped theatrically off the rostrum, with little Amey following behind. She strode down the hall between the guests and halted in the centre.

"No clues whatsoever," she responded beaming her delight at the many onlookers. "But I will say it will be - different."

A loud round of applause accompanied Madam's exit from the hall.

***

From the terrace in the fading light and rapidly advancing darkness, lights could be seen. Two long rows of patio lights twinkled on the grass to form an illuminated pathway that led all the way to the copse. In the trees in the distance floodlights could be seen giving a ghostly hue to the thick canopy of foliage. This all added to the excited chatter as the guests offered suggestion after suggestion as to what the main event could be.

"One thing is certain," a woman guest said loudly. "Arabella can always be relied upon to provide the best and most varied entertainment."

"Agreed!" a man stated firmly. "I just wish she would let me at that tiny slut of hers."

As if prompted, Arabella moved close, Amey stood dutifully by her side.

"My little slave appeals to you then Ronald?" she asked smiling proudly. "The little slut has a body that is a delight to bed down with."

206

The man stood in his dark Victorian gentleman's outfit, his cock jutting stiffly out of the opening in the front in erection.

"I could have her suck you," Arabella teased.

The man smiled broadly and his cock twitched in excitement.

"Prefer to fuck the little bitch. The size of my cock would make the little slut wail that's for sure."

To Claire, standing close by, the word 'fucking' seemed alien to his polished and upper class accent. The meaning was certainly the same but in a way it seemed more sensual and horny, more emphatic.

She watched as Amey squatted, her knees parted wide and her down covered pussy on view to all. Her tiny little hand grasped the man's cock gently and she moved her head close to the tip of his cock. Amey's sweet little fingers with the red painted nails circled around the huge shaft and her glossy red lips moved closer still.

"God!" the man gasped in pleasure. "She has the touch of an angel."

Her little pink tongue lapped at the velvety glans, circling lovingly all around and under the great bulbous head. It flicked and teased, stabbing momentarily into the little slit at the tip to draw great sighs of delight from the man. Her tongue tensed, the very tip drilling down hard into the eye-hole of his cock.

The man's body locked rigid, his head threw back and his eyes closed. He groaned loudly as time after time the little tongue pressed in.

"Sweet little bitch isn't she?" Arabella observed casually. "You should see her in full school uniform."

He came instantly, his thick seed squirting out over Amey's red lips to coat her nose and chin then to drip down onto her naked breasts.

Claire squeezed her thighs tightly together as she watched, it put pressure on her throbbing clitoris to send shards of exquisite pleasure rushing through her. That was what she needed so very desperately, a cock. To hold and to suck, to have up inside her but the bitch Madam would not allow it. Such an erotic sight it had been, the act of her friend teasing and pleasing then accepting the sperm so readily was so very exciting.

Another man pushed his way through and stood before Amey offering his cock to her willing mouth. As he was being sucked Arabella sidled slowly over to Claire.

"Is your backside still warm?" she asked brightly.

Claire watched the repeating scene before her and didn't avert her eyes as she replied.

"Agony, it is burning like hell and I doubt that I will sit down for a week."

Arabella's wisdom came to the fore, her voice low and knowing.

"It tunes the senses though doesn't it? Heightens the excitement and increases that burning need in your sweet pussy. Anticipation and the waiting, two very strong elements of the emotions that bring you close and leave you to hover there wanting so desperately."

Claire realised at that moment that Madam was right. Her need was greater than it had ever been, a dull throbbing ache that gnawed away at her insides. A tingling excitement mixed with gripping little ripples of extreme sensation that was accentuated by her pain. A glow filled her body as never before, she felt in control and yet so helpless in her need, a conflict of emotions that simply raised her level of arousal to its highest pitch. She could only nod in agreement and drew breath as Amey's cute little face received jet after jet of warm sperm spraying over it.

***

In the centre of the copse a large area of the clearing had been roped off in a square. Rough wooden benches had been placed around and the whole area was illuminated as daylight by the powerful floodlights. Trestle tables were strategically placed

208

and loaded with drink and food, bundles of canes and riding crops hung from the surrounding trees for any guest that might care to use them.

It was a slightly eerie atmosphere that existed in the copse, the chill of the night air and the location, the shadow casting lights and the sheer naughtiness of the situation. The guests sensed it as they began to arrive and settle themselves around the central arena. Usually brash individuals were more passive, the usually more reserved of the guests sat silently awaiting the show to begin.

***

Madam had been right Louise felt, she had recognised in herself the need to be mistreated and made to suffer but this! This was the ultimate humiliation, ridiculous and obviously designed as further payment for the unkind words she had written.

She had been in the small hut to the side of the roped off area for over an hour now. Left there in darkened loneliness and uncertainty to await her fate.

Rigid handcuffs held her wrists together in front of her, the palms turned downward. Her elbows had been strapped to her sides so as to keep her hands up and out at waist level and her ankles were bound tightly together. The silly suit that she wore was the real humiliation though. Made of a furry fabric, it was like a one-piece swimsuit, her thighs and legs were bare as were her arms and shoulders. The crotch had been removed to leave access to her pussy and anus but otherwise the tight suit hugged her slim body. The long floppy ears attached to her head made the rabbit outfit complete and they had even drawn whiskers on her cheeks with an eyebrow pencil.

Brilliant light hurt her eyes and as the door wrenched open, her sight blurred by the dazzling floodlights.

"Out!" the gruff voice commanded.

Louise hopped, both feet having to make tiny little jumps that added to the silly rabbit like manner, she blushed heavily at the thought. It happened all at once, her eyes adjusted to the light and her vision cleared as a thunderous roar went up from the surrounding crowd.

She wanted to die, to just curl up and never awake, Louise blushed deep red and hung her head in shame as the laughter echoed around her. So many people! To be the focal point and the butt of their mocking laughter was simply too much. She felt her stomach grip and her cheeks burning red as she listened to the taunting. She stood at the edge of the arena on full show to all; the servant behind her prevented any escape and with her ankles tethered it would have been a futile attempt anyway. She had no choice but to stand and to endure the deep humiliation and embarrassment that Madam had designed for her.

The noise lessened as Arabella stood, she positioned herself at the edge of the arena.

"First servant please," she announced formally.

A naked servant, still sporting his Arab strap and the hard erection it created for him stepped into the arena. He stood on the opposite side and waited for his Mistress to start the game.

"You little bunny," she addressed Louise, "will try to outrun the buck."

A loud cheer went up and the excited crowd jostled for better viewing positions.

Louise's mind was in turmoil, she couldn't run but then the bitch Madam knew that. What they would do to her once caught? It was anyone's guess and she shuddered at the thought.

Arabella raised her arm in readiness.

"Run rabbit run," she screeched in laughter and dropped her arm smartly to her side to start the proceedings."

Louise began to hop, clumsily and frantically as the servant on the other side of the arena began circling around the roped perimeter. Panic welled up in her, her mind filled with

210

the thoughts of her ridiculous situation and lumbering attempts to escape.

He was running towards her now, his thick cock jiggling as his body moved and was on her in an instant. Louise felt herself pushed forward onto her knees, her face pressing down on the dirt-covered floor of the arena. His big hands gripped her hips, the head of his cock poised at the entrance of her pussy.

"You may release the Arab strap now," Arabella yelled above the chanting crowd.

The servant quickly unbuckled the tiny strap and gave a loud groan in relief. He pulled on Louise's hips to drive his cock fully up inside her. Her face was rubbed into the dirty soil as he rammed frantically into her. Her slim body was pounded brutally by the excited servant, urged on by the baying crowd. He came, squirting his seed deep up inside her before pulling out and lifting her to her feet.

Louise's mind was a blur of confusion, the cock and the sex had been very welcome but not exciting, her position and the audience detracted from any pleasure she might have received. The man had been gorgeous; his fit young body under normal circumstances would have been welcome indeed but it had all happened so quickly.

A second servant stepped into the arena, discarded his Arab strap and advanced on Louise. His fist held his cock ready as he broke into a run, a great smile on his face.

One hop was all Louise could manage before she felt herself bowled roughly off balance and was rolling on the floor. He was straddling her head and sitting on her chest, the terrific weight pressing down to make breathing a difficult and laboured action. He fed the head of his cock into her gaping mouth and forced inward.

Her feet pounded the ground behind him, her knees striking in his back to ease the pressure on her chest. Her mouth full and the terrific weight combined to make her fight for air.

The crowd were on their feet, shouting and clapping their delight at her demise. A thunderous roar went up as the servant shot his come into her throat to make her gag and splutter.

Louise rolled onto her side, gasping for air as the man lifted his weight and walked away. Sperm dribbled from her mouth and pussy as she lay on her side fighting to cope with the numbing sensations in her head. She was only given a moment before she was aware of a third servant entering the arena. It was only then that it dawned on her that she would have to take all eleven of them. She was hoisted unceremoniously to her knees and a cock pushed hard against the tight puckered entrance of her anus. She wailed a pitiful pleading as he pressed in to stretch her little ring of muscles wide and then screamed loudly into the soil as he pushed up inside her.

The crowd was chanting, urging him on in time with each brutal inward thrust of his hips.

"Fuck her! Fuck her!" The cry went.

She knelt there, her body battered brutally by his great bulk as she sobbed her misery to the ground. The raw burning sting in her backside and the humiliation of so many people witnessing the defilement of her most secret place made her sob even more. The wash of his sperm up inside her was welcome relief; the burning pain remained long after he withdrew his cock and walked away to the loud cheering of the crowd.

Two this time, a hand gripped her hair to lift her head and the cock forced straight into her mouth. A second cock pushed hard into her pussy from behind and both began a rhythmic thrusting into her two orifices.

All of the servants in turn had her, her backside was used again and again, the deep humiliation and shame simply got worse for her. During that time though her body had responded, her mind too perhaps, for sexual pleasure began to come from her humiliation. Louise found herself now welcoming the crowd being there. To be had, so brutally and so many times before them all filled her with a thrilling glow. Her helpless position and being bound simply heightened those feelings and tuned her senses acutely.

Each cock was welcome now inside her, the thought of so many different men being inside her, their sperm being injected into her over that of the man before. A sense of perverse pleasure came to her, and she began then to play to the crowd for all she was worth. She panted and sighed as each inward thrust jarred her. She cried out in urgent pleading for more and none of it was playacting, her feelings were real. She came several times, rippling and stifled orgasms at first but then they grew in intensity. To the delight of the crowd she screamed as a terrific orgasmic surge passed through her as a finale.

Louise knelt there in the centre of the arena, alone and highlighted by the floodlights. She moaned her pleasure as the waves of sensations gripped her in little convulsions of sweetness.

Arabella entered the arena and strode over to the kneeling girl to tower over her.

"You learn well bitch," she said in a hushed tone and then raised her voice to address the crowd.

"This bitch insulted me, insulted her madam!"

A low moan of disapproval rippled through the audience.

"She will now display her subservience to me by licking my boots."

The crowd fell silent, waiting anxiously to see if the girl would comply.

Louise lifted her head and kissed the toe of Madam's boot, her tongue then lapped at the polished leather as she muttered her thanks to Arabella.

She raised the cane and brought it down hard on Louise's backside as she licked. Again and again the cane stung at her buttocks in a torrent of cruel blows designed to inflict the maximum pain. At length Madam paused, turned and raised her voice.

"The slut has paid her penance, I now declare her worthy to serve me."

Amidst the loud applause and cheering, Natalie and Claire stepped into the arena and walked to stand either side of Madam. They both wore their tight latex suits and carried riding crops. Little Amey skipped sweetly over to kneel in front of Arabella.

Madam raised her foot and rested it on the back of Louise's head to press her face down into the soil.

"My girls!" she announced proudly. "Now we are five at the manor. Future parties here, I feel will hold much entertainment for you all."

A rousing cheer went up and wild clapping and shouting followed for minutes afterwards.

"My two girls, Claire and Natalie will now administer punishment to any guest or guests that might like to feel the bite of the crop on them. Little Amey however," she paused to stroke Amey's hair lovingly. "Remains out of bounds to all but me."

A groan of disappointment was heard from the crowd.

Winding up her speech, Arabella's voice became sincere and loud.

"I feel sure that you will all see many happy times here at the manor and will be hearing from we five Madam's again."

As Arabella turned to leave there was a surge in the audience as they scrambled to be first to kneel before Claire and Natalie.

And now for the opening of next months title, "SLAVES of the SISTERHOOD" by Anna Grant.

CHAPTER ONE

Boston, USA, 1953.

The freckle pattern on their pert little bottoms was the only way to differentiate between the willowy blonde twins. Apart from themselves only their father had ever noticed this when he had put them over his knee and thrashed them with his broad belt. Their pretty oval faces were almost identical and their deep blue eyes perfectly complemented their hair, which reached down almost to their impossibly slim waists. No one could tell them apart, not even their parents.

The sisters stood where the local bus had deposited them, outside the entrance to the college, taking in the scene before them.

At first sight the building was large and imposing but the Virginia Creeper across the red brick Gothic frontage reminded them of the town hall back home in Iowa and, set as it was amongst acres of rolling hills and lush green farmland, their hearts soon warmed to it. Ma and Pa would definitely have approved, the twins felt sure that they would settle down here and grow to love it.

After another quick look at their surroundings they smiled reassuringly at one another, picked up their suitcases and headed towards the grand entrance to the college. A polished brass plaque on the tall granite archway gleamed in contrast to the dull grey stonework; the twins read the words carved neatly into it. It confirmed to them the name of their home for the next three years - 'Flemmings Academy for Young Ladies.'

The girls looked at each other and giggled, both trying to imagine themselves as ladies, even though they were both only just eighteen. Overcome with the vanity that seems to affect all teenagers, they swiftly checked their appearance in the reflection of the polished plaque. Automatically they smoothed their hair down, straightened their dresses and inspected the seams of their stockings to ensure that they were straight down their long shapely legs. They may have been tomboys at heart, but they had seen ladies do this before they entered church and figured that it was the correct thing to do before entering a public building.

Satisfied with their appearance they pushed aside the great oak doors and entered a strange new world. The twins both shivered involuntarily as they entered a large corridor, the high vaulted ceiling of which was supported by ranks of tall stone pillars. The clicking of their heels on the polished marble floor echoed down the hall, they looked around in wonder as they walked along taking in the sheer magnificence of the entrance. The twins gazed in awe - if this was what the doorway looked like what must the rest of the place be like? Finishing school was not what the twins had wanted for themselves but they were dutiful girls and always obeyed their parents; except for the occasions when their teenage pranks had led to their father tanning their pert behinds with his belt.

A notice board, which curtly welcomed new arrivals, informed them that all freshmen were required to attend the welcoming ritual in the Great Hall. Directions were given and, once they were sure of their bearings, the twins found themselves leaving the entrance hall and walking across a spacious open-air quadrangle. Freshly cut grass covered the open area in the quad and the smell reminded the girls of home, a tinge of homesickness for the lives that they were about to leave behind.

Some other girls were in the quad, enjoying the late summer sunshine, laughing and talking with one another. Their gazes followed the twins' progress as they made their way to the archways at the far side of the quad. In turn the twins noticed that the girls were all wearing the same regulation uniform; given that the girls must all have been at least eighteen this fact came as a bit of a shock to the twins. They had spent most of their high school years wearing dungarees and pigtails, as the pupils at Des Moines High were not expected to wear uniform. The twins had always been tomboys, growing up on their father's Iowa farm and so they were athletic and even statuesque, but had never been young ladies in the proper sense - the very reason they had been sent to Flemmings Academy. To be trained and educated as ladies, acceptable then in polite society.

As the twins had not been told to wear their uniforms they were still neatly folded in their suitcases. The twins felt conspicuous in their own pale blue dresses, dainty white gloves, high-heeled court shoes and pretty white bows in their hair. Ma had sent them off in their best clothes to give a good impression on arrival but they realised with a sense of foreboding that they already stood apart from the others. Their own outfits were in almost complete contrast to the other girls, their uniforms consisted of dark blue pinafore dresses, with very short pleated skirts, worn over crisp white blouses with bright red neckties. Seamed stockings were the order of the day so at least the twins had that part right and most of the girls wore high-heeled shoes complete with little ankle straps and tiny buckles. It was both worrying and exciting for the twins to think that they too would soon be expected to wear the uniforms they had brought with them.

After what seemed like an eternity under the gaze of the staring school girls the twins reached the other side of the quad, climbed a broad staircase of dark stained wood and walked down another corridor towards what they hoped would be the Great Hall. They stopped by the door, nodded reassuringly to each other and both knocked tentatively. There came no reply so they opened the door and walked in. To their horror the room was already full of girls, all sitting in rows facing away from them. As they entered the vast room all heads turned to look at them and deathly silence fell over the large hall.

Self-consciously the twins stood looking around them, again their distinct dress making them feel different from the rest. All the twins could do was stare back but another figure standing on a raised dais at the front of the hall was glaring at them through half moon glasses. She was not in uniform, but instead she wore a severe dress of dark grey, which was tight fitting and clung to her ample and curvaceous body. This was no schoolgirl, but clearly a woman of some distinction and authority. Judging by her withering stare as she regarded the twins she was displeased with them, for some as yet undisclosed reason.

"So, young ladies, you have finally decided to join us have you?" said the woman with a voice as hard as steel and as chilling as ice. "I presume that you are Brigit and Imogene Schloss and I also presume that you have a perfectly good reason for being late!"

After an embarrassing pause one of the twins plucked up the courage to reply

"We're sorry, but the bus out from Boston took longer than expected!" blurted Imogene.

"I fail to see how the bus can be blamed for your tardiness and for your interruption of my welcome speech to your colleagues here," the woman replied sharply. "And for the record, my name is Miss Stevenson but you will refer to me as Ma'am from now on!"

"Yes, Ma'am," retorted the twins in unison.

They didn't wish to offend this woman any further for in her hand she held a long and thin rattan cane that worried them even more than the woman's piercing blue eyes.

"And how is it that you are not wearing the regulation uniforms like all your colleagues here?" Miss Stevenson asked, a decidedly dangerous and threatening tone in her voice.

"We did not realise that we were supposed to wear them today, ma'am," stammered Brigit taking her turn to speak to the woman.

"You wear your uniform at all times, unless instructed to

218

do otherwise," said Miss Stevenson sternly. "And that includes travelling to and from college."

"Yes Ma'am, sorry Ma'am," said the twins once more in unison.

"Well, I'm afraid that your apology just does not cut the mustard, young ladies," said the Miss Stevenson, with a definite note of relish in her voice. "And I will take this opportunity to punish the pair of you as a lesson to you both, and as an example to the others."

"But, Ma'am," pleaded Imogene, "we did not know the rules!"

"Ignorance of the rules is no defence here," said the stern Miss Stevenson. "so stop wasting my time and get up here!"

The twins could hear sniggers from the ranks of girls as they ran down the hall and scampered up onto the small stage. Miss Stevenson gestured to either end of a large table that dominated the front of the stage and without being told what to do they stood at either end. Miss Stevenson instructed that they should bend over and the twins found themselves sprawled across the table with their breasts squashed against the hard wooden surface and their bottoms sticking up invitingly in the air. The twins blushed with shame for the girls were now openly laughing at them but Miss Stevenson flashed a look of rage and the pall of silence returned in an instant.

"You will now observe a mild punishment, young ladies which, I will administer with this light cane," said Miss Stevenson ominously. She proceeded to role up the skirt of one of the twins and then, slowly and deliberately, she pulled back the waistband of her flimsy white panties and began to peel Imogene's panties down her smooth thighs.

"But Ma'am, you can't do that," Imogene whimpered, "not in front all these girls!"

"Silence, you disgraceful slut!" shouted Miss Stevenson, "you do not speak when you are being prepared for punishment, unless spoken to first!"

Miss Stevenson continued to pull the silky material over

the stocking tops and cute white garters their mother had given them and down Imogene's long coltish legs. Once the panties had reached Imogene's ankles Miss Stevenson ordered her to step out of them; Brigit watched in disbelief as she held them to her nose briefly and slipped them into her pocket.

The lecturer then patted Imogene's buttocks ordering her to spread her legs and Imogene rather reluctantly complied. The whole procedure was repeated with Brigit at the other end of the table, although Imogene could have sworn that Miss Stevenson actually stared at the secret place between her sister's legs as she removed her panties. All eyes were now on the twins as Miss Stevenson turned to address the excited girls.

"Now we are ready to begin,"Miss Stevenson said to the girls. "Seven strokes each I think as this is a first time offence."

The twins gasped in horror for seven strokes seemed a lot especially with that wicked cane, a cane that Miss Stevenson retrieved from the table and raised menacingly above her shoulder. With a terrifying whoosh she brought it down in a fearful arc upon Imogene's butt to land with a loud crack, it echoed round the hall and made some of the girls near the front start in shock. Imogene screamed as she registered the sudden blast of pain and her hands instinctively flew to cover her backside and protect it from further assault. She briefly traced the tell tail tramline of vivid red lines, which were already appearing across her buttocks.

Brigit too felt a stab of pain as well when the cane fell because, as twins, they had shared sensations of joy and anguish from being little girls. She knew instinctively what was in store for her and she felt the agony that her hapless sister was experiencing.

"Get your hands away this instant, you naughty girl!" screamed Miss Stevenson angrily.

"But Ma'am it hurts so much!" pleaded Imogene, wishing that Miss Stevenson was using her father's belt and not her cane.

"I told you to be quiet," said the enraged Miss Stevenson, "And now your flagrant disobedience has earned you two extra strokes!"

Miss Stevenson then turned to Brigit who had witnessed her sister's reaction to the first stroke and who was now absolutely terrified. The cane was raised again and Brigit closed her eyes determined to keep her hands on the table in front of her. However, the agony that followed the familiar whistle and slap of the cane had her crying out in pain and uselessly trying to cover her stinging cheeks with her hands.

"You as well!" cried her tormentor, "Well, you'll just have to learn like your sister there - two extra strokes and so as to avoid this unfortunate behaviour in future you will grasp each other's wrists. The first one to let go and allow the other to cover her buttocks will receive two more strokes of my cane."

The girls did as instructed and held on for dear life for this woman was obviously not joking, she fully intended to carry out her threat.

As Miss Stevenson turned her attention back to Imogene, Brigit looked into her sister's eyes and tried to reassure her that things would be all right. Imogene screamed and jerked her hands as the cane fell again, but Brigit held on and managed to prevent her sister adding more strokes to her own tally even though once more, she shared her pain.

She noticed a tear in Imogene's eye and she smiled encouragingly for she knew instantly how much the last stroke must have hurt. Brigit took a deep breath and hoped that her next stroke would not cause her to extend her sister's suffering.

To be continued..............

The cover photograph for this book and many others are available as limited edition prints.
Write to:-

Viewfinders Photography
PO Box 200,
Reepham
Norfolk
NR10 4SY

for details, or see,

www.viewfinders.org.uk

All titles are available as electronic downloads at:

http://www.electronicbookshops.com

e-mail submissions to:
Editor@electronicbookshops.com

STILETTO TITLES

1-897809-99-9   Maria's Fulfillment *Jay Merson*
1-897809-98-0   The Rich Bitch *Becky Ball*

Due for release November 20th 2000
1-897809-97-2   Slaves of the Sisterhood *Anna Grant*

Due for release December 20th 2000
1-897809-96-4   Stocks and Bonds *John Angus*

Due for release January 20th 2001
1-897808-95-6   The Games *Jay Merson*

Due for release February 20th 2001
1-897809-94-8   Mistress Blackheart Francine Whittaker

Due for release March 20th 2001
1-897809-93-X   Military Discipline Anna Grant

Due for release April 20th 2001
1-897809-92-1   The Governess Serena Di Frisco

Due for release May 20th 2001
1-897809-91-3   Slave Training Academy Paul James